LAST SEEN LEAVING

BOOKS BY
KELLY BRAFFET

Josie and Jack
Last Seen Leaving

Kelly Braffet

LAST SEEN
LEAVING

HOUGHTON MIFFLIN COMPANY

Boston • New York • 2006

Visit our Web site: www.houghtonmifflinbooks.com.

Library of Congress Cataloging-in-Publication Data
Braffet, Kelly, date.
   Last seen leaving / Kelly Braffet.
      p. cm.
   ISBN-13: 978-0-618-44144-0
   ISBN-10: 0-618-44144-1
1. Mothers and daughters — Fiction. 2. Missing
persons — Fiction. I. Title.
   PS3602.R3444L37 2006
   813'.6 — dc22   2005037965

Book design by Melissa Lotfy

PRINTED IN THE UNITED STATES OF AMERICA

MP 10 9 8 7 6 5 4 3 2 1

For Owen:

Everything that I understand,
I understand only because I love.

— LEO TOLSTOY, *War and Peace*

prologue: crash

IT HAD BEEN A BAD NIGHT, anyway. He'd had too much to drink, she hadn't had enough, and they'd ended up in the parked car, having sex while fat summer raindrops spattered against the windows. He was fast and grunting and she felt that she may as well have been alone in the car, in the parking lot, in the state; impatience had welled up inside her like bad food, the same feeling she had in tight spaces. She'd wondered how he didn't notice.

Then they'd argued, and now she was on the highway, driving the twenty miles it would take her to be home. And the car was hers, the music coming through the speakers was hers, loud and aggressive, and the highway felt wonderful under her tires. She was on the new bypass, which cost a dollar, but it was worth it because the road was empty. The cops stuck to highways with more traffic, where they'd be more likely to fill their ticket quotas, and so she gunned it, cutting through the empty darkness and pressing the accelerator closer and closer to the Nova's dirty floor mats. Singing along with the music and pounding the steering wheel in time to the beat, with all of that frustrated energy to burn. Raindrops smacked hard off the asphalt, back up into the air, and that suited her, too.

When she drove, she liked to think she was plugged into a huge, powerful machine. Like science fiction: the car's nervous system joined with her own through the sole of her right foot. That was where the car told her to add more gas or take it away, when she had a low tire and was driving soft, when she was on ice and when she was on dry pavement. That was where she felt it when the car hydroplaned. She just had time to think *Oh, shit* before time unlocked and she saw the guardrail racing toward her. Her headlights lit the grass with surreal stripes of daylight as the car hurtled down the high, artificial embankment and then the grass was in the sky and the sky was in the grass, and inside her head there was only a high-pitched wail of impossibility. She was rolling her car. People died when they rolled their cars. *She* could die.

The wail intensified. She knew nothing else until it was over.

A man crouched next to her on the grass, rain spotting his glasses. "Are you all right?" he said. "Are you hurt?"

She was sitting halfway up the steep slope. The crumpled Nova lay at the base of the embankment, twisted into sculpture. She had no memory of unbuckling her seatbelt and pulling herself from the wreckage, of climbing this hill, of sitting down on the wet earth.

The man said, "You don't look hurt. You're not bleeding."

She was too busy taking stock of herself to answer. Her shoulder burned where the seatbelt had dug into it, and her knees ached from bracing her legs against the floor mat. Her jaw felt stiff and sore. But the man was right. None of her hurts seemed serious.

"Did you see me go over?" she asked. Her voice cracked.

He nodded. "I was behind you. We should get out of the rain," he added, pushing his dripping hair back from his forehead. "Do you have a mobile phone?"

She shook her head.

"Neither do I. But I can give you a ride to the nearest pay phone." He helped her to her feet. The world was finding its place around her, but her legs still felt weak and disconnected from the rest of her body. She stumbled, almost fell, and he caught her without hesitation.

"I'm not drunk," she said.

"I know you're not," he said, his hand cool on her bare elbow. Together they made their way up the rain-slick hill to his car, a silver Mercedes. He helped her into the passenger's seat, making sure her seatbelt was buckled before carefully checking two lanes' worth of empty blacktop and pulling onto the highway. Only then did all the advice she'd been given about how to behave when you were a stranded female motorist come back to her. She realized that she had done everything wrong. She had not stayed in her car with the doors locked. She had not asked a passing motorist to send help. A stranger had offered her a ride and she had taken it.

Then she thought, *Fuck that, I'm alive.* And her rescuer didn't seem interesting enough to be dangerous. He wore a button-down shirt, khakis, and loafers, all slightly soggy from the rain, and wire-rimmed glasses that he'd carefully wiped dry with a handkerchief before starting the engine. He was about ten years older than she was, and he needed a haircut.

Her hands still shook with the aftereffects of the crash, and her heart was loud and dire inside her chest, like the backbeat from music playing too loudly in another apartment. The world felt foggy and surreal, and she decided that she couldn't be paranoid, not now. It was too hard.

For a time they drove without speaking, watching the flat gray ribbon of road unfurling in front of the headlights. The Mercedes seemed to glide above it without touching the asphalt. Even the rain was hushed. She leaned back and rested her head against the soft leather seat. Gradually, she relaxed. Her hands stopped trembling, and her heart quieted. She felt as if she'd been crying, fiercely and for a long time.

A slow scowl spread across her face. Finally she said, "I can't believe I wrecked my goddamned car. What the fuck am

I going to do? How am I supposed to get to work tomorrow?" She lifted her hands and dropped them hopelessly. "They'll fire me. They'll completely fucking fire me."

He said nothing, and she saw that he was smiling. It was a simple smile, as if he'd just seen something small and pleasant, like a butterfly. Suddenly she was angry. "Yeah, funny, isn't it?" she said. "My car's a piece of modern art next to the bypass, by this time tomorrow I'll be unemployed, and by this time next month I'll probably be living in my boyfriend's mother's basement. I could die laughing."

The smile vanished. "I'm sorry," he said quickly. "It's the way you talk, like *die laughing*. You sound like someone in a crime novel."

"Oh." Her anger vanished as quickly as it had come, but it left a strange taste in her mouth. *Was that a compliment?* she wondered. She watched him carefully now, looking for — she didn't know exactly what she was looking for. Some sign that would tip things one way or another, into hazardous territory or out of it. "I swear like a goddamned sailor, is what you mean."

"I think it's quite wonderful," he said, and that was strange, but was it dangerous? It sounded like the kind of thing some flake New Age friend of her mother's would say, didn't it? Affirmation for affirmation's sake. *You hated your job so you quit, and now you live in your car? How* wonderful *for you.*

"Wonderful. Right," she said, and then, deliberately changing the subject, "This is a nice car." She meant it; the seats felt like real leather, and the soft glow from the dashboard was all digital. She'd never been in a Mercedes before.

He shrugged. "I travel a lot for work. I used to fly; now I drive. The economy," he said, as if he expected her to commiserate.

"My economy always sucks," she said. "What do you do?"

"I work for the government. It's not that interesting."

She tried to smile. "You want to hear not interesting, I'll tell you about my job." The smile disappeared. "Although I guess it won't be a problem after I get fired."

He nodded, not unsympathetically. "You're lucky I came along, you know. There's not a lot of traffic on this road."

"I can take care of myself. A few months ago I had a fan belt break not far from here. No big deal. I just fixed it with my bra."

"That's very resourceful," he said, with enough sudden interest to make her regret mentioning her underwear. "I always thought that was an urban legend. Like giving somebody a tracheotomy with a ballpoint pen if they're choking. How are you supposed to keep the person from bleeding to death while they're breathing through your pen?"

It was hard to tell if he expected an answer. "Duct tape," she said.

He took her seriously. "If you have some. I guess it's the sort of thing that you never think you can do until you actually do it. It's a common phenomenon. Where do you live?"

"What?" she said, instantly tense.

"Where do you live? Where am I taking you?"

She moved uneasily in the seat. "There's a truck stop off the next exit. You can drop me there."

"I can take you all the way home if you'd like. The company is nice. I spend a lot of time alone."

"The truck stop is fine."

"I actually enjoy driving," he said. "I find it meditative. I think about things I've never done, things I'd like to do."

"Like what?" she said, thinking that if he said anything else about tracheotomies she would jump out of the moving car, which was something that *she* had never done.

But instead he said, "I don't know. The standard things, I guess. Haven't you ever failed yourself?"

"You know, for a guy who spends all his time alone, you talk a lot," she said.

"I'm surprising myself. I don't really like people, as a rule."

"Great."

"Why?"

"Because I'm locked in a car with a strange man who doesn't like people."

"Oh," he said, and then, for the first time, he laughed. His laugh was all in his throat. "You're funny."

She turned and looked out the window just in time to see the truck stop fly past in a blur of yellow lights. "Hey," she said. "That was the exit. You just missed it."

"Did I?" he said.

I

DEEP PAINFUL
STIMULI

one

THERE WAS A SHORT bald man sitting on the floor in Astral Projection. He had been there for over an hour. The ghostly pallor of his skin said that he was probably a tourist; the thick turquoise and silver bracelet on his left wrist said that he didn't necessarily want to be perceived that way. He sat cross-legged, yoga-style, and tucked in between the curve of his spine and the cradle of his lap was an almost perfectly round potbelly that made Anne think of basketballs, and playgrounds, and keep-away.

She didn't bother him. Eventually, she knew, he would find what he was looking for in one of the dog-eared books on the shelf — or despair of finding it — and when she looked back, he'd be gone, and there would be someone else sitting on the floor in another section. Anne would drift over to Astral, reshelve what she could, and the day would continue.

When Anne started working at the Infinite Void soon after moving to Sedona, she had asked the bookstore's owner, Zan-

3

dar (not Zander, as in the trendy millennial shortening of Alexander, but Zandar, as in the reincarnation of a high priest of ancient Lemuria), if this sort of lingering browse was a problem. Zandar had just smiled his gentle, I-am-party-to-the-infinite-wisdom-of-the-Allbeing smile and said, "But that's why we're here, Anne."

Now Anne thought that moment spent sitting on the floor reading a book you haven't yet bought, when the Answer that brings it all together might be just on the next page — that moment was like buying a lottery ticket. You think you're paying your dollar for a chance at the $6.2 million jackpot on Saturday, but really you're paying for the pleasure of the car ride home, deciding which credit card to pay off first and where your kid will suddenly be able to go to college.

It was hope, that moment. On her cynical days, Anne saw in it the entire New Age industry and the millions of dollars it brought in every year from credulous people like Basketball Belly there in Astral. Other days, she reveled in the faith and human resilience that the answers represented. She wanted this to be an Other day. So she watched the hands move on the clock and let Basketball Belly read in peace, even though he sat for over an hour and broke the spines of the books he looked at, and she tried not to think of him as Basketball Belly.

Rhiannon returned from her break in a wave of herbal cigarette smoke and plugged in the electric teakettle behind the counter. "I have an idea," Anne said to her. "Let's open our own bookstore and call it the Lingering Browse."

"Zandar would be devastated," Rhi answered. "Besides, that makes me think of facial hair. He's still here?" Anne nodded. Rhi gave Basketball Belly a searching look and then said, "His aura's putrid. He should be in Holistic, not Astral."

Anne told Rhi that she should go tell the man that, and she did. Watching them, Anne thought that it would be a useful skill, being able to decode the health and moods of people around you by just looking at them. Basketball Belly appeared to think so, too; the look on his face as he listened to

Rhiannon was one of close attention. Anne squinted across the room at the two of them, closed one eye, tried to relax and let it flow — but all she saw was what she had always seen. Nothing.

That doesn't mean there's nothing there, she told herself.

Soon the wind chimes hanging from the doorknob tinkled as the man opened the door and walked out into the clear desert day, the two books that Rhiannon had sold him tucked under one arm. He disappeared around the corner of the store toward the small parking lot and was gone.

"What did you give him?" Anne asked Rhi.

"*Healing Yourself with Chakras,*" Rhi said, "and that new one from Astral with the bird on the cover."

Anne nodded and looked at her watch. It was ten minutes after two. The second hand ticked around the dial once, twice, again; on the third trip around, the time was thirteen minutes after two. The date was August 15. Twenty-eight years ago, on that exact date and at that exact time, Miranda had been born. Screaming; full of rage even then. It would take most of the day for Anne to work up the nerve to call her. For now, she lit a candle in her name.

"Mmm," Rhiannon said, laying a finger between the pages of her book to mark her place. "Rosemary. Who are you remembering?"

"My daughter," Anne said.

Rhiannon winced sympathetically, and let it go.

By the time Anne left the bookstore that night, the sun was already behind the mountains and the air was growing dim. Only one car remained in the parking lot, exhaust billowing from its tailpipe. She could see a figure behind the steering wheel, probably checking directions; Sedona's strict light-pollution laws forbade streetlights, making it easy to miss a turn. Ordinarily she would have stopped to help, but Miranda, in Pittsburgh, was three hours ahead of Arizona. If Anne didn't call her soon, it would be too late, and so she drove home.

Home was a small pink house with a scrabbly dirt yard. Other than the cottonwood tree that shaded the roof, keeping the house cool in summer, almost nothing grew there. Anne had no intention of ever trying to make the dusty red soil support a lawn. For years, people from icier climates had been moving west to Arizona to get away from the winter, then planting lawns and maple trees and generally doing everything they could to make their new home look and feel as much like their old home as possible. Now, to curtail the water usage caused by their landscaping, local municipalities issued tax credits to residents with "natural desert" landscaping. Anne didn't care about the tax credit. She had moved to Arizona because she actually wanted to live in Arizona. She loved her little pink house and she loved her grassless yard, with its lone cottonwood that shed downy silver seeds like warm snow every spring. She loved the mountains and she loved the vast blue sky that filled the world from horizon to horizon; she loved the rain that fell so rarely, and in those years when snow fell, she even loved the snow. In her other life, in Pittsburgh, she had hated the snow, hated the rain, hated everything other than the brief pleasant period between bitter cold and crushing humidity.

Inside the pink house, Anne dropped her bag onto the table by the front door, scratched her elderly cat, Livingston, behind the ears, and went into the kitchen, thinking about weather.

Pilots — and those who worked with them, and those, like Anne, who had been married to one — called everything but clear skies and sunshine *weather,* as if all the limitless possibilities of meteorological turmoil could be lumped into one annoying phenomenon. She had once been in the habit, herself: *Put the snow chains on the truck tonight, there's weather coming.* Back then, weather meant hassle. It meant salt and shovels and fog lights and everything slowing down; no flying and no money and Nick sitting around the house, grumpy, bored, earthbound.

Pulling a head of broccoli out of the refrigerator, Anne froze. The house was quiet; the air around her felt pregnant, tense. The wind chimes hanging from the window in the kitchen (which looked just like the ones hanging above the door in the Infinite Void, and had in fact been purchased there) swayed ever so slightly to and fro but made no sound. The shadows were deep in the corners of the kitchen, and on the other side of the arched doorway into the living room. She stood absolutely still for several minutes, listening.

"Are you there?" she whispered.

There was no answer. She sighed, put the broccoli down on the counter, pulled a knife out of the block, and started to chop, freezing several times midmotion to listen. But there was nothing.

When her daughter disappears, Anne Cassidy is forty-eight years old. She has long hair of a shade that she is accustomed to thinking of as middlebrown, now running slightly to gray, and usually twisted up loosely at the back of her head. She favors long flowing skirts, tank tops and sandals, and smells like coconut sunscreen and vanilla essential oil — like a macaroon, truth be told, but people respond well to it. Generally she eschews makeup for reasons of laziness and practicality as well as principle, but she can't resist the vanity of mascara on her already-long eyelashes. She was born in Latrobe, Pennsylvania, to Phil and Sally Hanify — both deceased, her father of heart disease after the Korean War and her mother of ovarian cancer just before Anne's daughter was born — and now lives alone, save for an arthritic twenty-year-old cat named Livingston.

Anne was married at nineteen; young, certainly, but by no means the first in her high school class to marry. She has one child, the aforementioned daughter, Miranda, to whom she rarely speaks. This distance is due partly to geography (Anne lives in Sedona, Arizona, and Miranda in Pittsburgh, where she was born) and partly to Miranda's disagreement with Anne's lifestyle choices. Which ones? Most of them, but particularly those requiring Anne to live near major sources of ley energy, and anything involving the third eye.

Anne's husband, according to most sources and definitions, is dead. According to Anne's, he is merely — elsewhere.

Anne Cassidy's last memory of her family together takes place in 1984, early April and early morning. Snow from the last blizzard of the year melts sluggishly into mud by the side of the road. Later that day the sky will lighten to a pale, washed-out gray; by evening it will be raining. But now, as the three of them drive to the airport, the air is dark and cold. The stars are gone, but the sky in the east has yet to grow light.

Nick is driving. There is a tape — Jim Croce — playing quietly, because eight-year-old Miranda is asleep in the back of the car. Anne is curled in the passenger seat, her cold feet beneath her and her hands tucked into her sleeves. Through her haze of sleepiness she watches him nod his head in time to the music. One of his hands rests on her knee. Sometimes he takes it away to shift; a moment later it is back again.

Nick is going flying.

This means that he has to drive to Allegheny County Airport — Agony County, the pilots call it, even though for a small airport it's not particularly agonizing — and Anne has to go with him, so that she can drive the car back. Nobody wants to baby-sit at five in the morning, so Miranda comes along as well, and it has become a family tradition.

Once, Nick catches a ride to the airport with one of the other pilots. Six weeks later, when he returns, he confesses to Anne that those weeks have been nervous and uneasy, and makes her promise that the three of them will always make the drive together. Flying is so dependent on chance — wind, weather, physics — that small habits and idiosyncrasies begin to take on a supernatural significance. Nick will never take off without a bar of Hershey's chocolate in his flight bag, and he will not fly anywhere, not even on a commercial flight, without the medallion he wears around his neck: Saint Joseph of Cupertino, patron saint of aviators. And so these drives, too, have taken on a ritual quality, even for Anne — the empty roads, the car blanketed in a heavy layer of quiet, the stop at McDonald's for coffee and watery orange juice.

Nick drives past the grand art deco entrance of the mostly abandoned main terminal to a side entrance with a scarred yellow barrier that lifts when he reaches through his window to press the button on the control box mounted on the fence.

He stops the car in the lot where the Western Mountain pilots leave their cars. Anne can see through her window that Nick's best friend, X-Ray, is already there, waiting next to his truck with an overstuffed duffel bag at his feet.

Nick and X have been flying together for years: first in the Marine Corps and then for the constantly evolving series of companies that eventually became Western Mountain Aviation. Anne knows that in a few minutes, as she backs the car out of the lot, she will glance in her rearview mirror and see the two men hoist their duffel bags over their shoulders and head toward the hangar. After that, she has no idea what happens to them. They talk about Panama City, about Tegucigalpa in Honduras and San José in Costa Rica, but they also talk about navigating Portuguese and Israeli airspace.

"What, exactly, do you *do?*" she has asked Nick more than once, and he only grins.

"Uncontrolled landing avoidance," he tells her, with the jargon-filled black humor that all pilots seem to share and that Anne suspects is an aftereffect of life in the military, where phrases like "targeted opposition elimination" meant "kill," and "catastrophic equipment failure" meant "crash." Eventually she stops asking. All she really wants to know is whether or not he's in danger, but he's a pilot. The answer is always yes.

Nick parks the car and calls a hello to X-Ray as he wrests his duffel bag out of the trunk. X comes over to the car briefly, throwing a friendly arm over Anne's shoulders and saying hi to Miranda, who is shaken awake only long enough to mumble her goodbyes. Then Anne promises Nick that she will take pictures of Miranda's school play. Nick promises Anne that he will be careful and come home. Then she says, "Get out of here. I'm too cold to stand around," and he answers, "Love you, too, babe."

She hugs him one last time, breathing deeply of the airplane smell of his flight jacket, and leaves. The next time she smells him, she will be opening a box filled with the clothes he wasn't wearing when he died.

. . .

9

Anne had not seen Miranda in the flesh in almost three years, but her phone number was on a postcard tucked inside Anne's address book. Every time Miranda moved she sent Anne a new postcard, and Anne would swap it for the old one. Anne had learned from experience not to bother transferring the addresses to the book itself; the postcards came too frequently. They were almost always ads for cigarettes or alcohol. Anne assumed that Miranda picked them up free in bars.

Mom — moved again — new info below — M.

Rarely was there as much as a full sentence in the blank space on the back of the card. Rarer still the times that Miranda actually called. Anne kept a careful tally of her own phone calls to her daughter, their frequency and duration — she didn't want to smother, didn't want to force — but now they hadn't spoken in three months, and it was the girl's birthday today. That was a good enough excuse.

After four rings, Miranda's voice mail picked up.

Hey, it's me. You know what to do.

Miranda's voice on the recording was full of her usual bravado, and Anne wondered, as she always did, why a person would waste bravado on their voice mail. After the beep, she left her message: *Happy birthday, thinking of you, love you. Do you still live here? Call sometime.*

After dinner she dabbed a bit of sandalwood oil onto the middle of her forehead and spread a meditation mat on the living room floor. Sitting, she folded her legs beneath her and closed her eyes. Her lips moved slightly as she said the mantra under her breath — *I am a part of the universe and the universe is a part of me* — over and over again, trying to empty her mind of all other thought.

It was hard to do. She almost never got it right. Harder still because Anne didn't meditate to find inner peace; she meditated to reach Nick. Sometimes she thought that she could feel him just on the other side of the stillness, but she could never wholly convince herself that it wasn't simply because she wanted to feel him there. It was true, however, that there were some days when the house felt full of — something — and other days when it just felt like four walls with space inside and scorpions outside, hiding under rocks with their stinging tails bent over their backs. Big ones, little ones — the little ones were the worst, because they were the most poisonous and the hardest to kill. You could step on them, crush them, microwave them even, and they still wouldn't die — not that Anne would ever actually put a scorpion in the microwave —

Damn.

She wasn't supposed to be thinking about scorpions. She wasn't supposed to be thinking about anything. Anne's eyes rolled impatiently behind her closed lids, her mouth tightened, and she began again.

When the ache in her legs started to intrude to a degree that she couldn't ignore, she opened her eyes. Livingston the cat waited patiently on the kitchen table for his dinner; she fed him, scrubbed at the oily place on her forehead, and went to bed, because the day was over, and there was nothing else to be done with it.

The problem with hope, she thought as she drifted off to sleep in the empty house, was that it got your hopes up.

The next morning when she arrived at the store, Anne was surprised to see a car idling in the parking lot. Neither Rhiannon's ancient Volkswagen nor Zandar's Jeep was there yet; she tried not to be annoyed about being the last to leave and the first to arrive once again, and squinted at the strange car in the bright sun.

It was a midsized sedan, only a little dusty. The dark blue-green color had been trendy recently, and something about the car's unblemished surface and lack of bumper stickers or parking permits said *rental*. The more Anne looked at it, the more certain she became that it was the same car she'd seen checking directions the night before. Someone still sat behind the steering wheel. Anne could see a head leaning against the window as if dozing.

She walked up to the car. The arm draped over the steering wheel was wearing a turquoise bracelet that looked a lot like the one Basketball Belly had been wearing the day before. The bald head resting against the window looked like his, too. Had he come back to return the book? But then what had he been doing there the night before? Had he been there all night? She tapped on the window. When he didn't respond, she pulled at the door handle.

Several things happened in rapid succession. *Healing Yourself with Chakras* fell out of the man's lap and landed on Anne's foot. A fierce blast of arctic air burst out of the air-conditioned car and hit her in the face. Basketball Belly himself fell sideways out of the car against her legs, and she moved instinctively to catch him.

It had been years since Anne had eaten meat, but she remembered what it was like to hold a dead thing in her hands. It was like this.

His eyes, already covered with a thin, dry film, stared blankly up at the soft-looking cumulus clouds that dotted the blue sky.

A fourth thing happened. Anne screamed.

Rhiannon arrived first and found Anne kneeling by the still-idling rental with the man's corpse in her lap. Anne looked at her with haunted eyes and said, "I can't leave him. Will you —?" And Rhiannon, who had been known to tear up at particularly soothing shades of blue, kept it together long enough to call 911, and then Zandar. Zandar made it there first; the paramedics and police were not far behind.

Basketball Belly's body was stiff and cold — what one of the paramedics called *dead on scene*. A policeman told Zandar and the two women to step back, holding his arms out as if to try to embrace them. Zandar's own arms were firmly around Rhiannon, whose composure had fled as soon as it was no longer needed.

Anne stood by herself a few feet away. Her heart was full of a hollow, shrieking horror.

The dead man lay on the hard-packed dirt of the parking lot, arms thrown out from his sides. Anne had lain in exactly the same position the first time she'd gone to the vortex at Bell

Rock. The guide had recommended it; he'd said that some people found it easier to align with the energies if as much of their body as possible was in contact with the earth. The dead man might have gone on the same tour, she thought. He might have had the same guide. But no guide told him how to lie in the dust in Zandar's parking lot. He lay where Anne had left him when the paramedic pulled her away. Anne wondered dimly if he was aligned with the energies now.

"What happens next?" Zandar asked the policeman nearest him.

In a calm, quiet voice, the policeman said, "The coroner has to pronounce him dead and take him to the morgue, so we can figure out who he was and what happened to him."

"Is," Anne said. "Who he is."

The policeman nodded levelly. "Okay. Who he is."

"Can't you take him to the morgue now?" There was a slight tension around Zandar's temples. One with the Allbeing or not, Zandar didn't seem to be crazy about the idea of having a dead man in his parking lot. "Or at least put him in the ambulance?"

"I'm afraid not," the cop said.

"Is there a reason why?" Zandar almost managed to keep the petulance out of his voice.

The paramedic who was sitting in the open passenger door of the white van with a clipboard on his lap said, "Because it's illegal to transport a dead body in an ambulance." He sounded bored.

The parking lot was so quiet, Anne thought. The lights on top of the emergency vehicles flashed silently and without any urgency, and the policemen and the paramedics seemed calm, even languorous. It seemed wrong that a human death could make so little impact even on the people who dealt with it professionally.

"What if he's not dead?" she heard herself ask. "What if he's just unconscious, or in a coma?"

The policeman and the medic exchanged a look. "There's a test that we do," the medic said. "You rub hard, with your knuckles, right here." He touched the tip of his pen to his sternum. "If the patient is anything other than dead, there's at least a small reaction. They call it deep painful stimuli. It's the safest possible way to inflict the most possible pain."

"Look at him, ma'am," the policeman said gently. "There's no way he's anything other than dead."

Meanwhile the dead man lay in the parking lot, in the dust. Anne went to the body and knelt down next to it. For a moment she gazed at the man's open and staring eyes. Then she picked up his hand. It was rubbery and heavy.

She felt a presence next to her. It was the policeman.

"Ma'am, we need you to stay back," he said. His voice was kind.

"Nobody should die alone," she said. "I want to be with him."

The cop touched her shoulder. "He's already gone."

Anne breathed deeply of the sage-scented air. "He could still be here," she said. "I want him to find his way."

Behind her, Rhiannon cried.

Anne's lost Nick has dark hair, thick and wavy and romantic — film-star hair, his best feature — and hazel eyes that seem to darken when he's angry or amused. His skin is decorated with several ridiculous tattoos dating back to flight school, none of which he can remember getting and all of which make him feel vaguely ashamed. His left calf is impressively scarred from a motorcycle accident when he was a teenager, and one of his eyeteeth is chipped from a softball-game-cum-melee that he took part in the weekend he and Anne met. He is always hungry.

They meet in a bar in 1974, when Anne is eighteen and her middlebrown hair shorter, more carefully styled. Everything about her is carefully styled: her eyes are so thickly lined and her long eyelashes so heavily coated with mascara that she looks like a character from a comic strip. They are femme fatale eyes, Girl Reporter eyes. The effect is only slightly unconscious.

14

During Anne's first barroom experience, she hovered awkwardly in a corner with downcast eyes, crippled by shyness. By the time she meets Nick she has been to four separate bars on four separate nights, and she feels frustrated and bored. This new thing, this *bar scene,* is not what she expected. She expected glamour, excitement, crowds of adoring men vying to light her slim cigarette so she could stare alluringly at them through her exhaled smoke; she did not expect that everyone would be smoking cigarettes and that the resulting haze would make her throat burn and her eyes water. She did not expect this loud, dark room, full of barely hidden desperation and loneliness. The air is tense with the aggressive anticipation of sex: it fills the eyes of all the drinkers — even Anne's, although she doesn't know it — and colors the set of their bodies, the way their gazes prowl the room as they sip casually at their drinks.

Anne, in her fifth bar, suffers from an almost palpable disappointment in the world, and a terrible nagging fear that it will be this way for the rest of her life.

But Nick, when he appears — unshaven, quite drunk, and just off the plane from Laos, where he'd traded his Pirates cap for the embroidered shirt he's wearing — has a confidence in his walk and a glint in his eyes that she has never seen before. Standing next to her, he orders a Jameson on the rocks — *Jameson on the rocks,* Anne thinks with admiration, relishing the cool, masculine sound of it — and then asks her, as if it is the most natural thing in the world, what she needs.

"A gin and tonic," she says, wishing that she knew how to drink something less — girlish — but thinking, *You. I'm fairly sure that I need you.*

A year later they are in bed in his apartment. He doesn't spend much time there, and the two small rooms are cluttered with pieces of disemboweled flying machines: altimeters, control sticks, a propeller. Nick tells her that the kind of flying he does won't make for a great life — he flies job-by-job contracts, most of them overseas and most of them for the company that will become Western Mountain Aviation.

"Are you running drugs?" she asks him. They are naked together, and she thinks he might tell her.

"Yes," he says immediately.

She surveys him through narrowed eyes, which he meets head-on. "Bullshit." She is learning to swear from him.

He shakes his head. "If I was hauling bullshit, you'd smell it on me."

She smiles and nuzzles her face into his shoulder. There is a smell to Nick: a rich, open smell, like gasoline but dustier, mellower. It is the smell of jet fuel and pressurized cabins, of riveted metal and soldered wires and altitude. It is the smell of flying, a smell she is coming to love.

"You smell like a dirty old airplane," she says.

His eyes widen in mock horror. "Dirty!"

"Dirty," she agrees.

"You want dirty," he says. "I'll show you dirty."

Afterward, he tells her that his job is important, but not the kind of thing he can talk about. With uncharacteristic gravity, he asks her if she can live with that, and she tells him that yes, she can. She is nineteen, recklessness is sexy, and although she will remember this conversation later and wonder if he was trying to warn her, right now that warning is more alluring than threatening. As, perhaps, he intends it to be, because the sudden grin he gives her is all mirth and sexy, confident satisfaction, and she knows that he never expected her to say anything else.

"That's my Annie," he says.

Anne likes when Nick calls her Annie. She even thinks of herself that way: *Nick's Annie. I am Nick's Annie.*

When he dies, the good people at Western Mountain — who turn out to be lying bastards, but she'll learn that later, too — tell Nick's Annie that the last plane he ever flew is most likely at the bottom of the Pacific Ocean, disintegrating into silt just off the coast of Panama, his body surely fully integrated by now into a million tiny and not-so-tiny marine organisms. No, Western Mountain cannot be positive, since they never found the wreckage, but whatever happened, they are sure that her

16

husband is dead. When his death is new to her and she is still numb, Anne spends no small amount of time wondering which got him first, the water or the sharks.

But as time passes, she realizes that Western Mountain is anything but forthcoming about the wheres, whats, and whys of Nick's life in the air, and she has no reason to believe that they are being any more straightforward about his death. She begins to wonder if the remnants of the last plane Nick ever flew lie in a dense chunk of Central American jungle, twisted and rotting, instead of in a million microbial pieces at the bottom of the Pacific Ocean. She is willing to bet that one or more pieces of the wreckage are pocked with bullet holes — or maybe just one enormous hole, from a surface-to-air missile or some other horrible weapon that she can't even imagine.

Bizarrely, as soon as she stops believing Western Mountain's story, she misses it. She would rather think of Nick being in the ocean — of Nick *being* the ocean — than as a corpse, lying in his plane in the jungle or, worse, in a shallow grave somewhere. Broken, with air passages packed full of dirt, because he'd been buried alive. She has heard of such things happening, stories half overheard from pilots in other rooms speaking in hushed tones.

It becomes too hard, after a while, to think of Nick every time she sees an airport, an airplane, the sky. The weight of his death begins to crush her, and she grows desperate. Western Mountain Aviation will give her neither a body nor an answer. When she comes across a book about spiritualism, she suddenly feels that she has found her own answer, and she clutches it desperately, vitally. Nick is not in a million pieces in the Pacific Ocean. He hasn't been buried alive in some awful jungle teeming with awful, devouring life — hasn't even been buried dead in such a place, because the part of Nick that matters has left the scarred cage of his body and come back to her. He is in her kitchen, her living room; he is with her.

And sometimes, when the silence grows thick and alive with possibility, she almost feels him there. She almost hears his voice, his footsteps, his cracked singing. She talks to him the way you talk to a loved one in a coma: not because you expect an answer, but because it keeps the connection between you alive.

The problem with hope, Anne finds through the years, is that it gets your hopes up. But hopelessness is worse.

At home, after a few glasses of wine, Anne wondered if the way that it happened with Basketball Belly was the way it had happened with Nick. Was his body tended by strangers, cleaned and buried? Did they find his wedding ring or Miranda's school picture and wonder about the people he'd left behind? Had witnessing the death of a stranger affected them the way it had her, driven them home and into a bottle; was his corpse a shock? Was it their hundredth, their thousandth? Did they tell jokes as they dug the hole that would hold him? Was their bottle deeper than hers could ever be?

Anne realized that she didn't even know if Nick had carried one of Miranda's school pictures.

She could call Basketball Belly's family, she thought drunkenly. She could call them and tell them all the things that they wouldn't otherwise know. *The policeman was kind and dark-haired, the paramedic jaded, the car a teal-green sedan,* she would say, giving them an image to counter the blank eyes and the slack jaw of the corpse that had been shipped home to them. She could ask questions that would show she'd paid special attention to him, that he hadn't been just a nameless customer: Was his turquoise bracelet new? Had he worn a hairpiece or a baseball hat for most of his life? Was that why his head was so pale?

They don't even know he's dead yet, she thought. *They're me, before X-Ray's phone call.*

Nobody — not Nick's boss, not his friends, not anyone — had done for her what she was thinking of doing for Basketball Belly's family, and those men *knew* her. They had eaten her food, joked with her daughter, and flown airplanes with her husband, and not one of them had bothered to come to her after his death and say the only thing she wanted to hear: *This is the way it was, Annie. This is the way it happened. I saw his body. I touched it.*

"But he was just a nameless customer," she suddenly said to the empty house. "He broke the book spines. He was annoying."

It was true: he had annoyed her, and now he was dead. Anne closed her eyes and took a deep breath. She imagined all the anger and grief inside her as dark greenish black fog, and the air coming into her lungs as clear and light; exhaled, and imagined all the dark, nasty stuff going out with her breath.

The wine helped. After her fourth glass — which she stared at in confusion, unsure what it was or how it had come into existence, since she never had four glasses of wine in one night — she picked up the phone and called Miranda again. Because she was drunk she could make the call without a second thought, without tallying the messages she had left and the time that had passed between them. *There was a dead man in our parking lot today,* she thought blurrily. Surely that was worth a phone call.

Hey, it's me. You know what to do.

Anne was surprised when what came out of her mouth was "Miranda. Call me. I miss you. It's your mother. Call me."

Anne dreamed.

In her dream, she watched as Nick's airplane, toy-sized, was rocked by bullets over a dense, frightening jungle. Giant Anne watched it happen, unable to reach out, to take the tiny plane in her hands and protect it from the hidden guns. As the battle raged in front of her, she heard Nick's voice, jolly and fearless, singing, *From the halls of Montezuma to the shores of Tripoli: we will fight our country's battles on the air and land and sea —*

And the plane exploded.

There's no way that he's anything other than dead, she heard a voice say. In the indeterminate way of dreams, Anne could not tell whether the voice belonged to Miranda, or Nick, or herself.

She jerked into consciousness. She stumbled to the window, her eyes wet with tears as she gazed out at the blue desert. She felt horribly alone.

An hour or so later, Anne's exhaustion overcame her unease, and she fell asleep. When she woke again at eight, the uneasy feeling was back. It stayed with her while she made tea, while she toasted an English muffin.

Anne wondered: what if she were hit by a bus; what if she went hiking and got lost in the desert? What if she died suddenly while sitting in a parked car in a strange town, from a stroke or a brain aneurysm or some other deep and secret injury? Who would call Miranda? How would Miranda even know her mother was gone? Would she sense the loss, like a flat spot in her hearing or a blurring of her vision?

Anne threw the last bite of her breakfast into the trash can, picked up the phone, and called Miranda again, as she had done the day before, and the day before that. But this time, her nerves twisted tighter and tighter with each ring until — after what seemed like an eternity — the line clicked and the machine picked up.

Hey, it's me. You know what to do.

But this time, after the message, instead of the single long beep that she expected, there came a short repeated beep, and a toneless, mechanical voice answered. "The voice mailbox of the person you are trying to reach is full," it said. "Please try again later."

Anne did so: tried again later, after she returned from work. In Pittsburgh, it was almost nine at night.

Hey, it's me. You know what to do.

All day long Anne had been thinking of her daughter, remembering things she hadn't thought of in years — birthday parties, childhood ailments, crude school art projects — and when she heard the message this time, she listened carefully, as if it were code. The voice sounded strong, arrogant; like Miranda. But it was only a recording on a machine. There was nothing else there.

She tried every night for almost a week. Despite all of the careful theories Anne had developed to explain the distance between her and Miranda — their life paths were temporarily divergent, Miranda was just going through a self-reliant phase — she suddenly felt that she had hit a limit. It had been three months since they had spoken, and that was too long. Hearing her daughter's voice on the answering machine was like standing outside a restaurant with an empty stomach. By the fourth day, Anne felt like she was waking up Miranda, going to sleep Miranda, and dreaming Miranda. She ate Miranda's favorite childhood sandwiches — grilled cheese with tomato and peanut butter with strawberry jam — and drank her favorite purple lemonade. She bought a hank of metallic green yarn and started knitting Miranda a scarf, and she remembered. Constantly, she remembered.

By the sixth day, her hunger turned to worry. She began to spin elaborate fantasies about all the terrible things that could have happened to Miranda — she'd slipped in the shower and was starving on her bathroom floor, she had adult-onset chicken pox and was near death in intensive care — telling herself all the while that her fears were neurotic and groundless. Still, on the seventh day, she called again. This time the phone didn't even ring. Instead, an emotionless voice said, "The number you are trying to reach has been disconnected. This is a recording."

Anne hung up the phone.

The air in the small pink house felt sick with anticipation and worry.

"Nick," Anne said aloud. "I'm concerned."

two

A PART FROM ANNE'S persistent feeling that perhaps she was overreacting by several light-years, there were no problems arranging the trip. She bought a cell phone and left the number on her machine at home, in case Miranda called. She lied to Zandar and Rhiannon and told them that Miranda had invited her to come for a visit, because she found their enthusiastic good wishes easier to stomach than she would have their attempts to share or alleviate her concern. Rhiannon happily took Livingston the cat in as a boarder, and Zandar even offered to loan her the money for the plane ticket.

"I don't need it," she said, and that much, at least, was true. The deposit from Western Mountain that had started appearing in her Pittsburgh bank account three months after Nick's disappearance had, the last time she checked, continued steadily every month since then. For many years she hadn't wanted Nick's parents to know where she and Miranda were — had they ever filed a missing-persons report? Hired an investigator?

— so she hadn't touched it. Now the account held several tens of thousands of dollars. She called the bank to make sure that her twenty-year-old checks were still good, and when she knew that they were, she gave one to her travel agent in exchange for a coach-class ticket from Phoenix to Pittsburgh.

Was she crazy? she thought, waiting for her documents to come out of the printer at the travel agent's office. Flying however many thousand miles on the spur of the moment, with no further justification than a full answering machine and a disconnected phone line — it certainly didn't seem like the act of an entirely healthy person.

But that phrase — "entirely healthy person" — only made her think of Basketball Belly. Bad things happened. They happened to ordinary people, on ordinary days. When you woke up and toasted your English muffin or grilled your daughter's cheese sandwich, there was no rash, no telltale whir, no suddenly ominous background music to let you know that this was going to be the worst day of your life, the last day of your life, the last day of someone else's life. There was no way to know but to *know*. And Anne would not be able to sleep until she knew.

The printer spat out her itinerary. The agent stapled it to the receipt and slid the whole thing into a brightly colored folder. She included, without being asked, several brochures on interesting things to see and do in the greater Pittsburgh area, for which Anne thanked her politely.

Then she went home and threw up.

On the plane Anne read an article in the airline's in-flight magazine about Pittsburgh's renewal. It said that modern Pittsburgh was a lovely city, far from the smoke, grime, and filth of its industrial years. Developers were even beginning to tear down the decaying steel mills that hadn't operated since the seventies, which the more heavily accented natives called *still mills* with unconscious irony. Suddenly Pittsburgh architecture existed to be appreciated: "You haven't lived until you've seen Pittsburgh's bridges," the article gushed.

When Anne left Pittsburgh, twenty years before, the only

thought that came to mind upon contemplation of Pittsburgh's bridges was jumping off them.

Her plane landed just before three. The airport had been rebuilt since she was last there, but she found her way to the rental car counter and rented a car. The Parkway West, the freeway that led from the airport to the city, was a bit wider than she remembered it, perhaps, but no smoother. More glossy office parks and shopping centers lined the parkway, but FOR LEASE banners hung across more than a few of them. Anne decided that the in-flight magazine writer had exaggerated Pittsburgh's New Tech Revival.

The steel mills by the river really had been torn down — and replaced by twenty-screen multiplex movie theaters, which seemed only a marginal improvement. But after she passed through the Squirrel Hill tunnel on the other side of the city, the roadside scenery grew more familiar. The turnpike turned out to be the same pocked, crowded mess that it had always been. By the time she stopped at a gas station outside Ratchetsburg for directions and Pepto-Bismol tablets — she was nervous, her stomach churning — the sky had darkened to the smoky gray of a coal-country autumn evening. Skies like that lurked in the back of twenty years' worth of Anne's memories. Strange, she thought, that they'd been happening for twenty years, whether she was there to see them or not.

Miranda's apartment building was a utilitarian brick cube just outside Ratchetsburg with nothing around it but a gravel parking lot. The cars parked in the lot were either cheap or inherited, and based on the LINKIN PARK and MEAN PEOPLE SUCK stickers in the car windows, she thought that the building's tenants skewed young. In Arizona, where a car didn't rust out after five winters' worth of ice and salt, kids spent real money on their cars. Here the investment clearly wasn't worth it.

Anne wondered which car belonged to Miranda.

She entered the building through an unmarked fire door that she found propped open with a brick. Inside, the hallway carpets were worn and stained, an unremarkable shade of brown that would easily forgive dropped beer cans and cigarette burns. Cheap reflective stickers, the kind sold in hardware stores to put on mailboxes, identified each apartment. When Anne found her way to number 15, on the second floor, she stood in front of the door and closed her eyes. She had no idea what was supposed to happen now.

In her imaginings, just as she raised a fist to knock, Miranda would open the door: taking the garbage out, perhaps. They would spend a moment gazing at each other, a moment during which Miranda would come to terms with her uprooted adolescence and Anne would forgive her daughter for abandoning her. (Since it was a daydream, Anne let herself be honest.) They would embrace. Later they would take the garbage out together on their way to the grocery store to buy fresh produce. (In Anne's mind, it was somehow spring.) They would bring the groceries back to the apartment and turn the tomatoes and basil into a simple, delicious pasta sauce. Miranda's apartment would be cozy and a little dark, the walls painted a rich shade of red or purple and every corner filled with charming furniture she had picked up at flea markets. As they sat and sipped tea together after dinner, Miranda would confess that when she'd bought the 1940s armoire that held her linens, she'd been thinking how much Anne would like it.

Now, standing in this bleak, cut-rate hallway that smelled like old pizza and confronted with the extreme unlikelihood of the cozy apartment, the richly painted walls, or the 1940s armoire, Anne thought, *She'll open the door. Her jaw will drop. We'll stare at each other, all right, and then I'll get to watch that old rebellious look surface on her face. Maybe she'll say, "I hope you don't fucking expect to stay with me."*

Well. She would fight through it. That's all.

She knocked, and waited. Waited for footsteps in the room beyond the door, maybe a toilet flushing. There was only silence. She knocked again.

Still nothing.

Not home? she wondered. She checked her watch. Five o'clock on a Thursday; Miranda could still be at work.

She tried the knob, not letting herself picture Miranda's reaction upon coming home and finding Anne not just on her doorstep but in her actual apartment. The knob didn't turn. Anne wasn't surprised. The doorknobs looked heavy and industrial, and probably locked automatically when the door shut.

"Okay," she said to the recalcitrant door. "So I wait."

And wait she did, outside, in the parking lot, on the rickety wooden steps that led to the door. The evening was cool, but not cold. Anne watched the first stars come out and thought about Pennsylvania.

It is near Christmas, 1984. Nick is nearly seven months gone, and Anne hates Pittsburgh. She hates the valley and the stinking, sludgy rivers. She hates the snow on the rooftops, the way it blends into the cold white sky. She hates the roads, twisting and potholed and switching back on themselves. She hates going to Christmas parties and weddings and seeing the same old goddamned plates of homemade baked ziti and rigatoni. She hates that the party guests don't know that the plural of *rigatoni* is *rigatoni,* and that they say things like "You taste 'em rigatonis?"

Not that she has been to many parties lately.

Anne and Miranda are living in a dingy townhouse that Anne hates because it's dingy and that Miranda hates because she had to switch schools when they moved there. The townhouse was supposed to be neutral territory, a fresh start; Nick has never been there, but his absence fills the house like concrete. His wife and daughter move through it as if they are two small, boring creatures who live deep underground — moles, maybe — and every inch of motion is a great effort. It seems to Anne that her entire life is the doctor's office where she works and the never-clean-enough apartment with her angry nine-year-old daughter. And Nicklessness, the flat unfeeling stretch of blank newsprint that is life without him.

The snow falls every night. It does not melt.

It becomes harder and harder for Anne to get up each day. Every morning when she wakes up, she fights off the urge to call in sick and spend the day lying on the couch under the afghan that Nick's mother crocheted as a wedding present; fights it off just long enough to make it into her car, and then it becomes easier — something about the motion — until she arrives at the office. Then her allotted corner seems smaller and smaller each day. She stops wanting to call in sick and begins wishing that she had.

Sometime during this vague, depressed haze, Anne's mother-in-law calls on her day off and invites her out "for a nice lunch." Anne tries not to sound as defeated as she feels when she says, yes, that would be lovely. She takes a shower, puts on a clean dress and, for the first time since Nick's death, makeup. Staring at herself in the mirror, coating her eyelashes with mascara and brushing color onto her cheeks — *warm spice,* although she feels neither warm nor spicy — she feels like she is painting a mannequin.

Agnes Cassidy is, and has always been, a stumbling block for Anne. As rugged and restless and exuberant as Nick is, his mother is equally as refined, sophisticated, and — Anne thinks — repressed. Nick told Anne once that when his mother spoke of him to her friends, she would say that he was in international business. Nick's father, Martin, if within earshot, would retort, "Bullshit, he is. He's flying for the government," and then add, proudly, "Can't talk about it. Classified."

Anne has always liked Martin, and she finds his overstatement of his son's job charming and a little sad. Martin, who runs one of the smaller steel mills in Pittsburgh, has always seemed slightly bored, and she senses that he lives vicariously through his adventurous son. It was Martin who encouraged Nick to join the military after college, to go to flight school instead of business school. But she thinks that Agnes is a silly, vain woman, comforted in her opinion by the knowledge that Nick shares it —

Shared it. Nick shared it.

Nick's mother has chosen a perfectly charming bistro in Shadyside, only a few blocks from the house where Nick grew up. For a while the two women perform the female ritual that

Anne thinks of as "chatting lightly," talking about Miranda's adventures at school and Agnes's skiing lessons. The clam sauce covering Anne's uneaten linguini congeals on her plate, and she grows more and more restless.

Agnes shakes her head. "Poor Miranda," she says. "That school really doesn't seem to be a good place for her, does it?"

Anne demurs, pointing out that the school isn't particularly bad or good, but that any child in Miranda's position — meaning any nine-year-old whose father had gone to work and never come back, and who had subsequently been uprooted from school and home and the few remaining notes of familiarity in her young life — would, naturally, have some trouble adjusting.

Agnes stirs her iced tea and seems to hesitate. Finally she says, "If you wanted to send her to the academy, Martin and I would be happy to take care of the tuition, of course. It would be nice to see her more often." She sounds a bit wistful. "She's all we have, now."

Agnes and Martin see Miranda almost every weekend, which is as often as Anne can make the hour-long drive into Pittsburgh to get her to them. Anne feels her jaw muscles clench and reminds herself that this woman, too, is mourning. No, no, she says; such a generous offer, but who knows, really, how long the two of them will be staying in the townhouse — she doesn't want to uproot Miranda again, but it really is *terribly* dingy, and Anne is certainly planning to find something better.

She says this with the intent of forestalling any questions or thinly veiled complaints about the townhouse, but Agnes jumps on her words like a dog on a bone. "Things are hard for you right now, aren't they?" she says.

Anne cannot deny that.

Agnes reaches across the table, lays her hand on Anne's. "We all miss Nicholas," she says softly. "I miss him terribly. Would it —" She hesitates again, and then pushes ahead. "Would it be easier to have Miranda come and stay with us for a while? We have the house," she adds, "and it's too big for us, really, and it's somewhere familiar, that she knows — it might be easier —"

And her voice sounds kind, but oh, the look in her eyes is pure greed, and Anne — whose face is suddenly afire, whose own eyes feel like two glowing hot coals — cannot speak. Her Miranda, her daughter; the part of Nick that is also a part of her, the thing they made together that is greater than both of them. God and Agnes both be damned if that ridiculous woman thinks that Anne would willingly let her precious, angry daughter be taken away from her and turned into one of those horrible field hockey academy clones: never, never, never. She will not allow it.

"No," she says. It feels like the first word she's spoken in six months. "Oh, no."

In her high school chemistry class, Anne learned about supersaturation, when a higher concentration of a substance than is possible under ordinary conditions is forced into a solution. For instance, air in the atmosphere can, under certain circumstances, hold more water vapor than it could at ground level; it has to do with temperature, and with pressure. Supersaturation is a tenuous and unstable state of being. One particle of foreign matter, one crystal of ice, and the molecular ties binding the supersaturated moisture break. The first fragment teaches the rest of the suddenly released molecules how to solidify, and the vapor coalesces into ice and falls to earth, where it melts into sprinkles and drizzles and showers and torrents. Or it finds an airplane wing to cling to and forms great sheets of ice that weigh the plane down, freeze the wing flaps, and pull it to earth.

Since Nick's death, the grief and anger have built up inside of Anne until she feels supersaturated with it. Every search through her purse for a stamp for the phone bill, every hunt for a parking space, every occasion when nine-year-old Miranda is tearful or defiant, threatens the tenuous equilibrium holding Anne together. When Anne sees that greedy look in Agnes's eyes, a single crystal of hard, bitter fury forms in the midst of Anne's grief, and her equilibrium is gone. During the long, furious drive back to the dingy townhouse, her grief coalesces into something solid, something fierce, and by the time she reaches home she has already determined that it will be the coldest possible day in all of the hells that ever existed before she lets the Cassidys take her daughter away from her.

That afternoon, waiting for Miranda to get home from school, Anne turns on the television against her rage and against the Nicklessness, and she sees a travelogue about Arizona. The show features aerial footage of pine forests, of crystal blue lakes and snowcapped mountains, of wide deserts with cactuses standing like sentinels in the rosy dusk. One segment focuses on Sedona, explaining that a growing contingent of New Age devotees believe that Sedona lies atop the convergence of ley lines, lines of power that carry the earth's energy like dry, invisible rivers. There is more aerial footage: high, majestic red rocks and rich green trees.

Anne says the word to herself: *Arizona.* It sounds fierce, wild, untamed. She imagines herself in Sedona, standing barefoot in red soil, mysterious energy thrumming up through the bottoms of her feet and welling up inside her, filling her with something pure and real.

Plans begin to form. Like crystals; like rain clouds.

Sitting on Miranda's stoop, deep in reminiscence, Anne didn't notice the pudgy young man coming out of the building, or the curious look that he gave her as he descended the steps and got into his car. By the time he returned a half-hour later, she was back in the present. Unaware that he had seen her earlier, she didn't understand why he looked at her so strangely as he unloaded two bags of groceries from his passenger's seat.

The boy approached warily, as if — Anne thought — she was likely to pull a snatch-and-grab, fleeing with his bags of potato chips and beer.

"Hi," she said with what she hoped was a friendly smile.

"Hi," he answered. He sounded uncertain. "Are you — are you okay? You've been sitting here a long time. Can I help you with something?"

"Maybe." Anne stood up, dusting off the back of her skirt. "If you know my daughter, Miranda. She lives in number 15."

The boy's wariness vanished. It was replaced by annoyance.

"You mean Andy," he said with disgust in his voice. "Did you come for the cat?"

"Cat?"

"Yeah, cat. Did she send you to get it?" He shifted his groceries.

"I don't know anything about a cat," Anne said slowly. "I was looking for Miranda."

He looked more closely at her. He wore a tiny patch of beard beneath his lower lip, a heavy silver ball nestled in the short dark hair like a bird's egg. "You said you were her mother?"

"Yes," Anne said, "but I haven't talked to her lately."

He laughed. "How lately, lady? Look, my beer's getting warm. You want to come in?"

His apartment was tantalizingly close to Miranda's — just down the hall. The only pieces of furniture inside were a table and couch that were probably castoffs from his parents' garage and an expensive-looking television on a milk crate. "Do you want a beer?" he said, starting to put his groceries away. "Or Coke. I have Coke."

Anne shook her head impatiently. "You said something about her cat?"

He put a package of bacon in the refrigerator. "Yeah, I would have thought she'd taken it with her, but it was still here after she'd split. I put food out for a while, but then I stopped."

"But Miranda," Anne said. "What about Miranda?"

"Haven't seen her in months," he said. He didn't sound concerned. "Not since Fourth of July. Sometime around then."

Anne's knees turned to water. She sat down hard on the couch. "That's two months ago," she said when she found her voice. "Has anybody called the police?"

The boy shrugged. "I haven't, and they haven't been around, so I guess nobody else has either."

Anne stared incredulously at him. "Two months?"

"Look, I'm just her freaking neighbor." The boy sounded annoyed again. "I feed her cat when she's not around. She leaves a window open, the thing comes and goes on the fire escape. A couple of months ago, I start to hear it meowing on my windowsill, like, constantly. So I put some food out, like I said."

Anne was silent.

"We're not really friends or anything. We play video games sometimes." He gave her a concerned look. "Jesus, are you sure you don't want something to drink? You don't look good."

"You just told me that my daughter has been missing for two months." Anne, who felt like somebody had just pumped her veins full of frozen gasoline, didn't care how the words sounded. "How should I look?"

"Well, I don't know about *missing*," the boy said hastily. "I mean, she hasn't been here. But I don't think she's *missing*, like milk-carton missing."

"You feed her cat," Anne said.

"Dillinger."

It took a minute for Anne to realize that this was the cat's name. "Then you must have keys to her apartment."

"Sure I do." His eyes narrowed. "You're really her mom?"

Anne reached into her purse and removed her driver's license. She handed it to the boy without a word.

"Arizona," he said, after examining it for a moment, and Anne nodded. He gave her the keys and said, with false chivalry, "I'd better go with you." The look in his eyes was suddenly too interested. She half expected him to say, *What if she's dead in there? What if she's gross?*

To which Anne would reply that she had seen dead people before, which was true. And at least then Miranda wouldn't be missing.

This time, as Anne stood alone in front of Miranda's door, her imaginings of what she would find behind the battered industrial steel were far different. Broken glass, overturned tables — and in some dark corner, slumped against the wall —

Or emptiness. The boy had said that the landlord required six months' advance payment, because the sort of people who lived in the building tended to leave without warning. Maybe Miranda had decided to move on, and Anne would open the door to see a nearly empty apartment, full of the sparse echoes of an unfurnished room but nothing else. That, she supposed, would be the best-case scenario. That was what she should hope for.

But abandoning a cat: it didn't sound like Miranda. A mother, an apartment, yes; a cat, no. Miranda had always been the kind of person who preferred animals to people.

The key turned. The door opened. The apartment faced away from the setting sun, and the space beyond was dark. She braced herself and took a deep breath.

Stale air. Abandonment. Nothing.

Anne felt on the wall for a light switch. Her groping fingers found the lever and flipped it up, causing bright white light to flood the apartment.

It was ugly. All the furniture looked as if it had come from a discount store, but that wasn't the problem. The problem lay deeper than that. The stained tan carpet and the chalky paint on the walls — Cheap Landlord White, the color of poverty — made the room look hopeless, depressing. The air smelled faintly like unwashed laundry and faintly like cigarettes and not really like either. Anne knew that smell, knew it permeated the walls and the drywall and the concrete of the foundation. It was the smell of desperation, and it didn't matter if the walls were painted a soothing sage green and the cheap wall-to-wall was replaced with hand-hewn bamboo; while the building stood, the smell would stay.

Anne recognized some of Miranda's things. The plaster skull on the coffee table came from a comic book convention that Miranda had attended in high school; the cheap metal goblet next to it had been given to her by one of her role-playing friends. Other items were unfamiliar, like the afghan lying in a heap on the couch and the faux medieval, screen-printed tapestry on the wall. Miranda had made only a cursory effort to bring life to the space. Anne tried to imagine coming home to this place every day, walking down the grimy, ill-lit hallway and then opening this door and entering this room.

She shook her head and began searching for signs of her daughter. In the refrigerator she found old eggs, a plastic bag of liquefying spinach, and a hard chunk of orange cheese with furry mint-green mold spread over it like moss. The milk had expired on the first of July, and if the neighbor was telling the truth had been outdated even before Miranda had vanished. The shelves in the door held ketchup, olives, soy sauce, and about half a dozen bottles of beer. In the bathroom, a toothbrush and an overflowing makeup bag sat on the counter. There was a second toothbrush in the medicine cabinet, along with a razor and shaving cream. So Miranda had a boyfriend.

The bedroom contained an unmade double bed, a taped cardboard box serving as a night table, and a white pressboard dresser with an attached mirror. Piles of clothes dotted the floor, and three empty glasses rested on top of the cardboard box, their insides coated with the faint scum left by evaporating water. A flat pink disk of birth control pills sat next to them. The prescription had been filled in June — there were two re-fills left — and seven days' worth of the pill slots were empty.

If Miranda had left town, she had done it without her tooth-brush, makeup, cat, or pills. It seemed unlikely.

On the mirror, Anne found a photograph stuck between the frame and the glass. The picture had been taken at a party or a bar, and the three people in it were all holding bottles of beer. Sitting on the right was a girl wearing a blue T-shirt and the wrong shade of pink lipstick. On the left was a big man with a blond goatee and one arm thrown possessively over the shoulders of the girl in the middle.

With a shock, Anne realized that the one in the middle was Miranda. Her hair, which had been long and dyed candy-apple red the last time Anne had seen her, seemed to be blond, and either pulled back or cut brutally short; she wore thick black eyeliner and a red tank top. Both straps of her black bra slipped down her shoulders, one strap resting against the dark tattoo encircling her upper left arm. She and her two friends all wore the same blurry, drunken leer, but on Miranda it looked confrontational, reckless.

It was the only photograph Anne could find of her daughter. It was the one she took with her to the police station.

• • •

34

Romansky, the detective, had the same closed-off, exasperated expression as every cop Anne had ever met, but he treated Anne kindly. He brought her coffee in a paper cup and took notes on a yellow legal pad while she told him about Miranda, writing down Miranda's name, address, and description — although there wasn't much Anne could give him in that regard, besides Miranda's height, identifying scars, and other permanent information. He took a long look at the photo Anne had brought, and wrote down *Fourth of July*.

Then he said, "Does she have a job?"

Anne admitted that she didn't know.

Romansky nodded. "Boyfriend?"

"I think so, but I don't know his name."

"And you don't know if she's been having money problems, or if she might have gone to visit a friend."

"For two months?" Anne asked in disbelief.

Romansky laid down his pencil.

"Forgive me for pointing this out," he said, "but you don't seem to know much about your daughter."

Anne felt her face grow hot. "Is your life perfect, detective?"

He smiled. "Far from it. But you have to understand that it's not illegal for an adult to move without telling anyone. That building where your daughter lives, it's —" He grimaced. "I don't want to say notorious. But it's not exactly the kind of place you make a home for yourself in."

"She left her *cat*," Anne said.

"I understand that, but —"

"My daughter once spent the night in a sleeping bag in our front yard because there was a stray kitten underneath the car," she said, swallowing the frustration that was building slowly inside her. "My daughter would no more leave a cat behind than she would leave her own arms behind."

"People change." His voice was gentle, and he spoke very slowly and calmly.

"People change," Anne said, trying to be equally slow and calm, "but they don't turn into teakettles. I lived with my daughter for eighteen years, Detective. Maybe I don't know where she works, but I know *her*, and I am telling you that she would not have abandoned her cat." Anne realized that her fists were clenched. She put her elbows on the table and pressed the heels of her hands into the sockets of her eyes, took a deep breath, and tried to pull herself away from her anger, imagining her body filling with clear, clean light. *I hear footsteps,* she thought. *I hear ringing telephones, and voices calling to each other. I feel the floor under my feet, the hard plastic chair that I am sitting on, the cold air from the vent above my head. I smell cigarette smoke and old coffee and bureaucracy and people who are* not *being helpful —*

She opened her eyes. The detective hadn't moved. The expression on his face was impassive but not unfriendly. "Are you okay?" he said quietly, and Anne suddenly felt very tired.

"No," she said. "I'm not okay. I came here to see my daughter and I can't find her. But I'm sorry I yelled at you."

"Well, that is the first time I've ever heard anybody make the word *teakettle* sound like an obscenity," he said, "but if it's the worst thing that happens to me today I'll still be pretty lucky."

She forced herself to smile. "That's a wise philosophy."

"Philosophy?" Detective Romansky laughed. "I guess so. I've always thought of it as more of a defensive strategy. No matter how bad you think it is, it could be worse."

She shook her head. "Sometimes it can't be. Sometimes it's as bad as it gets."

The detective didn't answer. When he spoke again, there was an air of finality to his words, and Anne knew that the interview was over. "I have to tell you," he said, "there's a strong chance that I'm not going to be able to do much to help you. I'll do what I can, but our chances of finding anything out about your daughter —" Anne's feelings must have showed on her face, because he stopped talking and sighed. "I'm just being honest."

He could have been less honest, Anne thought. "Well, what can you do?"

"I can run your daughter's particulars through our databases

36

— incident reports, motor vehicle registrations, that kind of thing — and see if we get any hits. I can also run a quick DMV search; maybe she's got a driver's license with a newer address on it. Other than that, the fact that nobody reported her missing seems to indicate to me that her friends" — he tapped the photograph with one finger — "aren't that concerned about her, which seems to indicate to me that there's no foul play involved." He shrugged. "She probably just moved on. Where are you staying?"

Anne hadn't gotten that far. "Can I stay in her apartment?"

"If you clear it with her landlord, sure, but not until we take a look at it."

"In case it's a crime scene?" Anne said, and immediately wished that she hadn't.

"Just — in case," he said.

In the month following Nick's death, Anne's grief is like a huge black ball of tar that she can barely hold on to with both arms, pressing her chin into the top of the bolus to keep it contained, but she has not yet entered the crushing depression from which Agnes will yank her. For now she is deeply immersed in Nick's month-old death, in trying to trace it, confirm it, deny it.

She calls Western Mountain.

What happened to my husband?

Poor Mrs. Cassidy. The calm female voice on the other end of the phone wants to tell her again on behalf of Western Mountain Aviation how sorry they all are about her husband. He was a good man. He'll be missed.

What happened to my husband's plane?

There's no way to know that, Mrs. Cassidy, without examining the aircraft. Which, as has no doubt been explained to you, is unrecoverable.

What happened to my husband?

He was on a supply run: sheet metal and pipe fittings (four and a quarter, copper, gasline approved) for renovation of Western Mountain's Panama City facility.

What happened to my husband's plane?

Western Mountain doesn't know, because Western Mountain's Panama City facility simply doesn't have the resources for that kind of large-scale marine search operation. The purpose of our Panama City facility is to provide a base of operations for our Central American programs, which include cargo services, personnel training and transport, and contract flying.

What happened to my husband?

If you'd like more information about Western Mountain Aviation's Central American programs, we'd be happy to send you out a prospectus. The new one just arrived in our offices. Shall we send one out to you?

Anne will not be stopped. She begins to call lawyers, trying to find somebody who will initiate any kind of legal action against Western Mountain: negligence, or some sort of safety violation. The first two, whose names she pulled out of a phone book, are initially enthusiastic and promise to investigate the situation further. Both of them call back the next day and say that there is nothing they can do.

The third, referred to her by a paralegal friend, is a pilot-turned-lawyer who specializes in aviation cases. His offices are in downtown Pittsburgh. Anne meets him there in September, when the air is just beginning to cool. But as soon as he hears the words *Western Mountain* he tells her that he is sorry, but he can't help her. "You're probably tired of being lied to," he says, "so I'll be straight. You're not going to find anybody who's willing to go up against Western Mountain. They're untouchable."

Anne asks how that can be.

The lawyer sighs. "Your husband — he was, what, Marine Corps? Navy?"

Marine, Anne says.

"He spent time in Southeast Asia, right? Got an honorable discharge and went civilian not long after he got there, and since then he's been all over the world. Africa, Central America, the Middle East — probably even flew some brushfires out west every once in a while, didn't he?"

Anne can only nod.

"Different company every time, but always seemed to work with the same guys. And I bet you never really knew what he was doing, did you?"

Feeling slightly dizzy, Anne asks what the lawyer thinks Nick was doing.

"For Western Mountain?" He shrugs. "If I had to hazard a guess, I'd say government contracts, although not the kind that Boeing is bidding on. But that's just a guess. Could be anything." He puts a slight emphasis on the *anything*, and Anne wonders through her daze exactly what he means by *government*.

He continues. "Outfits like Western Mountain fish in some pretty dark water. If I were you, I wouldn't look too closely. I know that's hard to hear," he adds, more gently. "And I'm truly sorry for you and your daughter. If a guy wants to live that life, that's his own decision. But he's got no right bringing anybody else along with him."

Finally, frustrated, Anne calls Herb Rushin, the only person from Western Mountain she has ever spoken with besides Nick and X-Ray and the other pilots. What the lawyer said had been accurate; the pilots did always seem to be the same, no matter how many times Nick changed jobs. But Rush she knows only as a voice on the other end of the phone, full of an avuncular cheerfulness that feels somehow thin and brittle. When he called the house for Nick, he rarely said more to her than *Hey, Annie, Nick around?* Sometimes he called Nick *our boy,* as if Nick were a project that the two of them were working on together. As if they shared him.

But when she speaks to Rush on the phone after Nick's death, the brittle cheer is gone. His tone is frank and honest as he explains that there is nothing he can tell her because no further information is available. Frankly, nobody knows exactly where or why Nick went down; honestly, nobody will ever know. By the end of the conversation, it is abundantly clear that during whatever mysterious training Rush has received in his capacity as Western Mountain's lead pilot, there was a whole unit on frank and honest.

"You're lying," Anne says.

Evenly, he answers, "I'm sorry to hear you feel that way."

"What if I came down there and sat in your office? What if I refused to leave until you told me what I wanted to know?"

"You're welcome to give it a shot. But it won't make a difference. Not if you sit there till Christmas."

There is a pause, during which Rush waits and Anne tries to fight through her anger and find the one thing she can say that will make a difference, the key phrase that will unlock a gate in the giant stone wall she is facing.

"I just want to know," she finally says in desperation. "He was my husband. Don't I have a right to know?"

"Generally, our men don't get married," Rush says. "We discourage it. This is why." There is something different in his voice now. Incredibly, it seems to be reproach, as if it were her fault that Nick is dead. As if all of this happened because she forced her way into Nick's life.

"How dare you," she says.

"I'm just calling it like I see it," Rush says. Frankly, honestly. "You might see things differently."

three

T HE ONLY MOTEL in Rachetsburg was part of a national chain. Anne's room was decorated with a floral bedspread and bland landscape paintings. She knew that, like Miranda's apartment, it would never feel like anything other than a holding cell.

If Miranda is dead, the person who killed her might some- day be in a holding cell, she thought, and then, in answer, *Not if nobody bothers to look for him, he won't.* It was the kind of thought that had been occurring to her fairly steadily since she'd left the police station.

What had she wanted? She supposed she had wanted the kind of full-scale search that she had seen on television, with sensitive, dedicated people working long hours to find her daughter: canvassing local bars, interviewing waitresses, show- ing pictures of Miranda to people on the street, and follow- ing leads toward an inevitable conclusion. Failing that, she had expected posters. News stories. Anything. Instead she had the anonymous motel room, with its sterile smell and rattling air conditioner, and a very nice detective who thought her daughter had just "moved on."

Anne forced herself to consider that he might be right; maybe Miranda had just moved to Cleveland or Altoona or Janesville. But the thought rang hollow, and did not comfort her.

Somehow she slept. When she woke up the next morning, she pulled aside the drapes that covered the room's window and looked out onto the parking lot. The glare of sun on asphalt hurt her eyes. There was no real horizon to speak of here — no rugged mountains, no towering clouds — and in the tiny cup that was left of the world everything seemed small and cramped. Across the asphalt, Anne could see the other wing of the motel and a housekeeper in a pale blue smock pushing a cart down the sidewalk in front of the room doors. From this distance the girl looked young, her hair a mixture of blond and hot pink. Anne thought of Miranda.

Just try to relax, Detective Romansky had said. *We'll call you as soon as we have anything.*

But Anne could not relax.

Romansky called late that afternoon, while Anne was watching TV and eating sunflower seeds from a plastic packet (they were the closest thing to real food that she'd been able to find at the gas station). As he'd expected, he said, he hadn't found any solid leads in Miranda's apartment. If Anne wanted to, and the building's manager acquiesced, she could stay there. The manager's phone number was in Miranda's address book. Romansky gave it to her.

Anne asked if he'd taken anything other than the address book, and he said, "Not much. Some pay stubs, a phone bill. That kind of thing."

"She had a job, then."

"Yeah." In the background, she heard the rustle of paper. "She worked at Boylan Distribution, did something hourly. They're pretty much the only thing going around here."

The managing company, when she called them, didn't object to Anne taking over Miranda's apartment. It was, as De-

42

tective Romansky had said, not the kind of building where people made homes for themselves, and the management was prepared for sudden, unannounced vacancies. "Six months' up front," the woman who answered the phone said. "No exceptions. Your daughter is only a month behind." Then, almost as if it were an afterthought, she added, "I hope she's all right. We get a lot of people who skip out, but nobody ever comes looking for them."

Anne thanked her, promised to make good on Miranda's back rent, and hung up. She made one more call, to the phone company to pay Miranda's bill and have service restored. Then she picked up her car keys and went to find Boylan Distribution.

She found it easily — the man behind the counter at the gas station gave her directions — but the twin glass doors leading into the long, low building were locked. So she drove back to her daughter's apartment, to live with her daughter's cheap furniture and her daughter's plaster skull. She put the skull in a cupboard as soon as she got there. There was enough death inside her head, and she didn't need it staring at her, in bad reproduction, from the coffee table.

She wondered if Miranda had ever looked at the skull and thought about the skin that should have covered it, the brain that should have been living inside it. Nick once brought a machete home from Central America, a long nasty-looking thing that was somehow nastier for its crudity: there had been no grace in the uneven chopping blade or the rough hilt. It was meant to cut and hack and kill. Anne overheard Nick proudly telling his friend X-Ray that he had given a guerrilla six Hershey bars for it. (She asked him later where in the world he had met a guerrilla, and he'd just said, "It's Central America, Annie. Can't swing a dead cat without hitting a homegrown militia.") He had never seemed worried about what the machete had done, where the blade had been.

As Anne searched her daughter's apartment aimlessly for some clue, some anything that the police had missed, she wondered if Miranda was a danger junkie, like her father had been. The last time Anne had lived with her, Miranda had been a teenager — angry most of the time, unhappy a lot of the time, and frustrated pretty much all of the time. Anne remembered feeling that Miranda had seemed more impatient with adolescence than her friends. For instance, during their senior year, Miranda and a few of her friends had decided they wanted tattoos. Anne had been the first parent to volunteer to go to the studio with her kid and sign the required consent form — she'd been fairly proud of it, really — but Miranda hadn't thanked her, just groused at a slightly increased volume about the unfairness of a world where she didn't even have control over her own skin.

So now Miranda was an adult. She had control over her own skin and everything else; how did she use it? What had happened to that old impatience? Did she drive too fast, drink too much, as Nick had? Did she always have to push just a little harder, the way he had? If she and her friends went skiing (did they go skiing?) was she always the last one out, racing down black-diamond runs in the dark while her friends drank cocoa in the lodge? Because Nick had done that, and more: rappelling, caving, skydiving, hang-gliding. She used to joke about it — half joke, really — *If there's a chance he'll die doing it, it's Nick's new favorite hobby.*

Before Miranda was born, he and Anne had traveled to California to visit X-Ray, who was flying out of El Toro. While they were there, Nick and X didn't just go surfing: they went surfing on the beaches with the heaviest surf, the biggest rocks, the most shark attacks. Anne had watched from the parked Jeep with her heart in her mouth. Nick only laughed. "If you worry when I'm twenty feet from shore," he said, "how the hell do you deal with me being twenty thousand feet from the ground?"

"I don't think about it," she'd answered. Lying, of course, since she dealt with it by waking up in the middle of the night to wonder sleepily where he was, what he was doing. Was he sleeping, drinking a beer, playing cards? Was he flying? Was the

44

view from his cockpit beautiful, with clear skies overhead and moonlit jungle below? Was he watching the stars, happy to be alive, happy to be himself?

And then she would wonder if there were thunderstorms that night, where he was, if lightning would strike his plane. Was this moment the one when Nick realized that his landing gear wouldn't come down? Was it five minutes from now? Would she know, would she sense it, when his plane hit the ground?

As it turned out, she hadn't. Then, as now, she had continued blissfully living her life for more than twenty-four hours after he was due to return and didn't; she had not felt the increased peril in the world until X had called her to tell her Nick was gone.

She hadn't known when Miranda vanished either. Perhaps this was because Romansky was right, she thought, and Miranda had just moved on. Maybe she had felt no horror because there was no horror to feel.

Anne found Miranda's makeup bag. No pink lipstick for this girl: Miranda's war paint sparkled. It shone. It glittered, splendid with illogical colors rarely found in nature and never on the unadorned human body. Not even Miranda would have worn the metallic purple lipstick out on a weekday, Anne thought; and in truth, none of the wild stuff looked like it had been used much. She imagined Miranda standing in front of the mirror, wrapped in a towel, admiring her glittering purple lips. Then wiping the lipstick off. Taking a shower in the chipped, rust-stained bathtub.

Anne tried the lipstick on. It felt as if her mouth were coated in school glue, and her lips instantly began to itch, so she quickly washed it off. Then, for lack of anything better to do, she turned on the television, and suddenly the room filled with loud electronic music. Grim red letters blazed on the screen: WANT TO RUN AND HIDE?

Video games. Miranda loved them. She had quit this one and turned off the television without turning off the game system, and in game time that had happened only an instant ago. The controller lay on the floor where Miranda had dropped it, covered in a thin layer of dust. Anne picked it up. The screen offered her two choices: *Yes, I'm a crybaby* and *No, I can take it.* Anne thought she was probably a crybaby, but she picked the other one anyway.

And then the music changed and she was back in the game — back in Miranda's game, in fact, maybe even from the day she disappeared. The screen showed a dark warehouse piled high with boxes, in one corner a tiny image of a man so heavily armored that only the shape of his body implied that he was human. Anne played with the controls, causing him to move back and forth and brandish his gun (which looked like nothing so much as a lethal vacuum cleaner) and launch bright explosive missiles into the electronic distance, where Anne could see another mechanized armor-man running toward her with his own vacuum cleaner uplifted. Anne pressed another button. The approaching man exploded. A nearly photographic representation of a human arm flew toward the screen, spurting blood from its severed end.

Anne, shocked, dropped the controller and turned the machine off. On the floor next to the television she found the game's case, the words *Hollow Point 4: Deep Cover* printed in faux military stencils across the top. *Nobody knows you're here,* the copy on the back said. *Nobody will know if you succeed. If you fail, nobody will claim your body. You have one directive: DON'T FAIL.*

"Spear of Everlasting Doom scores eighty-three hit points, Mom," Miranda says cheerfully. "You're dead."

She doesn't look particularly troubled by this news. In fact, she looks happier than Anne has seen her in weeks. Out of the corner of her eye, Anne is vaguely aware that Miranda's three friends, Jayce and Michelle and Glen, are suddenly staring at the floor in the awkward, don't-notice-me way of teenagers caught in a room with a hostile parent who's not their own. Crouched on her daughter's bedroom floor among the litter of dirty clothes and paperbacks with dragons on the covers, she meets her daughter's gaze.

Miranda is fifteen. Her hair is too long and usually unkempt, the same dark shade as Nick's. Pink acne mottles her skin and makes Anne feel guilty; it's her genetic legacy, after all, along with the hay fever that Miranda suffers from every spring. From Nick she has inherited the film-star hair, oversized ears, and a uniquely disdainful twist of the eyebrow. Once, annoyed at yet another swollen, painful pimple on her chin, Miranda asks Anne if she and Nick bothered to send anything good down the genetic line. Anne points out the long, thick eyelashes and heart-shaped face that she herself sees in the mirror, and the strong cheekbones and good vision that were Nick's. Miranda only twists her eyebrow.

But Miranda is more than just an amalgam of her parents. Anne has never ceased to be amazed by this. When she was pregnant, she imagined their still mostly hypothetical baby on good days as a perfect combination of the best things about its parents, and on bad days as a nightmare mix of the worst. Miranda was something else entirely, from her first cry in the delivery room. Anne's eyelashes, Nick's cheekbones — but the angry spark in her eyes is all Miranda. It always has been.

These, Anne knows, are what Miranda will think of in later life as her awkward years, when she is trying to bring together a body and mind that haven't quite sorted themselves out, let alone learned to work together. But as Miranda, sitting cross-legged on the floor with her friends, surrounded by the game's paper maps and miniature monsters, stares frankly at her mother — who has just been killed by an unfortunate confluence of a Spell of Fixing and the Spear of Everlasting Doom — the spark is still there.

"But don't I roll?" Anne wants to know, the bright blue die with the impossible number of sides cupped in the palm of her hand. "I thought he rolled and I rolled."

"You can, Mrs. Cassidy," says Jayce, the kid with the master's guide, which is stained with salsa and Coke and other substances that Anne doesn't want to know about. "But there's no way you could save for more than fifty-eight hit points. And since you've only got sixty-three points to begin with, you'd still lose." He is the one controlling the game, the one who decided that the Black Sorcerer would cast the Spell of Fixing just as the Ice Wizard threw the Spear of Everlasting Doom. His full name is Jayce Travis Cooper. It's a stupid name, Anne thinks; a stupid cowboy name. His mother should have known better.

"You were doomed from the start," Miranda says. "The Ice Wizard is level ten. You're level one. The multipliers are different, see?" This from a girl who can barely manage a C in algebra. "Plus, you're only a Wood Elf. A level-one Wood Elf has no chance against a level-ten Ice Wizard."

"Even without the Black Sorcerer or the Spell of Fixing," Jayce agrees. "Now, when I play, I'm an orc. A level-one orc would have a chance at winning that battle."

Goddamned cowboy orc, Anne thinks. *With your goddamned Spear of Everlasting Doom.* "So basically, what you're saying is that you set me up," she said. "There was no way to win."

The kids are squirming — they'd set her up, all right — and all at once she regrets ever knocking on Miranda's door. But she'd wanted to know exactly what went on in Miranda's bedroom every Friday night until midnight, and why when the four kids came out for chips and salsa, they called each other things like Loran of the Red Forest and Gleth-Toth the Invincible. One of them — she suspects that it is Gleth-Toth the Invincible, whose foolish mother knows him as Glen — sometimes fills the dry-erase board on the refrigerator with intricately gory cartoon depictions of the night's adventures, inscrutable speech bubbles floating near the characters' mouths: *Where's my Frost Sword?* or *Not another Fire Golem!* Anne doesn't get any of it, and the not-getting-it is a lonely, helpless feeling. So she had asked to play. Miranda rolled her eyes but said yes.

And now she, Anne, is dead, and Loran of the Red Forest — known in more mundane planes of existence as Miranda Cassidy — is standing over her imaginary corpse with bright, lively eyes and a satisfied smile.

Nick would have liked the game, Anne thinks. It is easy for

her to imagine him crouching next to Miranda, watching intently and occasionally whispering advice in her ear. The kids would have liked him, too. They wouldn't have sent him into a battle he couldn't win.

Jayce finally breaks the silence. "That's what makes the game good. It's so real."

"Well, what happens when one of you guys dies?" Anne asks, frustrated.

"Then you make up a new character," Miranda says. "Keeps the game interesting." She opens her bedroom door and stares at Anne, the expression on her face clearly saying, *Are we through here?*

"Thanks for letting me play," Anne says to the kids still sitting on the floor — *Thanks for nothing,* she thinks, not sure why she is so annoyed — and then rises and leaves. She is not entirely surprised when Miranda follows her, closing the door behind her so the two are standing alone in the hallway.

"Satisfied?" the girl says, her voice low but angry and bitter. "You've embarrassed the living shit out of me. Congratulations."

Exasperated, Anne glares back. "I just wanted to see what you guys do in there all night. I wanted to see what it was about. You could have just said no," she adds. "You didn't have to kill me."

Miranda's face is like a door slammed shut. "Don't try to be my friend, Mom. It's pathetic when you try to be my friend."

Then the door — the real, actual door — does slam shut, and Anne is on the wrong side of it.

There was a cat watching Anne through the window, a big tom with gray and white tuxedo markings. When he saw her looking back at him his mouth opened, and she heard a faint caterwaul through the glass. She opened the window. The cat slid through like smoke, leaping down onto the floor by way of the end table that he clearly knew would be there. He began to twine joyfully through Anne's legs, a loud, rickety purr emanating from his throat.

Anne leaned over to scratch his ears. The fur on his back

was the rich, solid gray of wet concrete. "You must be Dill-inger," she said.

The cat rubbed a fierce figure eight around her ankles, looked up at her with pale green eyes, and meowed plaintively. His back arched receptively beneath her hand when she stroked it, and she could feel the vibration of his purr through his thick coat.

When she stood up, the cat darted past her into the small kitchenette. She found him sitting next to a bowl painted with a cartoon mouse, staring pointedly up at one of the cupboards. Anne smiled. "I get it," she told him, and filled his bowl with the food she found in the cabinet. Then she sat down on the kitchen floor to watch him attack his meal with gusto.

"You eat like Livingston used to," she told Dillinger, and then remembered that Livingston, back in Sedona, had once been Miranda's cat, too. The cat kept eating and Anne's eyes filled with tears.

She stood up, dashed them away, and called Nick's mother. An unfamiliar female voice answered the phone.

"Is this Agnes?" Anne asked.

"Agnes is asleep," the woman said. "I'm the home nurse, Roberta. Who's this?"

"Anne." Agnes had turned sixty a year before Nick died. Martin had thrown a banquet in her honor, a catered affair with tacky, baroque, silver-plated bud vases filled with hya-cinths — Agnes's favorite flower — at every plate. Agnes had offered Anne several of the vases afterward, and she hadn't been brave enough to refuse them; she'd thrown them away when she and Miranda moved to the dingy townhouse. Nick hadn't attended the party. He'd been flying. Anne and Miranda had gone alone and played lines and boxes for three hours straight. If that had been Agnes's sixtieth, she must be in her early eighties now, Anne thought. The home nurse made sense. "I'm sorry," Anne said. "It's been a very long time. I —" She stopped, unsure how to put it. "I was married to Agnes's son. Is she doing well?"

"You're Miranda's mother?" the nurse asked. There was something strange in her voice.

50

"Yes," Anne said, "and I'm trying to find her. Have you and Agnes heard from her lately?"

There was a long silence on the other end of the phone. Finally the nurse said, "We haven't seen Miranda since last Christmas." Her tone indicated that Miranda hadn't been missed.

For lack of any better response, Anne said, "Oh."

"She showed up on Christmas Eve," Roberta continued. "Asking for money. Agnes is a sick old woman. She doesn't need that kind of aggravation. I told her not to come back. If you're looking for money, too —"

Anne felt her anger rise. *Deep breaths. Calm breaths.* "I'm not here for money. I haven't asked Agnes Cassidy for money — for anything — in twenty years. Why would I start now?"

"I'm sure you're a perfectly decent person," Roberta said. "And I'm sorry to say this, you being her mother and all, but I believe in telling people the truth. That's just the way I am."

Anne hung up and glared at the phone as if it were broken, as if that was why the conversation hadn't gone better.

And then it came to her.

Telephones. Telephone messages.

Hey, it's me. You know what to do.

Messages. Miranda's voice mail had been full when Anne had tried to call from Sedona. Which meant that it was full now, wasn't it? When she'd called Agnes, she had been too busy to notice if the message signal had been working, but when she picked up the phone this time, the quick staccato beat that came before the dial tone told her she was right. She made a guess, called Miranda's own number — *Hey, it's me* — and hit the star key, which was how the voice mail system at the bookstore worked. This one worked the same way.

"Please enter your passcode," the voice said.

When Miranda was in high school and had opened her first bank account, she and Anne had used the same code for their ATM cards: 6284. June 2, 1984. The day Nick died. Anne still used the same four numbers. Perhaps Miranda did, too. She keyed them in.

"You have fourteen new messages," the voice said. "Press one to hear your new messages."

Hope bloomed in Anne. With a trembling hand, she pressed one, and she heard a long, tuneless beep.

Anne felt, as she listened to the messages, that she was living the last days of her daughter's life in this apartment. The cold female voice of the mail system was her ghost of Christmas past, reciting dates and times before each recorded human voice.

"Monday," the Voice said. "July. Seventh."

The first message is from somebody named Kim, calling to see why Miranda isn't at work yet; she calls Miranda *Andy,* as her neighbor had, and says that Dave's in a managers' meeting, so Andy should try to get to work before it's over, okay?

The next message is from Dave, twenty minutes later, his voice managerial and disappointed. Miranda was supposed to be there at nine. He presumes she's on her way. They talked about this, he says. He now sees that he was just wasting his time.

There are more messages: Kim again (Dave sure is mad) and again (she hasn't ever *seen* Dave this mad). In Kim's fourth message, she reported that she heard Dave on the phone, and she thinks he was talking to Human Resources. She thinks Miranda is out of a job.

The next is from a young man, clearly unaware of the day's drama. "It's Jay," he says, calling Miranda "babe," and asks if she wants to grab some food later, maybe a beer.

Listening to the message from Mary Sue Kowalski, from Boylan Distribution's Human Resources Department, Anne — who was by now thoroughly caught in this day from her daughter's past — found herself worrying, even though whatever happened to Miranda had nothing to do with Mary Sue Kowalski. Even though losing her job would seem to have been the least of Miranda's problems. Mary Sue's voice, as she points out that July seventh is Miranda's third unexcused absence in six months, is pleasant and blank. Anne wondered if the woman enjoyed her job.

"Tuesday. July. Eighth," the voice tells her.

That day began for Miranda's answering machine at 10:10

in the morning, when Mary Sue Kowalski calls again to tell Miranda that she is fired — except Mary Sue says *let go* — for excessive absenteeism. Kim calls that afternoon, because she has heard through the grapevine about Miranda's job. Getting fired sucks. And what's with her and Jay? Miranda hasn't called her either. She's not mad about something, is she?

That night, Jay calls to see if she got his message about dinner. Is she still pissed off about Saturday? She should call him, or whatever. Later he calls back. What is this crap, he wants to know, some sort of silent treatment? He calls Miranda a bitch and says that he doesn't need this and he sure as hell doesn't need her.

Then almost forty-eight hours passed in an instant of silence, and only Anne knew that those were hours when her daughter was missing.

"Thursday. July. Tenth."

Kim breaks the silence at nine that night. The girl asks what the hell Miranda's problem is, and goes on to say that this whole silent treatment thing is just *not* cool. "You know, Andy," she finishes, "you keep treating your friends like this, you're going to run out of friends." Anne fought the urge to scream.

"Friday. July. Eleventh. Nine. Forty-five. P.M."

There are voices and music in the background. Jay says he's sorry for calling Miranda a bitch. He was just mad. He drove by her place after work today, but her car wasn't there. He's at the Strike. He wants to buy her a beer. Call him.

"Saturday. July. Twelfth. Three. Thirty-two. A.M."

The bar noises are gone. Jay is extremely drunk.

"Hey, cunt," he says. "Just wanted to let you know, I'm not at the Strike anymore. I'm back at my place, and I'm not alone, bitch." To someone else in the room, he says, "Say hi to the cunt, will you?"

A female voice in the background squeals, "Hi, cunt!" And Jay says, "That's all, Andy. Just wanted you to know I'm home and I'm fucking this girl. I'm fucking her — right — now. How do you — like that?"

The drunk girl laughs and moans loudly, cartoonishly. Jay says, "You can — go to hell — Andy. Go — right — to fucking — hell."

"End of messages."

"Call her voice mail. That's her code," Anne said, throwing the scrap of paper onto Detective Romansky's desk. Her eyes were blazing, and the detective division, which Romansky shared with two other men, was filled with an unearthly animal howl coming from the cat carrier in Anne's left hand. She jabbed a finger at the paper. "His name is Jay. They had some sort of fight, and then she never came home, she never went to work, and nobody ever heard from her again."

Detective Romansky picked up the paper. Looked at Anne. Looked at the paper.

"Jay who?" he said, and Anne shook her head.

"Find him," she said. "He killed my Miranda."

The detective opened his mouth to speak, and Anne shook her head again. "No," she said. Her voice was trembling. "His name is Jay. *Find* him."

She reached a hand behind her. Fortunately, there was a chair there. Anne felt her knees go.

Detective Romansky started from his chair, his face concerned, and the cat carrier fell to the floor with a clatter and a yowl.

It is 1984. The end of the world has come.

Anne cannot blink. She cannot breathe. She cannot even cry.

The telephone receiver dangles at the end of a numb hand and then falls. Faintly, she can hear X-Ray on the other end of the line, saying her name, but all of reality has drained away and she expects time to *stop,* just freeze here forever with her on her knees on the kitchen floor because it cannot go back and it cannot get better and, oh god, she cannot go on, she cannot live with this for the rest of her life the rest of her life *the rest of her —*

There is a small sound in front of her.

She looks up, and of course it is Miranda, because that is

how these things work: four-foot-tall Miranda with summer-bleached hair just brushing the tops of her shoulders. Miranda in bright green rain boots and a green army vest with many pockets that Nick bought her. Miranda is staring with Nick's eyes at her mother, who is cowering gray-faced and trembling on the floor.

Her pink child's mouth opens in her sun-kissed child's face. "Mom?"

And Anne's vision is growing blurry and prismatic with tears, so she can barely see Miranda, Miranda who is eight years old, Miranda who is holding some small child's thing against her chest, Miranda who needs to be told that her father is dead.

Anne's own mouth opens.

"Go *away!*" she screams.

And little Miranda jumps. Frightened, little Miranda flees.

Anne continues screaming in the kitchen, wordless, broken. The end of the world has come.

"I was just about to call you," Detective Romansky told Anne gently, over cups of water in the interview room, while Dillinger prowled the corners looking for escape, "because I found your daughter's car in Impound. Picked it up on the ninth of July out on the county thruway — totaled, with the seatbelts locked. No blood. No body. No nothing."

Anne sat quietly for a moment before she spoke. "What does that mean?"

He shook his head. "It means she crashed her car and either walked away or got a ride with somebody." After a moment, when she didn't say anything, he said, "Can I ask you a question?"

She nodded.

He pointed a pencil in the general direction of the cat, now crouched angrily underneath a chair. "Why did you bring the cat?"

"I don't know," she said, and tried to smile. "It seemed like a good idea at the time."

But Anne was lying. She knew exactly why she had brought

the cat to the police station with her: because he had been Miranda's cat. Also because first Miranda had left him, and then her obnoxious neighbor had stopped feeding him, and who knew if cats felt abandonment as keenly as humans? Most of all, though, she had brought him because her panic had made the world feel tenuous and fragile, and she feared that if she let the cat out of her sight, he would disappear without a trace. Like Nick; like Miranda.

II

BURN IT DOWN

four

S HE SAT ON THE DARK BEACH with a beer
between her ankles, cold drops of condensa-
tion dripping down her skin to the sand. Faint music drifted
from the bar on the other side of the boardwalk. She knew the
bar, knew what it was like inside; knew the smells of aftershave
and fruity sweet shampoo mixed with beer and the salt breeze
from the ocean, knew the words to all the silly dance songs
on the jukebox. She knew the rich, chewy texture of the fried
clams the bar offered, a dozen for a dollar on Friday nights
like this one, the sticky alcohol taste of the shooters the waitresses brought around in test tubes and the ebullient crow that
rose from the crowd every time her roommate, Jenny, behind
the bar, convinced another sorority girl to let a stranger lick a
shot of tequila from her navel. She knew these things because
she had been inside ten minutes before, and because it was that
way every weekend.

But out here on the empty beach, that world seemed far

away. Somewhere offshore, a storm raged. The wind was up and flavored with rain, carrying on its currents a sense of hurry, the feel of an impending *something* just over the horizon. When she was a little girl this kind of weather had made her think of movies where something fantastic happens to somebody hopeless: lonely girls and fat boys and daydreamers, who venture out in stormy weather and find the door in the hedge, the magic ring in the gutter, the lost key to the secret attic.

Now she was older and she no longer looked for magic. But nights like this made her feel wistful and expectant, and that was why she was sitting here, as the waves stirred up by the storm crashed down on the sand. She wanted to be out on the beach in the same way that she sometimes wanted to be out in summer cloudbursts, to feel the world happening around her. On a moonless night like this one, the ocean felt like an animal crouching in the darkness — not threatening, just there. The beach was wide and the light from the boardwalk didn't penetrate far onto the sand. Normally half a dozen bonfires burned like signal flares up the beach, outlining the gentle curve of the water's edge against the absolute black, but the coming storm had kept people inside.

She heard the muffled sound of footsteps on the sand.

"What are you doing out here?" He sounded worried.

"Just sitting," she said. "I got tired of being inside."

He dropped down next to her with a soft thump, pulled her beer from between her ankles, and took a long drink. "You know it's not safe to be out here by yourself."

"My first night here, I slept on the beach," she said coolly.

"Yeah, well," he said. "Not on my watch."

She shrugged and took back the bottle. "I can't quite bring myself to worry about being murdered. Psycho killers are like flesh-eating viruses. How many can there really be?"

"It only takes one." He reached for the beer again.

She moved it away. "You know what I heard? I heard this guy likes to kill skinny grad students from New Jersey who drink other people's beer without asking."

"That's funny, because I heard he killed pretty girls who

hang out on the beach by themselves." He put his arm around her and pulled her close. "Maybe I should leave you here. Then when he comes for you, I can rescue you."

His breath on her face was hot. She pulled back. "My fucking hero," she said. Then she stood up and started to brush the sand off the back of her thighs.

He scrambled to his feet next to her. "You want to go?"

"Yeah," Randa answered.

She had met Seth in a bar — not the Clam Shack, across the boardwalk, but another just like it. That had been in late July, just a few weeks after George had picked her up in Pennsylvania and driven her to Virginia, to Lawrence Beach. She no longer remembered who had spoken first, or what they had talked about, but she did remember Seth suddenly leaning over to smell her hair. He had inhaled deeply and with no inhibitions.

"Hey," she'd said, feeling that she ought to protest.

"I like the way your hair smells," he answered. "I know that's a stupid guy line, but I do. Most girl hair smells like candy, or flowers."

"What does mine smell like?" His own hair was dark, deliberately cut to look messy. He wore heavy, dark-framed glasses and a T-shirt with a diet soda logo on it; the soda was long defunct, but the shirt looked new.

He leaned over to inhale again — closer to her ear this time, close enough for her to hear the warm rush of air he drew in. "Crème brûlée," he answered, and she had never heard that one before, so she smiled.

Seth had his uses. He bought her drinks on the boardwalk, cheeseburgers, fried clams. Afterward, they would go to his apartment on England Street — which was too nice for what he made waiting tables, yacht club or no yacht club — play video games, and have sex. Then she would walk back to the motel room she shared with Jenny, or he would drive her there.

Once, early on, he had convinced her to stay the night, promising her breakfast and a ride to work. In the morning he woke up early, brought croissants that she was too hung over to eat and espresso that she couldn't bear to drink, and she lied and said that her shift at the chair-rental place, where she'd worked then, started two hours earlier than it actually did because being around him was making her feel like she was wearing wool underwear. Itchy.

That had been three weeks ago. There were things she still liked about him — his long, lanky arms, the way his shoulders looked under his T-shirts. He was, more than any guy she had been with, genuinely, effusively kind. She wanted to want that. But his kindness came in espresso and croissants; it came in five-disk shuffles of quiet acoustic music that all sounded like the same unending song. It came in questions. *Tell me about your parents, tell me about your childhood, tell me about your life,* he would say, and Randa would itch.

And so she balanced the itch against the niceness of having a someone, the security of going into a bar and knowing that she would not go home alone, knowing exactly whom she would be going home with. She balanced, and she itched, and she waited.

Now they were naked, stretched out across the bed on their stomachs playing Death Prix III on Seth's computer. On the screen, Seth's avatar in the game — a blue cartoon car with a vicious-looking spoiler and oversized tires — suddenly sprouted knives from both its sides. Her red car, which lacked a spoiler but had a shark's grin painted across its digitized front end, was impaled on one of the spikes and disappeared in an electronic fireball.

"Ha," he said. "Gotcha."

She tossed her controller down and rolled over on her back. He reached out to run a hand along her stomach, lingering over the tattooed dragon twining around her navel. She had five tattoos and he liked them, kissing and touching them obsessively while they had sex, as if proving to himself that they were a part of her. In Seth's real life, the nonsummer part that had nothing to do with waiting tables or brushing sand off his sheets so that he could crawl into bed with her, he was a graduate student who read thick books with tiny print and no characters. He taught eighteen-year-olds about Heidegger and Nietzsche. He ate sushi, went skiing in Vermont, and was writing a dissertation about *Being and Time*. She didn't think that any of the girls he knew in that life had dragons tattooed around their bellybuttons.

"I should go home," she said. "I have to work tomorrow." Her clothes lay where she'd thrown them over the one chair in the room. She could feel him watching her as she dressed.

"I wish you'd stay over," he said.

She shook her head. Seth picked up the controller. On the screen, the little blue car reappeared, and the game's electronic music started up again. "You're just mad because you lost," he said. "Come on, let's go again."

Randa reached around her back to fasten her bra. "No."

"At least let me drive you home," he said without looking away from the game.

"I feel like walking." She pulled her tank top over her head and ran her hands through her hair.

"It's not safe," he said, the same dogged refrain. Just because he knew one of the girls whose bodies had turned up on the beach; just because the dead girl had worked in the bar where the yacht club waiters hung out and slept with some guy's brother. Randa doubted that any of them, Seth or his friend or the friend's brother, would have remembered the girl's name if she hadn't been murdered, but now they all recited it like a litany. *April Agostino, age twenty-five, blond hair, blue eyes.* "I said I'll drive you," Seth told her now. "Just let me finish this game."

Randa slipped her feet into her flip-flops and then stepped in front of the screen and stood there until she heard another electronic fireball. "Game over," she said.

Seth rose to his knees so that they were face to face, put his palms flat against her stomach, and then slid them around to her back. "You screwed me up on purpose." He leaned in to kiss her.

She pulled away — the itch was almost unbearable — and said, "Doesn't matter. I'm walking."

"Like hell you are."

"Seth," she said, trying not to grit her teeth. His eyelashes were so long. When they met, she had thought his eyes were pretty. Now, with those pretty eyes gazing at her, she felt like he was a child and she spent all her time fielding constant demands for Band-Aids, a story, more cookies. "I'm going home. You're staying here."

He shook his head. "And waiting for you to wash up dead on the beach tomorrow? No way."

"Christ." She picked up her backpack from the floor and slung it over one shoulder. "People die, you know. It happens all the time."

"Randa," he said. But she kissed him quickly, before the thing in his eyes could make its way to his mouth, and then put a hand on his forehead and pushed gently so that he fell back down to the bed.

"I might not see you tomorrow," she said. "I'm working an extra shift." And she left.

But on her way down the stairs, she decided that she would not see Seth again, ever, and the itchy feeling instantly disappeared.

The boardwalk had always been her favorite part of Lawrence Beach. On that first morning, when she had walked its length with George, he had bought her breakfast, a fruit smoothie and fried dough smothered in powdered sugar. Half delirious with sleeplessness and caffeine and the ocean breeze, she had said that she wanted to stay there forever.

"Why don't you?" he'd said.

And so perhaps that was part of the attraction, because the boardwalk was where her life in Lawrence Beach had officially begun. But she loved it for itself, too. She loved the crying seagulls, the way the washed wood under her feet glowed pale in the sunshine or orange under the streetlights, the smells of saltwater and drying kelp mixed with the fried sweet aroma of boardwalk food. She loved the days, when the boardwalk was all rainbow-colored commerce and good clean fun, and she loved the nights even more, when everything became wilder and faster and further away from reality. The balloon-animal twisters and sidewalk artists shed T-shirts and wacky hats like outgrown skins and revealed heads shaved or dyed in elaborate patterns and unnatural colors, skin pierced and tattooed and branded. The fire breathers used more kerosene; the jugglers switched from bowling pins to power tools. The chalk artists put away the pictures of dolphins and apple-cheeked children and replaced them with portraits of Jimi Hendrix and Tupac Shakur, evil wizards and bare-breasted sorceresses. And night was when the freaks came out — the *real* freaks, the ones with physical customizations they couldn't hide and disturbing tricks involving razor blades and six-inch spikes. Like the guy on Shore and Fifteenth, who had a lizard-ridge implanted under the skin of his forehead; he drove nails through his hands. Not fake nails, either.

Lawrence Beach was perfect. It was exactly the way she wanted it to be. Like that first night, after George had continued on to Langley to do whatever mysterious government thing he said he did, and left her alone. By nightfall she'd found a bar and had a beer and danced with some guy from Maryland. When he'd asked for her name, she'd told him it was Randa, and it had been that easy to step out of one life and into another. Randa had been drifting since high school: she'd drifted into college, drifted out of it again, and spent the five years since drifting from job to job. Staying in Lawrence Beach felt like the first decision she'd made since leaving her mother in Arizona that had mattered. Some people, she thought, lived their whole lives and never did anything that mattered. Lived their whole lives, and died a meaningless unit in a meaningless statistic: car crashes, contaminated ice cream poisoning, elevator-related fatalities, victims of serial killers.

One of the reasons Randa refused to be afraid of the beach killer was that he was ruining her perfect world, and it pissed her off.

As she walked from Seth's apartment to the room she shared with Jenny, she considered April Agostino. Age twenty-five. Blond hair, blue eyes. April's had been the third and most recent body to wash up on the beach that summer. It had started in June, before Randa had arrived in Lawrence Beach. The first corpse was that of a girl who had worked at one of the seafood shacks. She'd been left alone to close down at the end of the night, and that was the last time anybody saw her alive. After they found her body two days later near the pilings by the park, Jenny told Randa that her boss quit letting her close up the bar alone. Which was annoying at first, Jenny said, because she had to share her tips.

The next girl, a chambermaid like Randa, had been found on the Fourth of July. The local newspaper buried the story by the classified ads, trying to keep it away from the tourists, but by the time Randa got to Lawrence Beach a few days after the Fourth, people were nervous. Just nervous. Not scared, at least not until they found April at the end of July. By then, Randa had noticed, Jenny didn't seem to feel so bad about the tips.

Suddenly everybody on the boardwalk was scared. Scared and pretending they weren't, scared and pretending they didn't care, scared and pretending none of it was happening. April and the girl from the seafood shack had been identified as drifters, seasonal workers like Randa without permanent addresses or local family, and the chambermaid hadn't been identified at all. None of the tourists cared; it was a shame, sure, but the dead girls were working, not vacationing, and thus not of their tribe. But somebody had to rent the tourists beach chairs, to sell them snow cones and bus their tables and pour their frozen melon-flavored margaritas. And all the people who did these things were very much of April Agostino's tribe. To the workers, her death was real.

But behind the fear, Randa could feel the real Lawrence Beach in all its low-rent, hedonistic glory. The summer was short, and the places where the worker tribe spent the rest of the year were cold and hopeless. So they drank cheap keg beer and had bonfires on the beach, just as they would have during a normal summer, and everybody on the boardwalk claimed to have known at least one of the dead women, or to have been the last to see her alive, or to have stood on the beach behind the police tape watching the coroner load her body into the van. As Randa had told Seth, people died — it happened all the time — but the murders were so singular, so unexpected, that everybody felt like a part of them, and everybody wanted to be able to stake a claim. *I knew her,* people would say, voices dark with drama. *I saw her, I saw her body. I was there.* Everybody knew that someday the cops would catch the son of a bitch, and they all would have lived through something and come out on the other side. Then, maybe, it would seem worth it.

But Randa, who had more experience than most people with sudden, unexplained death and the havoc that it could wreak on the hearts of the living, didn't indulge. The rush to claim pieces of April's death reminded her of the old theory about maggots growing out of pork chops like trees grew out of acorns — what did they call it? — spontaneous generation. She knew that Seth and his friends hadn't thought twice about April when she was alive, and it seemed like a betrayal of her memory to claim a profound, intimate connection with her now just because she was dead. Randa found it ghoulish, the worst form of armchair quarterbacking, for people to take April's death — which had been lonely and sad, sure, but which had also been something that only April and her killer truly understood — and make it somehow about them. Their fear. Their suffering. Not April's.

In her own way, though, Randa was as morbidly consumed by the murders as everyone else. She walked alone on the boardwalk at night, half congratulating herself on her refusal to be cowed by fear, but men with casts on their arms still made her think of Ted Bundy, and men with glasses of Jeffrey Dahmer. She collected rumors: April's blond hair had been freshly dyed red when she washed up, her nose painted with Magic Marker freckles. She had been wearing clothes that didn't belong to her. The rumors said that all of the bodies had been changed like that post mortem, in cosmetic ways drastic enough to confuse even the mothers flown in from the heartland to identify their dead children. If that was true, Randa wondered, what did April Agostino's family do about her hair when they got her body back home? Did they dye it back the way it had been? Were they able to get the shade exactly right? Or did they just leave it, and hold a funeral for a body they didn't recognize? It was bad enough that your last memory of somebody was of a corpse — worse still to have it be an unfamiliar one.

Randa's route home from Seth's apartment took her inland, away from the ocean. As she walked, the boom of muffled bass from passing cars replaced the roar of the ocean in her ears. It was late now, after midnight, and the discount swimwear shops and liquor stores she passed were closed. Despite the occasional drunken laugh that drifted through the darkness from a hotel room or a bar, the empty streets made her feel lonely. A passing car would probably stop for a person who seemed to be in serious trouble, she thought. All the same, she walked faster.

Randa and Jenny lived in a building called the Oceanside Arms. Once it had been a motel — the empty pool still lay like an abscess in the courtyard, collecting rainwater and dead bugs and empty beer cans — but it had been converted to the cheapest kind of apartments. Their room was just big enough to hold a miniature refrigerator, a hot plate, and a double bed, which the two girls shared. Randa's shift at the motel where she worked lasted from seven in the morning to three in the afternoon, and Jenny worked the bar at Jimmy's Clam Shack from eight at night to four in the morning. When Randa came home from work, she'd wake Jenny up and the two of them would eat pasta or rice or ramen noodles, and then they'd go sit on the beach until it was time for Jenny to go to work. Randa's final meal of the day was often provided by Jenny's unknowing employer: baskets of free chicken wings and barbecued shrimp on Friday or Saturday night, popcorn and packaged snack mix otherwise. Somebody at the bar usually bought her a drink or two. Rarely was it the same person twice.

When Randa opened the door that night, the smell inside the apartment instantly reminded her that the garbage needed to be taken out. She sighed and threw her backpack on the bed without bothering to turn on the light.

68

The bed moaned and mumbled something, of which the only intelligible word was *fuck*. Randa hit the lights.

Jenny lay sprawled sideways across the bed on her stomach. One of her high-heeled sandals lay on the floor, her bare foot dangling over the edge of the bed above it. Her eyes were closed, her lipstick gone, and her hair, carefully styled earlier that night, a tangled mess.

"Didn't think you'd be here," Randa said. "What happened to the guy?"

Jenny opened one bleary eye and managed, after some apparent effort, to focus it on Randa. She smiled faintly. "Cute, huh?"

Randa paused over her friend's nearly inert body. "You okay?"

Jenny was too drunk to talk. She waved a hand. *Yes, fine.* Randa went into the bathroom to wash off her own makeup. When she came out again she had thought of something else. "Where's your car?" she asked, because she didn't like to think of Jenny driving home so drunk.

The girl moaned again. "Took a cab. Geddit tomorrow."

Randa, knowing that the next day Jenny would be hung over and angry about having to walk to work, said, "Is it at the Clam Shack, or —"

Jenny pushed herself upright. "*Randa*. Shut the fuck up and let me sleep."

Randa shrugged. "Move over, then."

But Jenny was already asleep again, her legs still sprawled over Randa's half of the bed. With some effort — Jenny's lax body was heavy and unwieldy — Randa managed to shift the girl until she had room to curl up near the pillows. As she waited for sleep, it occurred to her that whoever had left April Agostino on the beach must have been both strong and patient, to get her dead head into the sink and dye her hair.

The storm blew in sometime during the night and hung sullenly over the town by the next morning. Even the rain falling against the window sounded placid and lifeless. When Randa woke up, Jenny was still asleep, a puddle of drool soaking into the sheets by her head. Randa found a sweatshirt that smelled cleanish, put it on over the pink polyester smock she had to wear to work, and crept out of the room.

By the time she got to the motel — a cheap motel, too far from the beach, called the Pink Pearl — the sweatshirt was soaked through. Tom, the owner, greeted her at the office when she signed in and said, "Wet enough for you?" She thought he was kind of a jerk, but she smiled anyway, because even though the so-called guests were filthy pigs and she got paid crap, this was still the best job she'd ever had. She had been there for almost two and a half weeks. When the phone rang, she didn't have to answer it, and the only people she had to deal with were Tom and sometimes his wife, Angie, whom she saw twice a day at most. She could listen to music while she cleaned, and if she worked quickly enough, she could grab a nap in one of the empty rooms when she was done. She put towels down on the bed first, though. She knew exactly how often the bedspreads were — or weren't — washed.

The work was hard, but all work was hard, and she'd grown used to it. She'd never been much for cleaning before, but she had discovered something satisfying about taking a used motel room — that was how she thought of them, *used* — and erasing its history. Emptying the garbage, rinsing the whiskers out of the sink. She doubted that the rooms she finished with would ever be what you'd technically call clean, but at least they were clean-looking. Sometimes while she worked she thought of the last apartment she'd had, back in Pennsylvania, and wondered if someone had come in after she left and erased her, too. The thought felt good, like slipping into a bed with clean sheets.

Such a bed would never be found in the Pink Pearl. Or at least not in any of the rooms Randa cleaned.

A wan Jenny found her on the first floor at around half past two. Randa was done, but her shift didn't end until three and she got paid by the hour. They killed the last thirty minutes in the public parking lot behind the motel. Jenny hunched down on one of the concrete parking barriers, smoking a cigarette with trembling fingers. Randa, who would rather have smelled the salt air, wished that her friend would put the cigarette out, but didn't say anything. "Tell me about what's-his-name," she said instead. "From last night."

Jenny smiled dreamily. "Seward. From Louisiana, or Kentucky. Somewhere like that. Had a sexy little accent on him." She groaned and put her head down on her knees. "God, I'm sick."

"You like him?"

"What I remember, sure."

"When's he leaving?" All the men in Lawrence Beach were leaving, sooner or later.

"Four days." Jenny's head was still down, her voice muffled by her legs. "It's too bad. He's actually kind of nice."

"Four days isn't really enough time to be an asshole," Randa said without much emotion.

Now Jenny raised her head, propped her chin on her hands, and squinted up at Randa. "Ouch. Should I ask how Seth is?"

Randa just shook her head, and Jenny laughed. It was a thin, queasy sound. "You're the asshole, Randa. He was crazy about you. What'd you tell him?"

"Nothing."

"Nothing at all?" Jenny dug her cigarette against the concrete barrier to put it out. "That's kind of cold, don't you think?" Randa shrugged, and Jenny laughed again. "You, my friend, are one heartless bitch. In a way, it's kind of impressive."

Randa, who didn't at all mind being thought of as a heartless bitch, smiled.

At three she stuffed her smock into the bottom of her backpack and found Tom reading the newspaper in the office. He was an old guy with no hair and a round stomach. He and Angie had retired to Lawrence Beach to run the motel, which didn't seem like much of a retirement, but they paid Randa in cash and didn't ask any questions. As he counted out her money — five bucks an hour — he asked how many rooms she'd cleaned that day.

"Seven," Randa answered. "The others were all empty." She

was looking at the paper in front of him, where she could see a photograph of a motherly-looking woman holding a framed picture and several bright award ribbons. The face in the frame was April Agostino. The headline read "Murdered Woman Loved Horses, Math."

April Agostino had died waiting tables in Lawrence Beach, and suddenly she was both a math genius and an Olympic-level equestrienne. Death, Randa thought, elevated people.

Meanwhile, Tom was shaking his head. "Getting close," he said.

"To what?"

"End of the season." He shrugged. "Might be able to get a few more weeks out of it."

"Maybe the weather'll hold."

"Never has before. I won't need you anymore once we get down to fifty percent occupancy." Tom handed her a stack of bills. "Almost forgot. A friend of yours came by today."

Counting, Randa said, "She found me."

He waved a hand dismissively. "Not that one," he said, not seeming to feel that Jenny merited any more specific designation. "Some middle-aged guy."

Randa, already on her way out the door, froze.

"Middle-aged guy?" she said.

"Yeah. Glasses, dress pants — looked like an accountant or something." He laughed. "Baby doll, you need an accountant, I must be paying you too much."

Gritting her teeth — *Hey, baby doll, fuck you* — Randa asked, "What did you tell him?"

"I didn't tell him anything." Tom slammed the cashbox shut and put it back in the drawer. "He just said he'd meet you when it started to get dark. Didn't say where."

She stuffed the money into her backpack and said nothing. When she got outside, she must have looked distracted, because Jenny asked, "You okay? You look a little funny."

"George is back," Randa said.

Jenny looked blank for a moment, and then laughed. "Oh, right. Double-oh George. Your super-spy sugar daddy."

"Double-oh this," Randa said. "He's not my sugar daddy. He gave me a hundred bucks. Once." Although she'd wondered at the time, and wondered again now, exactly what the hundred bucks had meant. "I never said he was a spy, either."

"Liar. You told me he worked for the CIA."

"No. He told *me* that he worked for the CIA. Hell, people do have normal jobs there, you know," Randa added, with more conviction than she felt. "Secretaries and janitors and shit."

Jenny gave her a look. "You know all about it." Then, seeing Randa's expression, she said, "Oh, come on. You don't know shit about the CIA. Anyway, you did too say he was a spy. All that secret identity, *remaining anonymous* crap. Remember? When you were looking for a job?" Randa said nothing, and Jenny laughed. "Oh, you can just go to hell. See if I ever believe anything you say again."

Sunset, when George wanted to meet her, was still hours away. The weather was too gray for the beach, so they ended up in the Clam Shack. "I'm crazy," said Jenny as they walked in. "I only spend every fucking night here, now I'm spending my days here too?" But soon she was drunk and dancing by the jukebox while Randa sat at the bar. Three tourist boys sat in a booth nearby with a pitcher of Coors Light, eating barbecued shrimp and watching Jenny appreciatively. One of them offered her a cigarette and a light, and Jenny accepted both. She gazed up at the young man with eyes that were, if slightly bloodshot, the same crystal blue the sky should have been. He gazed back. Men usually gazed back at Jenny, a warm, sunny blonde who wore bikini tops instead of T-shirts. She was thin and deeply tanned, and Randa supposed that, what with the sun and the drinking and the cigarettes, in not too many more years she would look like ten miles of bad road. Watching her dance, Randa thought that probably it was worth it.

On another day, maybe Randa would have let the tourist boys buy her drinks. But today she was thinking about George, who had told her almost two months ago that he'd stop by on his way through and check up on her sometime, although she hadn't believed him. She'd figured that picking her up had been a good way for him to pass time on a boring drive. It'd make a good story to tell all his friends around the Secret-Government-Agency-That-May-or-May-Not-Be-the-CIA water cooler: *My last trip out, I picked up this crazy chick who'd totaled her car — started out taking her to the nearest phone and next thing we know we're in Lawrence Beach and I'm telling her how to go off the grid.* Maybe he'd add a hot but totally imaginary sex scene in some roadside motel. She would have.

Although, come to think of it, she hadn't. She'd told Jenny just enough so.the girl wouldn't think her homeless, jobless prospective roommate was a complete loser, and dropped a couple hints about George's job, maybe. But she hadn't said anything concrete, because she didn't know anything concrete. *He works for the government,* she'd said. *Secret stuff. Super hush-hush.* Thinking back on it, it sounded like bullshit even to her.

And hell, maybe it had sounded like bullshit at the time too. They'd driven ten hours in the dark car together from Ratchetsburg to Lawrence Beach, and while she'd never really expected mousy, reserved George to have the cojones to do anything crude like pull the car over onto the shoulder or into a motel, she had expected — something. A guy like that, who spent a lot of time alone, who didn't think he liked people: he'd be a romantic, she'd thought. He'd want to fall in love with her. If she'd been him, that's what she would have wanted.

So she'd figured the CIA stuff was designed to impress her, and she'd been slightly tempted — it also made a good story from her end — but George himself hadn't quite been sexy enough to sustain the fantasy, and in the end she'd been relieved when he'd dropped her off in Lawrence Beach with a handshake and a folded hundred-dollar bill. Whatever he'd been hoping for when he'd said *You can come with me if you don't want to go back,* it hadn't happened. She'd never expected to see him again. Not really.

But now he was in town, and that made her feel — what? Interested, because it was an interesting thing to happen. Flat-

74

tered, because he'd come back to see her. Nervous, because she didn't know what was going to happen next. She ran through scenarios in her head, all of the plausible and implausible reasons that George might be there. He wanted her to pay back the hundred bucks he'd given her. He was working the serial killer case, and wanted her to go undercover. He was planning to go undercover himself and needed her help integrating with the locals. He'd been pining with love for her and wanted to enact a hot, nonimaginary sex scene in some roadside motel. Or he actually did love her, full-on, hearts-and-flowers, some-day-my-prince-will-come love, and while Randa sort of wanted to be somebody's romantic fantasy, she didn't really want to be George's, so what the hell would she do about that?

Or maybe — and Randa had to admit this seemed most likely — he was just driving through, on his way back to Cleveland or Chicago or wherever he'd been coming from that last time.

Although that still didn't explain how he'd found her at the Pink Pearl.

Deep in thought, she sat by herself at the bar and nursed a beer while Jenny drank from the tourists' pitcher. Around four-thirty a tall, dark-haired guy came in. Randa recognized him: Jenny's cute boy, originally from Louisiana or Kentucky but most recently from last night at the Clam Shack. Jenny stopped dancing instantly and went to him. Bringing him to the bar, she fell onto the stool next to Randa, sweaty and out of breath, and asked the bartender for two drinks. "Seward," she said while she was waiting, "have you met my roommate, Randa?"

"I have not," Seward said. From the smell of him he had been drinking already. His accent was thick and a little blurry around the edges from the alcohol. "But I'm awfully pleased to."

Jenny threw an arm over Randa's shoulders. "Randa just broke up with her boyfriend, but she hasn't told him yet."

"I'm sorry to hear that," Seward told Randa.

"He was very fancy," Jenny said, rolling her eyes toward the ceiling. "He was getting a Ph.D. in philosophy."

Seward laughed and said, "I'm real sorry to hear that," just as Randa said something obscene.

Jenny looked at her with mock disdain. "How crass. Now, Seward is *very* polite. Seward is a real live southern gentleman."

Seward slid his arms around her thin waist. "Don't count on it."

"Where are you from?" Randa asked without interest.

"Kentucky." Seward gave Jenny a significant look. "Only one state north of Tennessee, darlin'."

Confused, Randa said, "Tennessee?"

"Fuck." Jenny threw her head back dramatically. "Don't mention Tennessee to me. I don't even want to think about Tennessee until I absolutely have to."

Randa raised an eyebrow. "How often do you absolutely have to think about Tennessee?"

"That's where I'm going when the season ends." Jenny rolled her eyes again. "My sister lives there. I *hate* Tennessee," she added plaintively.

"So why go?"

"She's a teacher. And she has a baby. She lets me stay for free if I watch the kid while she works." Jenny shrugged. "Gotta go somewhere."

Seward bit at Jenny's ear and Randa noticed that his teeth were crooked. "This year will be different," he said. "I'll be there to take you away from it all." He picked Jenny up, as if she were a child, and kissed her again. Then he seemed to remember another person was there and asked Randa where she was from.

Before she could answer, Jenny said, "Randa is a woman of mystery. Don't ruin it."

"Really?" Seward gave Randa a curious look. "What's so mysterious about you?"

"Everything," Jenny said, throwing up her hands in mock exasperation. "I live with this girl, and I don't know anything about her except her name. You want to know where she's from? *I* don't even know where she's from. I don't know a single damn thing about her. She could be the psycho killer, for all I know."

Randa laughed. "I promise you I'm not the psycho killer."

"But you could be," Jenny said, and Seward said, "Well, if you're not the psycho killer, who are you?"

Randa suddenly found herself thinking of George again. She picked up her beer and drank the rest of it quickly. "I don't know," she said when it was gone. "Just me, I guess."

For her eighth birthday, the little girl who will someday become Randa requests a lemon meringue pie and chicken with dumplings for dinner. Her mother will comply, but since meringue is difficult to decorate and the little girl's father hates lemon-flavored anything, she will also make a chocolate cake. The little girl is currently going through a phase where she wants to be called Randi, with a star scrawled over the *i* in place of the dot, and so the cake will be decorated; but according to her birth certificate, the little girl's name is Miranda.

At eight, Miranda is already an accomplished daydreamer and a consummate fantasist. In the coming year, as in the last, most of her daydreams will involve her favorite television show, *The Emerald Idol,* which chronicles the adventures of a jaunty South Seas smuggler with a seaplane. The montage that opens every episode starts with a shot of the words painted on the side of the plane — *Mike Finn, Pilot for Hire* — and continues with images of Finn's trusted-but-drunk mechanic and spunky-but-frustrated girlfriend. Interspersed among these are luscious scenery shots: sugar-sand beaches and turquoise oceans, the battered plane flying into fiery mai-tai sunsets, dense green jungles through which Finn must inevitably hack his way with a machete. (Miranda has seen photographs of her father, unshaven and tanned, sitting on gleaming beaches in front of similarly lush jungles, and among the souvenirs he has brought back from his travels is a real live machete. Just like Mike Finn's.)

The Emerald Idol is on every Wednesday night at eight o'clock. Miranda is normally in bed by eight-thirty, but the show lasts for an hour. So every Wednesday night, there is a bedtime exemption in the Cassidy household. Provided that Miranda's teeth are brushed and her pajamas donned, she is allowed to sit in front of the television right up until the end of the closing credits. The extra half-hour makes *The Emerald Idol* seem even more magical.

During the long, dull intervals between episodes, Miranda's favorite game is, of course, Emerald Idol. During school recesses, she can be seen corralling as many children as she can to play various bit parts from the show: *Let's play you're Hibachi the bartender, and you're Lukey the mechanic, and you three are the bad guys, okay?* The children who are willing to go along with her are the left-outs: too slow for kickball, too scared for baseball, too uncoordinated for jump-rope, and somehow just *wrong* in that ineffable way that children instinctively sense. At Miranda's school, kids like these have three choices. They can sit against the wall reading and risk having their books kicked, slapped, or torn out of their hands. They can stand with the teacher, which even they recognize is the coward's way out, and which is only a short-term solution to a long-term problem — said term being anywhere from twelve years to the rest of their lives. Or they can play Emerald Idol with bossy Miranda Cassidy.

Most of them choose Miranda.

At school, Miranda is always Mike Finn. Of course she is; as the left-outs soon learn, Mike Finn is the only really good part. One day in the not-too-distant future, a little boy named Douglas — who, to his social detriment, will actually be called Douglas long after he should have shortened it to Doug — will have the temerity to suggest that there is something mismatched about Miranda, whose mother still occasionally pulls her hair into two pigtails and ties them with plastic bead ponytail holders shaped like flowers or cherries or kitty faces, playing the role of the scruffy but dashing Mike Finn.

"You can't be Mike Finn," he will say, in what he will think is a fairly reasonable tone. "Mike Finn is a *boy.*"

When Miranda hears this, she will be hanging from the

monkey bars by one hand, pulling a pretend gun from her pretend shoulder holster to fire at some pretend bandits, one of whom is Douglas. Fixing him with a steely glare, she will drop to the ground and tackle him instead. And although she will tear her favorite T-shirt with the parrot on it, end up with an ugly scrape on her cheek, and earn a three-day suspension from school for fighting; although her mother will give her a thorough scolding after picking her up from the principal's office and won't let her ride her bike for the duration of her punishment, Miranda will float home on a cloud of ecstatic pride. Had Mike Finn been dangling from the monkey bars with her, she does not doubt that he would have done exactly the same thing.

The Douglas Incident will happen to fall during one of Nick's at-home times, so when they get back to the house her mother will say, "You go tell your father what you've done," in a tone that will make Miranda glad that Wednesday was the day before, because her precious hour of *The Emerald Idol* is seven safe days away and in no danger of being taken from her. She will go and find Nick in the upstairs bathroom, where he will be trying to figure out why the toilet keeps running, and tell him that she has been suspended.

"For three days," she will say, trying to sound mournful.

Nick, up to his elbows in the toilet tank, will twist an eyebrow at his daughter, fingers still searching for the leak in the gasket. "What'd you do to deserve that?"

She will explain that Douglas Showman told her she couldn't be Mike Finn because Mike Finn was a boy.

"Mike Finn, huh?" Nick will say musingly, as the rotten rubber of the gasket crumbles in his fingers and the toilet begins to flush uncontrollably. "Shit. Goddamn it. Randa, honey, hand me that thing right there on the counter that looks like a flying saucer. Yeah, that's it." Not until the flushing situation is under control will Nick remove his arm from the toilet tank, dry it on a towel, and sit down on the closed lid of the bowl. "Now. You're talking about that guy from television? With the monkey?"

Miranda will nod. Mike Finn has a pet monkey that can pick pockets.

"So what'd you do?"

Shrugging, Miranda will try to play it cool. Mike Finn is always cool under interrogation.

"I did what I had to do," she'll say.

And she will be so small and fierce, with her torn T-shirt and disheveled ponytail and scraped face — like the world's smallest, pinkest gangster — that Nick will throw his head back and laugh. This, in turn, will prompt Anne to emerge from the hallway where she has been eavesdropping and say, "Nice work, flyboy. Next time, *you* get to go talk to the principal." But Miranda won't care, because even after Nick chokes back his laughter she will still see approval in his eyes — as will Anne, incidentally. The adults will fight about it later in voices that are not as quiet as they think. From her bedroom, Miranda will be able to overhear key words and phrases, including *undermine, consistency,* and *fucking relax, for Christ's sake.*

But no matter. Little Miranda knows whose side her father is on. She also knows that when her next schoolyard battle comes along, Nick will probably be flying, anyway.

Despite her passionate defense of her right to play the role, when Miranda plays Emerald Idol alone she does not pretend to be Mike Finn. Instead she has broken with the show's script and invented another South Seas smuggler, whose plane is just as fast·and light as Mike Finn's and whose fists can hit just as hard. This smuggler's name is Julia. Miranda thinks that Julia is the toughest, most beautiful name she has ever heard, and often mourns the fact that it is not her own. Sometimes Julia works with Mike Finn and sometimes they're in competition, depending on how at odds with the world Miranda feels. Sometimes they kiss; sometimes they shoot guns. There is usually at least one fist- or firefight.

But her favorite scene, the one she plays over and over again, is the one where Mike and Julia meet for the first time in an island bar. The police come in search of Mike Finn to arrest him for smuggling ammunition to the honorable rebels, and Julia leaps to his defense. The two of them outwit and outfight the authorities and escape together into the dark jungle; thus does she prove herself brave and true, and thus begins the process of her unique and special acceptance into his confidence. Because in Miranda's version, Julia is the only person Mike Finn trusts, and he is the only person she trusts. Poor Mike Finn's girlfriend.

One year after the Douglas Incident, Nick will be dead. Miranda will still play Emerald Idol, but her games play out on the hard-packed dirt playground of her new school in Phoenix, Arizona, instead of on lush Pennsylvanian grass. The scene she plays will always be the same: it's one in which Mike Finn's seaplane suddenly develops mechanical trouble, or is shot down, or he is in prison, and it is up to Julia to save him. Over and over again, she will save him. The other children in Miranda's class will sense (rightly) that there is strangeness here. They will leave her alone, and she will play by herself, always.

Years later, when Miranda's mother tries to explain her theories about Nick's job, and why they will never know more than they already do about his death — *Probably CIA,* she says, *although I suppose it could have been DEA or anything, really* — Miranda will accuse her of finally losing it, finally going insane. In Miranda's eyes, all the problems of her short life date back to her father's death, which was not a fantasy, not a game, not an adventure. CIA or not, he is dead. She could not have saved him.

five

IN THE PARK at the northern end of the board-walk, Randa lay on her back next to the duck pond with one arm thrown over her eyes. The rain had stopped. The air was warm, the breeze cool, and the leaves of the trees rustled pleasantly overhead. Beneath her, the ground smelled damp and rich from the rain.

She was still a little drunk, and part of her wished that she could fall asleep. Instead, though her eyes were closed, she was hyper-aware of the people around her: their voices, their foot-steps. She heard the slap of flip-flops against bare soles, the soft rustle of tennis shoes in the grass. She heard the quick foot-falls and panting breath of a jogger on the path nearby; she heard the small squeak of a bicycle's wheels, and the low, sibi-lant *thok-thok-thok* of a skateboard moving over the cracks in the sidewalk. Each new noise almost made her flinch with tension.

And then, after a time, she heard two feet in hard-soled

dress shoes approach her, and slow, and stop. All at once she had a queer feeling in her stomach. She listened for the person's breathing but could not hear it.

It's him, she thought. *It's not him. I don't care. Why do I care?*

"You dyed your hair," George said.

She opened her eyes and shaded them with her hand as she squinted up at him. "Not all of it."

"Sit up. Let me see."

She sat up and shook her head so that her hair — mostly black, the top layer shot through with wide blond streaks — fell back into place. "My roommate did it," she said, and was about to ask if he liked it, but decided she didn't care.

George crouched down next to her on the grass. His gray slacks were out of place in Lawrence Beach, where *formal* meant both shoes and a T-shirt. His shirt was open at the collar, and sweat rings stained the fabric under his arms. "It's okay, I guess. But you don't look like I remember."

Randa felt her hands wanting to go to her head. Instead she laced her fingers together and stretched her arms out in front of her, palms toward the ocean. "Nothing's changed but the hair."

George frowned slightly. "I'm not sure," he said. Then, "Are you hungry?"

She said yes and let him help her up. His palm felt cool and damp. For the briefest of instants after she stood up, she thought he was going to try to hold her hand. Then he let go.

"I was surprised to hear you were in town," Randa said as they set off down the boardwalk.

"I told you that you'd see me again. I said I'd check up on you."

"I figured you were just being nice." She felt like she was on a date with an ex-boyfriend, somebody who simultaneously knew her too well and not at all. "How did you find the motel?"

He shrugged. "I asked around. None of the chains would have paid you under the table, so that narrowed the list. It was a bit of a challenge, though, because I didn't know if you were using your own name. Are you?"

"How did you ask about me without using my name?" As they walked, Randa couldn't help looking at the passersby for somebody she knew, but for the first time in weeks she didn't see a single familiar face. She felt strangely betrayed by this, as if the boardwalk had cut her loose, set her adrift. She was nervous and unused to feeling that way around men. It would have calmed her to see *somebody*. Even the guy who drove the nails through his hands. Even Seth.

George reached out and touched the thorny black vine circling her upper arm. There was a matching bracelet around her wrist. "Your tattoos," he said, answering a question she'd almost forgotten she'd asked. "They're memorable. So what should I call you?"

Randa looked out at the crashing surf and scratched — almost unconsciously — at the tickling place where he had touched her. "Just Randa. I'm using a different last name. It doesn't matter," she added. "Nobody's looking for me."

"I was looking for you. I found you."

"You knew where to start."

"You look good," he said. "You look happy."

That made her smile, and some of her nervousness dissipated. "The last time you saw me, I'd just totaled my car. It's not hard to top that."

"Are you happy?" he asked.

She didn't answer. It was strange, she thought, how people changed in your memory. He didn't look like she remembered him either. Of course, his hair had been wet and too long then, and now it was recently cut — very recently, judging from the tiny snips of hair still stuck to the skin around his ears. He had blue eyes. If she'd ever noticed that, she'd forgotten it. "Something's different," she said, and then: "I know. You're not wearing your glasses."

Suddenly he smiled, a quick, brilliant smile that seemed to shine out of every part of his face. It was a nice smile, and she thought, *Maybe this will be okay.*

"You noticed." George sounded pleased. He pulled down his lower eyelid with one finger and rolled his eyeball up. "Contact lenses. Can you see them?"

They stopped. He was taller than Randa, enough so that she had to raise onto her toes to peer at his eyeball. "They're new," he said. "The way I see it, I'm nearly forty. If not now, when?"

Randa, looking for the telltale rim around his iris, could smell him. He smelled like laundry detergent and coffee. Suddenly she realized how close her face was to his; *kissing close,* she thought, and then wished she hadn't. Quickly she stepped back. "You got a haircut, too," she said.

George's eyes went to her scalp again and his smile vanished. "I wish you hadn't done that to your hair," he said as they began walking again. "It looked better when it was its real color."

She gave him a grin she did not feel. "My hair hasn't been its real color since I was seventeen," she said lightly, "but I appreciate the thought."

"It's not blond?"

"Brownish. I think," she added. "Like I said, it's been a while." This, like the grin, was just for effect. Her hair, left to its own devices, was dark and wavy, like her father's.

"You had such nice blond hair," George said. "Like Marilyn Monroe." He sounded disappointed, and Randa couldn't help thinking, *Last weekend, I picked up this crazy chick who'd totaled her car — she had blond hair, just like Marilyn Monroe —*

Goddamn it, she told herself. He was just a guy. He got haircuts like any guy, he had a thing for blondes like any guy, he probably told bullshit stories to his friends like any guy. What was she so nervous about? She could handle him. Hell, she'd been on worse dates than this, and still gone out with the guy a second time if he'd sprung for a nice dinner. Like Jenny always said, if the fish were biting, only an idiot didn't dangle a little bait. "So," she said, "what did your friends at work say when you told them that you'd started picking up hitchhikers?"

"Why would I tell them that?" he asked, blinking and looking surprised.

"You didn't tell them about me?" Her voice was playful, but she was watching him closely.

"You?" He laughed. "Why would I tell them about you?"

His tone was so amused and mystified that she had no choice but to believe him. She felt slightly amused and mystified herself to find that his words stung. "Good point," she said. "Why would you?"

George stopped. "Oh. You're offended."

"No, I'm not."

"Yes, you are," he said. "You think that I didn't tell them about you because I didn't think you were worth telling them about. But it wasn't that at all."

Randa considered, decided what the hell, and told the truth. "I just figured you lied, told some wild story about us getting it on in the backseat or something. I would have," she added, forcibly cavalier.

He shrugged. "I'm not you."

They continued walking. To her left, the ocean turned gray as the sun moved toward the western horizon. She kept looking back at the ocean. The water was warm, she knew it was — this was the last month of a hot summer, and today had been warm despite the rain — but the Atlantic always looked cold. During her first week in Lawrence Beach, when she had been working at the Clam Shack with Jenny, she had gone on a date with a boy whose father kept a yacht at the marina. He had taken her out on the open ocean and given her champagne, and they'd gone swimming in the deep water, so she knew that no matter how warm and friendly the water was on the Virginia coast, twenty miles out to sea the ocean was icy, dark, and unforgiving.

It had been cheap champagne anyway, she thought now, and the yacht had been on the small side. "George," she asked suddenly. "Have you ever been to California? Or Florida?"

After a moment George said, "Florida, yes." He had a way of pausing when she changed the subject; she remembered that

86

now. Like an old-fashioned telephone switchboard, with the plugs that switched from one jack to another.

"Is the water different there?"

"What do you mean?"

"It's cold here," she said. "The Atlantic. Is it different in California? Or Florida — you hear about people all the time, floating over from Cuba on rafts and inner tubes and old cars. You couldn't do that here."

"The Cuba-Florida crossing is very dangerous," he said. "Lots of people don't survive. But it's further south, so warmer, maybe. Is that what you mean?"

She shuddered. "I couldn't do it."

"If it was important enough to you, you could. Some people might say that they couldn't imagine picking up and walking away from their entire lives. You did that, didn't you?"

"Yeah, well. There wasn't much chance that I was going to get eaten by a hammerhead on the turnpike."

George cocked his head, considering. "Hammerheads are actually very shy. People always assume that the grotesque is menacing. But you never said whether you were happy or not."

"Sure," she said. "Sure, I'm happy."

It is early morning, late spring, 1993. Miranda — little Miranda no more, now she is teenage Miranda — is asleep. Her hair is long and luscious, a deep, vibrant green. She has dyed it just the night before, and a fine mist of dark green has bled across the white cotton of her pillowcase.

Next to her bed is a table that holds an alarm clock and a small CD player. When the alarm clock goes off, Miranda's hand — the fingernails painted glossy jet black — will reach out even before her eyes are open and slap it quiet before fumbling for the play button on the CD player. The disk loaded into the player is Nirvana's *Nevermind*. In just under a year, Kurt Cobain will kill himself, and Miranda will make much show of sarcastically fluttering her eyelashes and falling into feigned grief-stricken swoons. She will buy all the special issues of *Rolling Stone* and *Spin*, but she will resent their insistence that something tremendous has happened to her, because her life will go on exactly as it always has, and Miranda knows that anything truly tremendous leaves a scar. Like, for instance, the day her father vanished.

But all that is a year away. Kurt is still alive, and Miranda has dyed her hair forest green. She lives with her mother in a suburb of Phoenix, where the sun-baked city hunches in the valley underneath a wide desert sky. This is where they moved after Nick disappeared, to this city of concrete and stucco and nothing at all that is soft. This is the landscape that nine-year-old Miranda viewed for the first time with immense, bitter skepticism, because she knew that her lost father would never be able to find them in this place. But that was all long ago and far away. Miranda has grown out of the belief that her father will ever come back; her early skepticism has hardened into cynicism. She is in high school, and this is the way her day will be:

The alarm will go off, and her pale, black-tipped hand will flail desperately for the alarm. She will hear her mother moving in the rest of the small house, getting ready for work, and she will lie in bed listening until she hears the front door closing and her mother's car starting in the driveway. Miranda and Anne do not talk in the morning. Neither of them has the disposition for it, and recently their conversations are halting and strange, anyway.

When her mother is gone, Miranda will climb out of bed, dress (a Nine Inch Nails T-shirt, black fishnet stockings, cutoff army pants, and her beloved combat boots), and then sit in the front window, waiting for whichever of her friends has agreed to drive her to school that day. Today it is her old friend Jayce Cooper, who used to be the QuestMaster and currently thinks that he is in hopeless, impossible love with her. When he sees her hair his eyes will widen and he will tell her that she is the most beautiful thing he has ever seen. Miranda will blush and tell him to go to hell.

At school, the principal, the teachers, and most of her fellow students will pointedly ignore the green waves spilling over

Miranda's shoulders — *she's just after attention, let's not encourage her* — but a few will not. The young chemistry teacher, who fancies himself one of his adolescent charges, will jocularly suggest that it might be time to wash that hair, because it's looking a little moldy. Chad Ott, who drives an oversized American truck with a Confederate flag flying proudly from the antenna, will spit on her in the hallway and call her a freak. In gym class, Amanda Ryerson, one of the Perfect Girls — in fact, the alpha Perfect Girl — will lead a small gaggle of acolytes across the hockey field to the spot where Miranda is apathetically playing defense and, with a predatory glint of confidence in her eyes, will command Miranda to tell her what, exactly, she thought she was trying to prove with that hair anyway.

Miranda will take all this in stride. The persona that she attempts to cultivate at school is mysterious, disdainful, superior; today maintaining this air will be easy, because she will feel as if her spine has been replaced by iron. All she's done is buy a bottle of GangGreen dye at a head shop in Tempe and follow the directions on the back, but she's *done* it. In truth, her feelings about her hair are not unlike Chad Ott's feelings about flying the stars and bars on his antenna, although she will never admit it — during the Civil War, Arizona was still technically Mexico, so what the hell does Chad Ott's flag even mean, anyway? But in the end it's a matter of choice, or rather of the desire to choose to deny something that they feel has been chosen for them: a lifestyle, a future, an identity. For Miranda, it is also a matter of self-defense. If she cared enough to explain to Amanda Ryerson exactly what it was that she thought she was proving with that hair anyway, she would say something like this: *You don't like me, and you think it's because of my hair. But you wouldn't like me anyway, would you?*

Would you?

By the end of the school day Miranda will be exhausted, worn out from the weight of walking around with a symbol sprouting from her scalp. And so she will be quiet as Jayce drives her and her friends back to her house, which is the only house with a working, and thus absent, mother. The four of them — Jayce and Miranda and Michelle and Glen — have been friends since junior high and are united not so much by what they have in common with each other as by what they lack in common with everyone else at school. Until Anne comes home, they will sit in Miranda's bedroom, burn incense, and listen to music on her CD player. A few years before, they would have spent the hours playing Sword & Sorcery — in fact, all the books and miniatures and maps are still safely tucked away in their place beneath Miranda's bed — but at the ripe old age of seventeen they fancy themselves to have cast aside such escapist diversions. They think of themselves as creatures of the world, hard and brutal and unflinching. They listen to dark angry music, watch dark angry movies, collect dark angry comics. They read Neal Stephenson and William Gibson and William S. Burroughs and Philip K. Dick and Mervyn Peake. The modern world, to them, is but a pale imitation of the dystopian universes that they read about. They are under the impression that they live in a time that hasn't yet grown interesting enough to write about.

So they wait. In the meantime they jealously guard their disillusionment and its trappings, because as far as they're concerned, you either get it or you don't, and if you don't you'd better not act like you do. Their disillusionment is all that they are sure of, and they do not want it used casually.

Secretly, of course, each of them has fond, longing memories of their Sword & Sorcery years. Deep inside, each of them knows that slaying Fire Dragons with the Sword of Unhinging in the Goblin Caverns is a hell of a lot more interesting than listening to the same Jane's Addiction album on endless repeat. Take sickly, nervous Glen, who suffers his days like other kids suffer pimples, who has just shaved his head and whose screeching, disappointed mother won't let him take his driver's test until his hair grows back. Some of the best moments of his life have been spent in this room, slaying were-beasts as Gleth-Toth the Invincible. Small, pudgy Michelle was once Rana the Magistrix, and would that she could magic away the extra twenty pounds that have dogged her since puberty. Even

Jayce, whose dark good looks have made him the closest thing the group has to a success story — who even Amanda Ryerson has been heard to admit is "cute" — even he misses his days as QuestMaster: the glory, the tragedy.

And would Miranda step into Loran of the Red Forest's Boots of Traveling without even an instant of hesitation? Would she be deliriously happy to suffer attacks by an entire legion of the Zombies of Agony and Despair rather than face another game of field hockey or another of Amanda's disdainful little smirks? Only in a red-hot instant, but the opportunity has yet to present itself, and on that air-conditioned spring day in Phoenix, Arizona, none of the four teenagers — Miranda included — will remember that Loran of the Red Forest's most distinguishing physical characteristic was her long, rippling waves of green hair.

Hair as green as ivy, as green as a lush tropical jungle. Anne will cry when she sees it. Miranda will try clumsily to comfort her, but the distance between them has grown too great. She will end up sitting quietly on the couch, watching as her mother sobs.

"You had your father's hair" will be all that Anne can say, but Miranda will come, eventually, to believe that the true tragedy of her hair-dyeing experiment is this: nothing changed. She expected it to. It didn't.

But she's young and cannot truly conceive of being old, and on some level she will think that there is still time. It will be years before she begins to feel the shadow of hopelessness falling over her pained attempts to drive her life somewhere interesting; years before she begins to sense time biting at her heels, the Zombies of Boredom and Death close behind her in hot, mindless pursuit.

For now, though, she sleeps, convinced that when she wakes up, the world will be hers.

George bought her a taco. He had wanted to buy her fried dough, the way he had that first morning, but she said no, she wanted something that was close to real food. They sat on the seawall while she ate. Randa sat cross-legged, her left ankle with the tattooed black cat twining around it resting on her right thigh. She caught George's eyes on her as she licked a spicy drop of grease from her hand and wiped it self-consciously on her cutoffs. "What?" she said.

"I didn't remember that you had so many tattoos," he said.

Randa gave him a hard look. "Well, I do."

"That's not what I meant," he said quickly. He always assumed that he'd offended her, she thought, never actually giving her a chance to decide how she felt about the things he said. She found it a little hard to keep up with him. "They're fine. Memorable, as I said earlier. Can I ask —"

She interrupted him. "Seventeen, no, yes, no, and yes."

Blinking, he said, "What?"

"Everybody asks the same questions." She ticked them off on the fingers of her left hand, the one that wasn't holding the taco. "I got the first one when I was seventeen. No, I don't regret it. Yes, I have others. No, you can't see them, and yes, it hurts."

George reached over and picked up her wrist. He held it gently and inspected the thorny tattooed bracelet the same way that the artist who had etched the design into her body had inspected it, tracing the contours of bone under thin skin. "How much does it hurt?" he asked, running his thumb over the filigree of blue veins on the inside of her wrist.

What a question. She shivered and pulled her wrist back. "More than a skinned knee, less than a broken bone."

"I didn't phrase that right," he said. "I meant, what kind of pain is it?"

Randa had to think about that one. She stared down at her reclaimed wrist, comparing — as she always did — the inked skin in front of her with the unmarked skin in her memory. "Sharp, I guess," she said. "When it's happening. Electric-feeling. Afterward it's like a sunburn. Stings, and sort of — nags at you. Some people say it feels good."

"Are you one of them?"

She shrugged. "I don't really think of it that way."

"How do you think of it?"

"Like coming here," she said simply. "Making a change. It's like dyeing your hair or quitting your job or something. You feel like it'll make everything different. The pain is just a way of proving how much you want it." She let her flip-flops fall off and then stretched her legs so that the tips of her toes were buried in the sand. It would be nice to have a drink, she thought. If she were drunk — not too drunk, but just drunk enough for the boundaries to blur — navigating this conversation would be easier.

"Does it make everything different?"

She laughed, hearing and not liking the bitterness in her voice. "Sure, until it heals."

George looked thoughtful. "Dyeing your hair, quitting your job, coming here — did they make everything different?"

"Coming here did. Like a clean start." She didn't look at him. "Nothing dragging at my heels."

"When I was a little boy," he said, "my father decided to build me a clubhouse. I don't know why, since I certainly wasn't in any clubs, but he said that a boy needed a clubhouse. He drew up the plans and bought the wood, but he had no real talent for building things. No matter what he did, the clubhouse came out crooked and rickety. One day I came home from school to find nothing in our backyard but a pile of smoking ash where it had been. My father was inside at the kitchen table drawing new plans. All he would say was that sometimes you had to burn it down and start over."

Wine, Randa decided: red wine, rich and dark. After this was over, she thought, she would go to the Clam Shack and find some guy who'd buy her a bottle of wine. They'd sit on the seawall like this, and drink, and listen to the ocean. She would kiss him; it would be good. Clean, simple. Not like George. Not like this.

Double-oh George, she thought; *super-spy George and his arsonist father.*

But the real George was still talking. "That's what you did. Burned it down and started over. I respect that."

Still thinking of her imaginary beach paramour, Randa raised an eyebrow. "Arson?"

"No. Independence. A sense of adventure." He smiled at her. "You must have gotten that from your father."

Had she told him about her father that night? She couldn't remember. "Yeah, well," she said. "He was better at it than I am."

The sun was almost all the way down now. The ocean and the sand looked flat and hard, the sky flat and gray. She asked him if he'd mind going back to the taco place and getting her a bottle of beer, and he said that he thought there were fairly strict open-container laws on public beaches and he didn't think she'd like being arrested. She reminded him that her sense of adventure was one of the things he admired about her, and he said that he thought it would be severely stifled in prison. Then he wanted her to tell him about her friends, and she said she would if they could walk while she did it, because she was getting cold, but also because she wanted to move, because the dream of sitting on the seawall and kissing an imaginary boy had made the reality of sitting on the seawall with George an impossibility.

So they walked up the beach, Randa's flip-flops dangling from her hand, and he listened while she talked. There was something about him that made her want to talk, as if he were empty space waiting to be filled. She told him about the room she shared with Jenny, working at the Pink Pearl, drink specials on the boardwalk. The bodies on the beach. Seth. George listened to all of this as if it were the most interesting story he'd ever heard.

"So you're not going to see him again," he finally said. "This boy."

"He wouldn't leave it alone," Randa said. "He wouldn't leave *me* alone. Always staring at me, asking questions, like he was trying to get inside my head." Which, now that she thought about it, was familiar. "It was all bullshit, anyway," she added. "He was just going to leave at the end of the summer."

"You're going to leave at the end of the summer, too."

She shrugged. "Seth was different. If we'd just been hanging

94

out, not letting it mean anything — but it was like he thought he was in a movie, having his big summer adventure, and I was the Girl." Suddenly she laughed. "Hell, he even had a murderer to protect me from."

"You're not the kind of woman who wants to be protected," George said.

She didn't like the way he told her about herself. "Is that so?"

"Are you offended again? I meant it as a good thing. It sounds as if he cared about you, that boy."

Randa thought about Seth, the croissants and espresso he'd brought her when doughnuts and coffee were all she'd wanted, and laughed again. "Well, he didn't want me dead."

"I've heard people talking about your beach killer, you know."

"People?"

"At work," he said, "in Langley."

"Langley. Of course." With some effort, Randa kept from rolling her eyes. "And what are they saying about our serial killer in Langley?"

George looked away from her. "You know I can't talk about that."

Caught you. "Then why did you bring it up?"

George's ears turned red. "It's not being ignored, that's all. There are people paying attention. Even if it doesn't seem like it." He coughed. "I suppose the police are trying to wait out the tourist season. When does it end? Labor Day?"

"Sometime around then. You know what I heard? I heard he changes the way they look, so they're hard to identify."

"How do you know it's a he?"

"Because serial killers aren't women."

"Sometimes they are," George said. "I could name half a dozen female serial killers. Of course, usually they blame the men in their lives — but dead is still dead."

Randa stared at him. "You know a lot about serial killers. What is it, a hobby?"

"A person picks things up. What happens to your job when the season ends?" George asked.

"Depends on the weather." Randa wondered if George had

been the kind of boy who'd worn Charles Manson T-shirts in high school, and had a brief vision of an adult George — she couldn't picture him as a teenager — sitting in the back row of a high school health class, scribbling *Helter Skelter* on a notebook cover and peeking at the textbook chapter on human reproduction. It almost made her laugh. "Sometimes it holds for months."

"But it won't hold forever." He paused. "You're running out of time, you know."

She sighed. "Remember when you picked me up on the highway? You were going to take me to the truck stop, right?" He nodded. "And I was going to call what's-his-name, my boyfriend, and he was going to come and get me. But instead I came here."

"Because I missed the exit."

"Exactly. If you hadn't missed that exit, I would have stood there in the stupid rain and waited until what's-his-name came and got me, and the next day I would have gotten up and gone to the job I loathed, and that was what I was planning to do. Great plan, huh?"

George didn't say anything.

"Now, here," she went on, "I show up, and inside of twenty-four hours I meet Jenny, who gets me a job and a place to stay."

"I thought she worked at a bar. You're not working at a bar."

"I quit. Turns out I hate people." Randa shook her head. "My plans suck, George. They always have. So I don't want to talk about what happens after the season ends. You want to talk about serial killers, CIA bullshit, my sex life, fine. But not that."

He was quiet for a moment. Finally he said, "I think you're amazing. I wish I could convince you of that." His voice was serious.

"I think I'm not." She tried to make it a joke. "I wish I could convince you of *that*."

"I could do something for you," George said.

"You already did," Randa told him, instantly uncomfortable. "You brought me here."

He smiled. "You told me that your mother thinks your father worked for the CIA."

"My mother also thinks that mountains talk to her."

"Maybe she's right."

"About the mountains?" Randa shook her head. "Secrets don't keep. Somebody gets drunk or bought off, or swears their best friend to secrecy, and the next thing you know it's all over."

"I could look into it," George said. "There might be a file on him."

"Where?"

"Langley."

This time Randa did roll her eyes. She was getting tired, she realized; she wanted to be away from him, to be alone and easy in her own skin again. Or she wanted him to do something, say something, that would give her something to hold on to, some reason for him to be here. Hell, even sleeping with him would be better than this ever-present not-knowing. "Sure, George. Look him up. Let me know what you find."

She saw George swallow hard. "You don't believe me."

"Of course I do," she said, and suddenly her patience was gone. "You're a total badass CIA operative who just happens to talk constantly about it to people you hardly know. Just because my mom has spent the last twenty years asking questions and hasn't even been able to find out what happened to my dad's extra socks after he died, that doesn't mean you won't be able to."

"I never said I was with the Agency." George wasn't looking at her again. "There are a lot of auxiliary companies in Langley."

"Bullshit, there are," she said. "Why are you so interested in my dad?"

"I'm not. I'm interested in you."

"Since you bring it up," Randa said, and stopped. She'd been about to ask why he was so interested in her, but she'd abruptly decided that she didn't want to know. In the same way she'd decided that she did not want to see Seth again, she knew that she did not plan to see George again after tonight either.

George seemed to know what she'd been going to say. "Does that mean you want me to look into your father's death or not?" His voice was cold. "He might not have been anything," he added. "He might have been just a plain old civilian mercenary."

"No doubt," she said, although the word *mercenary* felt ugly to her. "I guess if you can really do it, then knock yourself out." She dropped her flip-flops back to the sand and slid them on.

"Wait," he said, reaching out and grabbing her wrist. "I'm sorry. I didn't mean it. Where are you going?"

Home, she almost said — but even now, in the orange light from the streetlights that had just come on, there was something in George's face that stopped her. The set of his jaw was stoic, but his eyes were filled with an almost childlike desperation.

Hell. She'd always felt sorry for those Manson guys in the back of the room. "Just over to that bar to use the bathroom. I'll be right back." George was smiling now, but something about it felt wrong, and his fingers gripped her wrist tightly. She shook him off with some difficulty. "George, relax. I'll be back."

The bar was one she'd never been to before. She didn't know anybody there. As she made her way through the crowd she realized that she still hadn't seen a single person she knew, and her earlier feeling of having been abandoned by the boardwalk returned. She felt as if she'd been swept into some alternate reality, some place where the things that were familiar to her had never existed. Like an old science fiction movie from the late sixties, with the quiet, doom-filled atmospherics and the hero who dies in the end. She wondered if April Agostino had felt the same way when she'd realized what was going to happen to her, but decided that the dead girl had probably had other things on her mind.

She found the bathroom in the back of the bar and resisted the urge to look in the mirror. She could feel with her hands that her hair was tousled and hanging in clumps; she had a tendency to run her hands through it when she was tense. She used the toilet, washed her hands, and dried them. Only when these things were done did she look at her reflection.

Her hair *was* a mess, her eye makeup worse. She looked like she had been crying. She licked a finger and ran it under each eye, wiping away the smeared mascara and remembering another mirror, in another bathroom, somewhere between Rachetsburg and Lawrence Beach, the night she'd crashed her car. She remembered standing in the fluorescent-lit room, surrounded by the unique unreal emptiness of a public space at four o'clock in the morning, looking in the mirror at the hollows under her eyes, feeling the trembling of her caffeinated heart (there had been a lot of coffee on that trip); knowing that George waited outside and thinking, only half consciously, of the door in the hedge, the magic ring in the gutter, the lost key to the secret attic.

Civilian mercenary, she thought at her reflection, and then shook her head.

When she rejoined George outside, she told him that she had to get home and used the same lie she'd told Seth about working early the next day. George offered to drive her, and because she wanted to prove to herself that it was no big deal — remembering their car trip, which had felt sudden and adventurous and *good,* if slightly bizarre, while it was happening — she said yes. The car was exactly how she remembered it: sleek and silver, cool lines and soft leather seats. When he turned the key, the air conditioning came on almost immediately, icy and smelling like rain. In the darkness the hum of the engine was lulling, nocturnal.

She leaned back and the seat held her as if it were the palm of a giant hand. The sensation of memory was strong: the sound of wheels on the road, the dim glow of the dashboard lights. George next to her, silent. Driving. Only the lights of Lawrence Beach passing by the windows were definitively of the present.

After a long time, George spoke. "I shouldn't have said

that," he said. "About your dad being a mercenary. I apologize."

"George," she said, "why are you here?"

"I'm here to see you. I told you that."

"Why?" She turned toward him now. He was gazing out at the road, and she remembered this now too, how rarely he had turned to look at her while he was driving. "You gave me a ride out here, and I appreciate that, but it was ten hours. Effectively speaking, we've known each other for less than half a day. I'm not sure what you want from me." George didn't answer, and so she decided to cut through the crap. Easier to get it out in the open; easier to know. "Do you want to sleep with me?" she asked. "Is that it?"

Suddenly he pulled the car over in front of a big hotel. In the glow from the street and the hotel's spotlights she could see that his cheeks were flushed and his eyes, fixed on her, were intense. "Don't do that," he said. "Don't make this into something cheap. Don't make it — ugly."

He stopped. Randa could see him shaking. "Is that a yes or a no?" she finally said, knowing that it was probably the wrong thing to say but wanting desperately to know. One way or another.

"Fuck," he said, and sighed. It was the only time she'd heard him swear, she thought, and then remembered that very first conversation, when he'd told her that her foul language was charming. "I imagined this differently. I'm doing everything wrong. I'm not good with people. I can never say what I mean." His expression was sad. "You want to go. You want to leave."

She almost said yes — *yes, yes, for god's sake, let me out of here* — but didn't. "I'm just tired, George."

"Then you should go," he answered, and then: "You're very important to me, Miranda."

And at once there was something about all this that made her feel tight and unhappy, as if she had done something that was both right and wrong at the same time. "George," she said.

"No, it's okay. Go." He smiled. It was a tired, pained smile. "Maybe next time, okay?"

She started to get out of the car. He touched her shoulder. "Please don't be afraid of me," he said.

"I'm not," she said, because it was not exactly fear that she felt, but something like relief mixed with guilt. She turned and walked away from him, listening for the sound of the car leaving. It was not until she heard it that she started to relax.

Not far from Ocean Avenue, she stopped to watch two men juggling knives. She knew the taller one; his name was Rainier and he had asked her out once, but she'd said no. When he saw her now he smiled and flipped a knife into the air, where it flashed silver and orange in the boardwalk light until he caught it neatly in one hand.

"Randy Randa," he said. "You want to learn to juggle?" His voice was teasing and rough.

Randa, still on edge, tilted her head and let her hair fall against her cheek in a way she knew was attractive — not because she felt like flirting but because it seemed like the sort of thing that the sort of person she was would do at a time like this. "You want to show me?" she said. When the words were in the air they sounded like a come-on.

Rainier grinned, revealing crooked and discolored teeth — one of the reasons she hadn't leapt at the chance to go out with him — and said, "I'd like nothing better." He balanced a knife neatly on the tip of one finger and winked. "First lesson: start with the balls."

She surprised herself by laughing. But before she could answer, the other juggler called out to Rainier — *Quit flirting and let's go* — and he shrugged. "Some other time," he said.

"Some other time," she agreed. As she walked away, hearing the calls of the two men behind her as they started another show, her head was full of the delicate silver knives, spinning and flashing in the orange glow of the streetlights, and the edginess that had been running up and down her spine since she'd left the car began to fade. Sure, she could juggle. That was something she could learn to do. Maybe she would even be good at it. Maybe she'd be so good that Rainier would want to make her his new partner. They could hook up with one of those concert tours for angry suburban high school kids on skateboards. Travel. Make money.

She worked this idea like a potter works clay, prodding and shaping it, stretching it and warming it in her mind. Pushing George back and away in her thoughts, she pictured the way her life would be on tour: the costumes she'd wear, the parties she'd go to after the shows, the looks she'd get when they stopped for gas in small towns. The daydream rolled, and grew. She saw the handsome rock star or pro skateboarder whose eye she would catch; at first she'd turn him down, of course, because who wanted to deal with that kind of ego — but maybe he'd keep trying. Maybe eventually she wouldn't say no.

As she walked, her steps lightened.

six

WHEN RANDA ARRIVED at the Pink Pearl
for her shift the next morning, there was a
vase of flowers waiting for her. Orchids, from a florist; not su-
permarket flowers, or the kind of roses that sad-looking women
sold at busy intersections. With them was an envelope with another hundred-dollar bill in it. There was no card. Randa knew
they were from George.

She didn't want to think about him. She tucked the money
into her shorts and gave the flowers to Tom's sour wife, Angie,
who always looked at Randa as if she suspected her of stealing
pillowcases and who responded to the orchids with suspicion.
"They're pretty," she said. "You sure you don't want to keep
them?"

Did she think the flowers were some kind of trick? Randa
wondered. They were just flowers; their capacity for evil was
limited. She shook her head. "I can't keep a plant alive."

"You don't have to keep them alive. They're cut flowers.

They're already dead." Angie tore the small packet of plant food off the plastic wrapped around the flowers and opened it with a box cutter she took from her desk. She held the box cutter like a weapon, as if it might be needed for self-defense at any moment.

Randa shrugged. "I'm not here enough to enjoy them and I don't want to carry them home. You keep them."

Angie's eyes glittered. "Must be a nice guy, to send flowers," she said. "You going out with him again?"

Randa didn't look at her. "It's not like that," she said, and left.

The flowers hadn't improved Angie's mood, but the money improved Randa's. George might be a weirdo, but a hundred bucks was a hundred bucks. Any wariness she felt about taking it was pushed quickly away. From a certain point of view, maybe he actually owed her, right? He hadn't come to Lawrence Beach for just a seaside constitutional, after all: he'd wanted something from her, and since she didn't know what it was, there was no way to know whether she'd given it to him or not. Besides, she reasoned, even if she didn't want to take the money, even if she wanted to give it back, there was no way that she could. George was gone.

Later on she met Jenny at the beach. Her roommate was full of plans she and Seward were making for that fall, when they would both be in the South. Randa paid little attention until Jenny said finally, "Saw Seth last night while you were out with James Bond."

Randa, lying on her stomach, drew a line in the sand with one finger. Seth. Now there was a guy who knew what he wanted. She remembered her fantasy about kissing some boy on the seawall: clean, simple, imaginary. Could have been anybody. Could have been Seth. Suddenly she felt nostalgic for him. "How was he?" she asked.

"Seth, or James Bond?" Jenny shrugged. "Kind of pathetic. He's leaving in a few days, I guess. He really wanted me to tell him about you, but he didn't want to ask. You know how it goes. Hey, how was Double-oh George, anyway?" Jenny said, and giggled. "Did he take you to his secret spy cave in his invisible spy car?"

"Hey, fuck off," Randa said, matching Jenny's gleeful tone perfectly.

Laughing, Jenny said, "Did he buy you dinner with his secret spy credit card?"

Suddenly Randa sat up, turning to face Jenny. "I mean it." She was a little surprised at her own vehemence. "Fuck off."

Jenny drew back, eyes wide with surprise. "Jesus," she said. "Jump down my throat, why don't you. I was just joking."

Randa didn't answer. She lay down again, this time on her back, and threw an arm over her eyes so she wouldn't have to look at Jenny. "Sorry," she muttered. "Sorry." After a moment she said, "My hippie freak mother thinks my dad was in the CIA. George says he can find out for me."

After a beat, Jenny said, "So?"

"So that's it." Randa shrugged. "Whatever. Probably a load of crap, anyway."

Another beat. When Jenny spoke again, her voice sounded as if she was trying very hard to be open-minded. "Well, why does your mom think your dad was in the CIA?"

"Because she's a nut," Randa said, and sighed. "And because he was flying down in Honduras and Nicaragua, around there, and apparently a lot of CIA bullshit was happening in that part of the world back then." She flicked away an ant. "It's kind of interesting, actually. Back in the early eighties, there was a revolution in Nicaragua, right? And the side that won the revolution wasn't the side the U.S. wanted to win."

"What did we care?"

"Because the new government was communist, and we're historically obsessed with stomping the shit out of communism. And because the old government was pretty much in our pocket, and the new one wasn't. But we couldn't come right out and *say* that we wanted the old government back in power again, because that would make us look like assholes." As an afterthought, Randa added, "This was back when we still cared about that kind of thing."

Jenny shook her head. "What does this have to do with your dad?"

"Well, basically, what happened in Nicaragua was that the CIA started training the people who wanted the old government back and arranging for them to get guns — that was the whole Iran-contra thing, right? And according to my mother — who is a grade-A nutjob, as I've said before — the way the CIA operates is that it has these sort of phony companies that it sets up all around the world, so if it needs pilots or whatever, then they officially work for one of these phony companies and not for the CIA."

"And your dad worked for one of those companies."

"My mother thinks so. Of course, my mother also thinks that you can cure depression by burning candles and that dead people speak to us through crystals." Randa turned over onto her stomach again and laid her chin on her folded hands. "He did work in Honduras, though," she said. "I'm pretty sure I remember that. And the timing is right." She shook her head. "My mother is probably full of it, and George almost definitely is. But if they're not —" Randa shrugged. "I don't know. Either way, my dad's still dead, so I'm not sure it matters."

Behind her sunglasses — which had sky-blue lenses and thus hid nothing of her expression from the world — Jenny rolled her eyes. "God, who knew," she said. "Here I thought I was just getting a roommate, but you're surrounded by international intrigue."

Randa smiled. "I don't know if one dead father counts as being surrounded."

"What about Double-oh George?" Jenny said. "Can he really find out about this for you?"

Randa shook her head. "Who knows." And then, slowly: "I'm not so sure about him, Jenny."

"In what way?"

"Pretty much in every way."

Jenny considered, and then shook her head. "It is a little bit creepy, Randa. The guy gives you a ride down here, and a hundred bucks, and then shows back up again a month and a half later to buy you a taco — but never hits on you. Not even once."

"I asked him if he wanted to sleep with me," Randa said. "He said no."

Jenny shook her head again. "You know what it smells like to me? It smells like he's one of those guys that thinks he's too *decent* and *moral* to want to do anything like, oh, say, *fuck* you or anything." She wagged a finger. The nail was half-covered in chipped green nail polish. "And that, my dear, is the creepiest kind of creep, because that's the kind who's going to snap someday, and you're going to end up chained to a wall in his fucking root cellar."

Randa stared at the bright water. "Well, he's got a Mercedes — don't know about a root cellar."

Suddenly Jenny gasped, her mouth a round, shocked O. "Oh my god. Randa, what if he's the guy? Seriously. I mean, isn't it awfully convenient that he happened to come through town yesterday, and today they find another body on the beach?"

"They did?" Randa hadn't known about that. She stared at a sailboat out in the distance and thought again about the rich boy who had taken her out on his father's yacht, and how small the people on the beach had looked from the top deck of the boat, with all of that water between her and them. Finally she said, "Impossible. He was with me last night."

"So he did it during the day."

"Who the fuck ever heard of a serial killer who killed people during the day?" Randa said, annoyed.

"No, really," Jenny said. "I'm telling you, you should talk to the cops."

Randa shook her head. "Trust me. George is not the Beach Bunny Killer, or whatever stupid thing they're going to end up calling him."

"How do you know? Did you do a background check?"

"I know because I was alone with him in his car last night, and he didn't kill me, did he?"

Jenny made a noise of disgust and lay down. "Do what you want. I'm just saying."

"Well, stop saying." But Randa was remembering George's grip on her wrist the night before, the fevered look in his eyes. And she wondered.

After a moment Jenny said, "All that time together. Just you and him in the car, and he never hit on you once."

"Maybe he's a nice guy," Randa said, and Jenny shook her head.

"Dude," she said. "Root cellar."

Before the second semester of Miranda Cassidy's third year of college, the University of Pittsburgh sends her a letter informing her that she is being removed from active student status because of her poor academic performance. When she reads the letter, Miranda is drunk, and she laughs. It is easy for her to laugh. She is living in an apartment with three other students, all of whom she likes, and the expulsion means only that she will no longer have to feel guilty about sleeping until two in the afternoon and skipping her classes.

Even when she sobers up, it takes Miranda almost a month to realize the gravity of what has happened to her. She spends that month working twenty hours a week at a local coffee shop. At first it is a lazy, blissful existence. She can still use her student ID to get into campus concerts, parties, whatever, and she does not miss the boring, overcrowded lectures that she never particularly liked. But as time passes, she begins to feel disconnected from her roommates in a way that she does not understand. When one of them has exam results to mourn or celebrate, she feels oddly flat. When their papers are due, she feels awkward and in the way. At parties, she has to explain to people that she is not majoring in anything, not stressing over job interviews or internships or her GPA. After that, conversation tends to lag.

The month is almost over before she gets around to telling her mother that she is no longer technically a college student. As she dials her mother's house in Sedona, she expects a fight; the idea pleases her. For a month now, Miranda has done nothing but sling coffee and drink and sleep, and she kind of feels like a fight.

But Anne, when she hears the news, only sighs and says, "Well, Miranda, if you don't feel like being in school, what do you feel like doing?"

Miranda knows that her mother is trying to be understanding. It annoys her. "I was thinking I'd join the Peace Corps," she says, although she has no intention of doing any such thing. "Or go backpacking through India, or something. Haven't decided which yet."

"Really?" Anne sounds delighted.

Miranda only laughs. "Come on, Anne. Even you know me better than that." She's firing with both barrels at once — using her mother's first name while implying maternal failure — and the shots go home. When Anne speaks again, to say that it wouldn't exactly kill Miranda to see a little of the world, she sounds hurt and withdrawn, and Miranda feels the same savage mix of emotions she always feels after a direct hit: part relish, part vengeance, part guilt, part satisfaction. Scoring against her mother, she suddenly realizes, is like making out with a stranger in a bar bathroom stall. She always seems to need just one more kiss, one more hard word, before she knows for sure whether she likes it — and then suddenly it's over, and maybe she liked it or maybe she didn't, but either way it's not worth worrying about anymore. All at once she no longer wants to fight.

"Yeah, maybe," she says. "I guess I could travel, couldn't I?" An idea occurs to her. "I could go to Central America. I could go see where Dad worked."

"No," Anne says. "Not there. There's nothing down there."

"I'm not saying I want to go be an investigative fucking journalist." Now Miranda is annoyed again. God, these conversations with her mother exhaust her. "It just might be nice to *see* it, that's all."

"You wouldn't be able to. The government wouldn't let you."

"Sure. They're terrified of college dropouts."

"That's not what I mean," Anne says. "I'm not talking about black helicopter stuff or anything like that. I just mean that nobody would know anything. It doesn't work the way it does in the movies, you know," she adds. "It's not just a matter of being persistent and brave and bribing the right bartender or something. If you want to know about your father, I'll tell you about him."

That's exactly the problem. Miranda was old enough when her father died to have a sheaf of memories to flip through when she thinks of him — Nick lifting her into an airplane in a huge echoing hangar and carefully placing an enormous set of earphones on her head (they'd pulled at her hair, but she hadn't asked him to take them off), Nick fixing a tire on her bicycle, Nick and his friend X-Ray smelling like beer and shooting baskets with her in the driveway — but they're the memories of a child, low-angle shots in which all of the grownups are huge and mystifying and separate. She was not old enough when Nick died to remember his sense of humor or recognize his perspective in herself. For this, she's had to rely on Anne. In Miranda's freshman year English class, the professor had talked about the problem posed when a story is told by a character who was too close to the story to be trusted. Miranda had known exactly what the professor was talking about, because as far as she was concerned, that was Anne: an unreliable fucking narrator.

She sighs and tells her mother to forget it. She's not going anywhere. She knows it.

That night, after work, she finds two of her roommates sitting in the kitchen and arguing about *Brave New World*, which they'd been assigned for a British literature class. This was one of the books she and her friends passed around in high school, and she remembers it well. So she makes a cup of coffee — even though she does not plan to drink it, since coffee is the last thing she wants after six hours of standing at an espresso machine — just so she can stay in the kitchen and listen to what they are saying. If she were taking that class, she thinks, as she would have if she were still in school, she would write her Huxley paper about how predetermination eradicated hope, and how human beings were hope addicts who'd go to all sorts of stupid lengths to get it, hold it, keep it. Just look at her mother: dead husband, no body, no hope — until she'd started chanting over crystals and hovering over Ouija boards. She would have liked to write that paper, she realizes; she would have bitched about it, sure, but secretly she would have enjoyed it. She opens her mouth to speak, to see what her two roommates think of her idea — and suddenly she realizes that there is no reason for her to have any ideas about *Brave New World*, that nothing in her life demands ideas anymore. In fact, she can't think of a single thing that her life *does* demand, other than a blood alcohol level just low enough to work a cash register.

Standing at the sink and listening to her roommates discuss the nature of predetermination in a pragmatic society, she realizes that her life can be divided into neat segments: the years before her father's death, those after her move to Phoenix, and those after her return to Pittsburgh. Each, of itself, can be neatly encapsulated, with no strings leading from one to another except those in her head. She could have started over each time, leaving all the grief and disappointment behind her. Only Anne would be able to follow the threads down through her history, and that afternoon's conversation notwithstanding, Miranda and her mother hardly have anything to do with each other, anyway.

And just like that, she feels the strings holding her to this chapter of her life dissolve like spun sugar in water.

She dumps her coffee in the sink.

"Hey, M'ran," one of the roommates says. "Where you going?"

"To bed," Miranda says. The next day she begins looking for a full-time job outside the city. Within a week, she is gone.

The weekend after George's visit, the Clam Shack threw a going-away party for one of the bartenders, who was leaving early to take a calculus class. Everybody Randa and Jenny knew was there — except Seth — including Rainier, the juggler. He asked Randa when she was leaving. There was no point — and no money — in hanging around after the season was over, he said.

She told him that she didn't know. She was going to see where the cards fell and play them as they lay. He grinned and said, "Well, hell, Randy Randa. As soon as I get up the money to get my van fixed, I'm headed down to the Keys for the winter. Have you ever been to Florida?"

"No," she said.

"You'd love it. Blue water, white sand — nothing like this dump." Rainier's expression was enthusiastic, his eyes bright. "All I got to do is make enough money to pay the man, and we're out of here."

"We?" she said, looking at his crooked teeth and thinking about the Keys — which sounded a lot like Lawrence Beach, sure, but might be different in some crucial, indefinable way. She wouldn't know until she got there.

"Yeah, sure." His smile was a little leering, maybe, but not predatory. "If you want. The only catch is, you'd have to contribute to the van-fixing fund."

Randa chewed her lip. "How much?"

Rainier considered. "Well, it needs a new transmission, that's a definite. Probably new brakes too. And if we're going to drive it all the way down to Florida, we'd better get all the belts and whatnot replaced — the whole nine yards. Let's say two thousand."

"That's a lot of money."

He shrugged. "So kick in what you can. I don't care. If you throw in twenty bucks, that's twenty bucks less I have to come up with." Randa didn't say anything. "Well, think about it," he said finally. "Option's open."

Later that night the party moved to somebody's apartment — Randa never knew whose — and she and Jenny went to the all-night grocery store to buy mixers. Inside the bright white space, full of soothing piped-in music and comfort foods in friendly packaging, they decided to split up: Randa toward the refrigerated-juice aisle, Jenny toward the tortilla chips. Randa made an additional request for anything covered in orange nacho-flavored powder and headed juiceward, singing along with the song playing on the in-store speakers.

This was a good song, she thought, slightly drunk. She remembered it from her childhood, from early morning drives to the airport to drop off her dad. Why weren't there good songs like this anymore? With melodies and words, not just beats. Songs you could sing along to in your car. Nobody played old songs like this these days. You had to go to a grocery store, for god's sake, and hear them on the in-store speakers. It shouldn't be that way. Songs like this were universal. They were — she reached back and found a college literature word, a Seth word — *anthemic.*

But hell, nothing was really universal, she thought as she turned a corner into the juice aisle. She liked this song because it made her think of her dad; if she'd been ten years older, it might make her think of heartbreak and unhappy love affairs, some jerk who'd dumped her at a junior high dance. Perspective all depended on where you were standing.

"Miranda?" a voice said behind her.

She turned around. George stood in front of the cheese, dressed — as usual — as if he had just stepped out of a staff meeting. Her jaw dropped.

"I thought that was you. I saw you come in with your friend." His tone was one of pleasant surprise, and just as she thought that he said, "What a nice surprise."

"George," she said. "What the hell are you doing here?"

He gestured vaguely at the orange blocks of shrink-wrapped cheddar. "Shopping," he said.

"For cheese?" she said. "In the middle of the night?"

He shrugged. "I'm driving. Sometimes I stop by here for road food."

"Like cheese. Sure." Randa started to step past him toward the orange juice.

He moved out of her way, but said, "How are you?"

"Drunk." She was being short with him. She didn't care.

"Yes," he said, nodding. "You look drunk."

113

"Thanks," she said, and then remembered something. "For the flowers. And the money. And you never said what you were doing here."

"You're welcome," he said patiently, "and I did. I'm shopping."

Randa shook her head. "George," she said, "this is weird."

"What's weird? Meeting here? If you ask me, it's a happy coincidence."

"No." Randa was emphatic. "Finding a stamp when you need one is a happy coincidence. A quarter in the pay phone coin return slot is a happy coincidence. You being in this exact grocery store at the same time that I am — that's weird."

He shook his head. "Miranda," he said, "you overstate your own importance. I'm not following you. I've been driving through Lawrence Beach for work for years. I have patterns, things that I do when I'm here. One of them is stopping here to buy raisins and —"

"Blocks of Longhorn cheese?"

"— yogurt," he said, and gestured. The yogurt was, in fact, right next to the cheese. "Coffee is my favorite, but I'll take cherry vanilla if I have to. It's the only grocery store in town that's open twenty-four hours a day," he added. "Where else would I go?"

"Coffee yogurt is foul," she said slowly.

"But I like it," he said. "There's no explanation. Just like I like you, even though you seem convinced that I have some sort of sinister ulterior motive. What exactly is it that you think I'm going to do?"

Randa thought of George as he had been the last time she'd seen him: in the car, his eyes intense and his body stiff. But now he seemed completely relaxed. His expression was mild, and faintly amused.

"Okay," she said. "But last time was weird, right? I'm not making that up."

"I work with a woman," he said. "She talks about something called — second-date jitters? The first time you're with somebody, it's easier because you don't know if you like them or not. The second time, it's harder, because there's an expectation to live up to."

"See, *no*," Randa said, exasperated. "George. We aren't dating —"

"Of course we're not."

"— which makes that a seriously weird thing to say."

"But I think it works the same way with friends," he said. "Or maybe it's just like that for me. I don't like many people," he added. "So when I meet somebody I like, maybe I get nervous."

Jenny rounded the corner behind him, her hands full of two big bags of chips. She saw Randa and George and her mouth dropped open in surprise. She lifted her shoulders up, mouthed *What the fuck?*

"Jenny," Randa said to her over George's shoulder, "this is George. I told you about George."

He turned around. "Jenny? You're Miranda's roommate. She told me about you." His smile as he held out his hand was completely normal, completely appropriate.

Jenny's eyes flicked toward Randa, and she held up the chips. "Hands full. Can't shake. Nice to meet you, though."

"Likewise. Let me help you with that." He took one of the bags away from her, looked at it. "Remarkable," he said, seemingly to himself.

"Doritos," Jenny said, speaking slowly and clearly, as if George had never seen snack foods before.

George laughed. "No, I meant how you two manage to look so healthy when you eat so badly. Of course, I used to be able to do the same thing, ten or fifteen years ago."

He walked to the cash register, talking easily and constantly. What had they been doing that night? Was that what they normally did? Did they prefer paper or plastic? When he offered to pay, Randa said no, but then Jenny stepped hard on her foot and said, "That'd be great. Randa always says what a nice guy you are."

"Does she?" George gave Randa a smile she couldn't read. "That's good to hear."

Outside, he turned to Randa. "I guess this is goodbye for now. It was nice meeting you," he said to Jenny.

"Sure," she said. Giving Randa a significant look, she went to start the car. Randa watched George carefully.

He smiled. "Was this less weird than last time?"

"Reasonably unweird," she answered. "I wouldn't expect any awards for it, though."

"I'm not in the habit of expecting awards." He raised one hand and touched her shoulder. "Did you really say that? About me being a nice guy?"

Randa shrugged. "Yeah, sure," she said. After all, hadn't she said something like that, and hadn't he just bought their groceries?

"I'm sorry about that thing I said last time," he said. "The cheap and ugly thing. I don't think you're cheap and ugly." Then he walked away, toward his car.

When Randa got in the car, Jenny said, "That was Double-oh George?"

Randa nodded.

Jenny checked her lipstick in the mirror. "I take it all back," she said. "He's normal. Not exactly normal-normal — more like geeky normal — but normal."

"You don't think it was a little strange?" Randa said. "Him showing up like that?"

Jenny finished with her lipstick and turned the key in the ignition. As she pulled out of the parking lot, she said, "Honey, it was a little strange, you getting in the car with him and crossing three states. *Mee*-randa," she added, and laughed.

"I guess it's all relative," Randa said. She could see George's Mercedes in her side mirror. He was sitting in it, not moving.

Her brow furrowed. "He didn't buy anything," she said, half to herself.

"What?" Jenny said.

"Nothing," Randa answered.

A few days later Randa was walking down the boardwalk alone, thinking indistinctly about George and Rainier and the

116

summer that was almost behind her. It was late in the afternoon. End-of-season-sale signs hung from all of the store windows, even though it was still technically summer: T-shirts marked down from twenty dollars to ten, kites and beach toys practically free. Everything was shutting down. Randa found herself thinking that maybe Rainier had the right idea after all.

"Hey there," a voice said.

She looked up. A boy — a kid, really, he couldn't have been more than nineteen — was perched on the boardwalk railing. In one of his hands he held a mass of plastic key chains shaped like telescopes, all clipped together like a bunch of grapes and all with *Lawrence Beach, VA* printed on their sides. A camera dangled from a strap against his bare chest. "You want a souvenir?" he said to her.

He had long hair and a scattering of freckles across his nose. Cute. Randa stepped up to him, picked up the telescope he was offering her, and looked through it. The picture inside, backlit by the sun, was of three teenage girls, their blond hair twisted into braids with beads on the ends.

"Seven bucks," the kid said. He held up the camera and gave Randa a crooked smile that had probably been more than a little responsible for the sale he'd made to the three girls in the picture. She wondered how many of the pictures in the mass of telescopes he held in his hand were of pretty teenage girls, and how many of them had the sparkle in their eyes that these three did: they weren't looking at the camera, they were looking at the kid behind the camera, and every one of them probably thought he was looking back.

She handed the key chain back to him. "Been here all summer?" she said.

He looked surprised. "You live here?"

"I work in a motel."

She saw his eyes flick down her body and back up. "Yeah, I seen you around," he said. "I like your tats. Check this out." He turned around. His left shoulder blade was covered with the head and forepaws of a prowling tiger, its mouth hanging open to show huge incisors. The lines were clear and sharp,

117

like ink on paper. It was new, and skillfully done, but not very original, in Randa's opinion.

"Nice," she said anyway.

"Got it over at Mike's Body Art. Cost me two hundred and fifty bucks. Where'd you get yours?" He did something strange with his tongue and she saw the glint of a stud there, heard the faint clink of the metal on his teeth.

Randa shrugged. "Different places."

"I'm Jeremy," he said. "But people call me Jay."

"Randa," she said. "How long are you in town for?"

"Another week and a half," he said. "You want to hang out sometime?"

She laughed. "For a week and a half?"

He gave her the charming smile again. "Seize the day, you know?"

"That's a dangerous philosophy," she said, and he said, "Danger is my middle name," which she'd been hoping he wouldn't.

"Well, Jeremy," she said, "maybe I'll see you around in the next week and a half, and we can hang out."

"It's Jay," he said automatically.

Randa shook her head. She'd already been with a Jay. "I like Jeremy better," she said.

They took the space of four rounds to get to know each other — not at the Clam Shack, but a place just like it called the Great Shark Reef, which was Jay-Jeremy's hangout. Then they went to his apartment, which was in a converted motel, like Randa's. Judging by the scattered clothes on the floor, he didn't spend any more time in his than she and Jenny spent in theirs. The bed was rumpled and unmade.

Outside, the sun was going down. There was a bad landscape painting on the wall, some seagulls and a derelict boat on the kind of sunset-colored beach that, as far as Randa knew, was an astronomical impossibility on the East Coast. Another cluster of plastic telescopes, about twice the size of the one Jay-Jeremy carried with him on his daily rounds, hung from the picture's cheap frame. He was in the bathroom, and Randa could hear the loud stream of his urine in the bowl.

118

She turned on the floor lamp next to the bed. One by one, she held the telescopes up to the light so that she could look through them at the pictures within. She expected girls, buddies, sunsets — but they all seemed to be of him, shirtless on the beach with his muscles flexed.

Amazing. She laughed aloud in the empty room and began flipping through the telescopes rapid-fire, trying to find at least one that contained a picture of somebody else — then the toilet flushed and she heard him say, "You like those?"

Randa turned. "They're all of you."

He shrugged. "Yeah? So?"

"Well, what do you need so many pictures of yourself for?"

He jumped onto the bed, flopping down next to her. Reaching up and sliding a hand up the front of her shirt along her stomach, he said, "Don't you like the way I look?"

She said, "If I had your job" — he was on his knees next to her now, kissing her stomach, his hands moving her shirt up so that he could get to her breasts — "I'd take pictures of everything. The beach, the boardwalk, the buildings —" She was wearing her swimsuit underneath her T-shirt. He pulled one of the cups aside and bit at her nipple.

"You're so hot," he said. "So fucking hot."

She grabbed his face in her hands and forced his head up to look at her. "You think so?"

"Yeah." His mouth was open, slightly, his eyes dazed with the alcohol, but his hands were still moving on her back, her breasts, her stomach.

She kissed him then, feeling the stud in his tongue sliding against her own, and he tasted like beer and smelled like aftershave and suntan lotion. His hair in her hands was greasy and tangled. The last man she'd been with was Seth, whose hair had always been soft and clean — but Seth worked in a yacht club, and this kid worked on the beach. She touched his chest, which was smooth and hairless and well defined, and thought of Seth's body and its covering of crisp, dark hair. Body part by body part, memory by memory, she erased Seth; replaced him.

His hands were at her cutoffs now and she let him take them off, thinking not about the sex that she was about to have

119

with this person who was four drinks away from a stranger but about how odd it was that she was here, in this place, in this motel on this bed with this person. She felt as if she were outside herself, watching. It was some other person with black-and-blond hair licking at Jay-Jeremy's neck, somebody else's black-lacquered fingernails fumbling with the condom. Somebody else's ankle that parted from its fellow to admit his legs between them, somebody else's dragon-tattooed stomach that was moving gently against his. Somebody else who was entered, somebody else feeling the weight of his body on hers, somebody else who clutched his back as he grunted and sighed. Somebody else.

It is June, 1984. Second grade has just ended, and this is Miranda's first day of freedom. The morning's rain was a bad start to the summer, but it has since stopped, and Miranda is enjoying the day, overcast as it is. She is wearing her survival vest — a birthday present from her father — which is olive green with lots of pockets. She is also wearing a brand-new pair of bright green galoshes that she is enjoying immensely. Her mother called them rain boots, but she heard the clerk at the store call them galoshes, and she likes that word better. As she tromps from one puddle to the next she sings a little song she has made up: *galosh galoshes SPLASH galosh galoshes SPLASH!* She plans to walk up to the second stop sign and back in her new galoshes, and then she thinks she'll probably get her bike out of the garage and go for a ride.

The housing development where Randa and her parents live is so new that most of the lots are still patches of brush and trees. It has a generically bucolic name that she will remember in later years as being either Spring Brook or Sunny Brook, but the name of their street, she knows, is Foxglove, and the street that her friend Jessica lives on is Marigold. The streets between are Magnolia and Hyacinth. When she rides her bike to Jessica's house, she passes Magnolia and turns at the second stop sign, which is Hyacinth. But Miranda rarely goes to Jessica's house, because the truth is that she doesn't really like

Jessica. Jessica has told her point-blank that she thinks Miranda has weird ideas for games. Miranda thinks that weird is better than stupid, which most of Jessica's games are. Jessica's favorite game is My Little Pony, which she prefers to play very properly, using her My Little Pony Sweet Stable Playset and maybe the cute little ribbon-bedecked Sunshine Wagon. Miranda doesn't mind My Little Pony; she has a small collection herself, although she prefers the newer ponies, with unicorn horns or wings. But when she plays with them, she designs elaborate quests for them to complete. Miranda's quests are Fraught With Danger; Not Every Pony Comes Back. In fact, there are usually at least two death scenes — Miranda likes death scenes — and plenty of pony corpses to be loaded into the Sunshine Wagon and hauled back to the Sweet Stable Playset, which Miranda thinks serves admirably as a morgue.

But Jessica won't play this way, so Miranda goes over there only when Anne makes her. Which is usually on days like this, when there's not much to do and she is underfoot. So today she has made sure to get herself out from underfoot before Anne can ship her off to Jessica's. She has no specific plans, but the warm weather and the looming clouds, still heavy with rain, fill her with a tension that excites her.

Almost-stormy days are Miranda's favorite kind. They feel like days when anything can happen.

She walks up Foxglove, singing softly to herself and making sure that she steps squarely in the middle of every puddle. She is watching only the few inches of pavement directly in front of her toes. This is why she comes so close to the cat.

The cat has been hit by a car. It is dead, its body ripped open, a pool of blood collecting in the empty hollow of what used to be its stomach. Its eyes are staring and glazed over, and its mouth is frozen in a scream. When Miranda sees it, she sucks in her breath in shock and then immediately wishes that she hadn't. The cat does not smell good, and the taste is in her mouth now.

For a moment she stands frozen. She does not know what to do. Glancing over her shoulder at her house, she calls once, tentatively, "Mom?" and waits. But there is no answer. Distantly, in the still summer air, she hears a phone ring.

She will go home, she decides. She will go home and tell her mother, and her mother will help her figure out what to do next. Before she goes, she takes one last look at the dead cat. It has — had — one black ear and one white ear, and a white tip on the end of its tail, and Miranda realizes that she is going to have to throw up, because this is not just a dead cat that she found in the road: this is Patches.

Patches does not belong to the Cassidys. As far as they know, Patches does not belong to anybody. She appeared in their backyard a few weeks ago, and Anne began to feed her — because, she said, Patches was going to have kittens, and she would need all the food that she could get. Then one day Patches showed up for breakfast looking thinner, with swollen, dangling nipples, and after she'd eaten, Anne and Miranda had followed her at a safe distance to an old refrigerator box in one of the vacant lots. Carefully, they had looked in and seen the three little kittens writhing and mewling in their nest, their eyes shut and the tips of their ears curled down. Miranda had wanted to pick one up but Anne said she mustn't and —

The kittens.

Suddenly Miranda does not have to throw up after all, although her stomach feels a very long way from all right. She pulls herself up straight and tall, takes a deep breath — the smell of death is everywhere, will linger on her clothes all through that day, which will become the worst day of her short life — and begins to run. She runs past the second stop sign, past the lot where the new house is being built to the vacant lot where Patches's three little kittens are living in their refrigerator box; hating the new galoshes she was so pleased with just a few minutes before because they make it hard to run fast and she feels that she must run fast. This is a Rescue Mission. She has seen television shows about Rescue Missions. When you're on a Rescue Mission, Every Second Counts.

This is not a television show.

The refrigerator box is still there. Miranda sees it, dark and a bit crumpled from the rain, and pushes herself to run a little faster. When she gets there, she stops short of the opening. She is afraid to look inside. She already knows a little bit about death, and one of the things that she knows is that Patches has been dead for a long time. Since yesterday, at least. Maybe the day before.

This is a Rescue Mission, she tells herself sternly. There is No Room For Fear in a Rescue Mission. She steels herself and looks inside the box. In the far corner she sees a small pile of furry things. They do not appear to be moving.

Maybe they're sleeping, she thinks. Tentatively, she reaches out toward them — but the box is too long, and she can't reach.

Rescue Mission, she tells herself. Getting down on her hands and knees, she crawls into the box. It smells bad.

The first kitten that she touches is dead. There is no doubt. She is not thinking about temperature or stiffness or motion; it simply does not feel alive. She jerks her hand back and starts to cry. She wishes that she had gone home first, after all, and brought Anne back with her.

"Rescue Mission," she whispers, unaware that she is speaking aloud. Her father would not be afraid.

She forces herself to reach out, pick up the dead kitten, and put it aside. She will come back later, with Anne, and they will do something about it. The second dead kitten is not as bad, because she doesn't have to move it. And the third kitten —

The third kitten is alive. When she touches it, it lifts its head, weakly, and stares at her through just-opened bright blue kitten eyes. Its mouth opens and emits a tiny, squeaky *mew.*

Miranda cries out and scoops the baby up in her hands, clutching it close. It feels terribly fragile against her chest. She can feel its bones, soft and delicate inside its matted fur. And if she thought she was running before, now she flies down Foxglove, tears drying on her face: past the second stop sign, past the first stop sign, across her yard, and into the house, calling for her mother, calling again and again.

She charges through the house, the living room, the bathroom, and into the kitchen, where she stops short. Her mother is kneeling on the floor as if cleaning it. But there are no cleaning supplies in front of her, and she sounds like she is crying. Miranda has never seen her mother cry.

Heart beating hard, pounding away in her chest just a few inches away from the fragile, fragile kitten, she is confused, and she hesitates despite her urgency.

"Mom?" she says finally.

And then Anne looks up. Her face is as much of a horror as poor dead Patches was. It is ghastly pale and streaked with tears, and the look in her eyes is so very lost and alone and frightened that Miranda instinctively clutches the kitten harder to her chest, as if to protect it from that look.

She waits for her mother to speak, holding her breath, but Anne just stares at her with eyes so empty with shock that an awful thought occurs to Miranda — a thought so unthinkable, so terrifying in its badness that she is forced to take a step back, away from her mother, because Anne is looking at Miranda as if she has forgotten who she is.

"Mom?" she says again. Her voice is as weak as the kitten's.

"*Go away!*" Anne screams.

To Miranda, the world breaks in half. She runs. Outside, into the garage, to the long bench where her father keeps his tools. With one hand she sweeps away the spiderwebs crisscrossing the space underneath the bench and crawls inside. She makes herself as small as possible. She is crying again, and she holds the kitten close. It is crying too.

"It's okay," she whispers to it. "There's nothing to be afraid of. Somebody will come find us. *Daddy* will come." She strokes the kitten's nose, over and over again, and it begins to purr weakly. She holds it up against her cheek, kisses the filthy fur.

"Daddy's on a Rescue Mission," she tells it. "He's coming now. He's coming in a big plane and he'll land in the backyard and it will be okay, it will all be okay —"

• • •

When it was over, Jay-Jeremy said, "You're so wild," and in five minutes he was asleep. Randa gathered her clothes and left. When she got back to the boardwalk, the ocean was gray and cold-looking and she wished that she were in California, where she imagined that the sunsets turned the water into fire and set the sky ablaze.

III

AGONY COUNTY

seven

THE RECEPTIONIST AT Boylan Distribution had hair so shockingly bleached that it looked as though a touch would crumble it to dust. The woman glanced briefly at Miranda's picture and told Anne that she was sorry, but the police had already been there, and she'd told them everything she knew.

Had they, Anne asked, in her best will-wonders-never-cease voice.

They had; yesterday. The detective spent an hour in the warehouse talking to the workers. Anne shouldn't go over there. The receptionist was sorry about her daughter, but there was work that needed to be done, and it wouldn't get done if people kept hanging around asking questions.

Of course. Anne understood completely, she said (noticing the way that the receptionist's pink eye shadow caked in the folds of her wrinkled eyelids). So Miranda had worked in the warehouse —?

"The shipping office," the receptionist said. The phone rang and she picked it up, resolutely turning away from Anne.

The warehouse was a tall, cavernous space filled with shelves holding chest-high cubes of packed toilet paper and dog food. There was a smell: not a bad smell, sort of an inside-the-cupboard smell. Workers zipped around the concrete floor on machines that seemed part phone booth and part forklift. Anne found the office in back, behind a long plate-glass window; three people sat inside at a table piled high with paperwork. Taking in the huge shelves behind her, the dim industrial lighting, the smell of boxed food and dust, Anne thought, *This was my daughter's life. This was her view.*

One of the people sitting at the table, the one closest to the door, was the girl from Miranda's photograph. The tip of her tongue stuck out of her mouth as she concentrated on the bundle of paperwork in front of her. In the picture her hair had been pulled up, or back; in reality, it was dark, frizzy, and copious. She had a small pinched face and no makeup. Anne would not have picked her for one of Miranda's friends.

When Anne opened the door to the office, the girl looked up with the grim expression of somebody expecting to be confronted by yet another in a long list of problems. "Can I help you?"

Her voice was the one Anne had heard on the answering machine. "You must be Kim," Anne said. "You knew my daughter."

The girl glanced at the picture Anne held out and made no move to take it. "Andy," she said unhappily. "I already —"

Anne nodded. "Talked to the police. I know."

"Yesterday," Kim said, and shook her head. The other two workers in the office — an older man with weathered skin and a woman who looked like she shared a hairdresser with the receptionist — were staring, openly curious, and despite Kim's weary tone, Anne saw a flicker of self-importance in her eyes. The police had come here to talk to *Kim*, after all. Just like on television.

Anne asked if there was somewhere they could go for a few

minutes to talk. Kim looked at her pile of paperwork and shook her head: she had already had to stay late last night because of this, and —

"Just a few minutes," Anne said. "I promise."

Kim sighed, sounding put-upon. "All right," she said. She reached under the table and grabbed her faded denim purse, which was decorated with a handful of plastic buttons that said things like *Life's a bitch and so am I* and *What part of NO don't you understand?* Then she led Anne through a maze of corridors behind the office to a door that opened onto one of the loading docks. There was a small patch of dying grass nearby, and a scarred picnic table surrounded by a thick carpet of cigarette butts.

"Andy said you two didn't really talk," Kim said as she sat down at the table. "How did you know she was gone?"

"I came to see her and she wasn't here," Anne said. The air around the loading dock smelled like burned carbon. "I was the one who reported her missing."

Kim pulled a pack of Virginia Slims and a lighter from her purse. She put a cigarette between her lips. "I haven't seen her since the day after the Fourth," she said as she lit it. "I didn't even know anything was wrong. I feel really bad." Her words were muffled by the cigarette, which she sucked noisily and then held between two fingers. When Anne asked how long she and Miranda had been friends, Kim shrugged. "I don't know. Since she started working here, so — six months?"

"Were you close?"

Kim didn't seem to want to look Anne in the eye. She flicked her ash onto the ground and said, "We'd go out. Get drunk. Me and Andy and Jay, sometimes this guy Tom I hang out with."

Anne took out the picture again and pointed to the goateed man on Miranda's left. "Is this Jay?" she asked. Kim nodded. "What's his last name?"

"Miles. He used to work here. I introduced them. They had some stupid fight that night," she added.

The fight. The voice mail message. "What was it about?"

Kim shrugged. "Who knows? Sometimes Andy was kind of

a snob. Jay told me he tried to call her and apologize, but she never called him back." She looked down at the surface of the picnic table and traced a long scar in the wood with one strawberry-laquered fingernail. "I guess now we know why."

A touch of drama colored the girl's voice, as if this were the way Kim thought the scene should play out. Irritation nagged at Anne like a rash. "Can you tell me about that night? Where did you go?"

Kim eyed her with suspicion. "You know, I already told the cops all this."

"I know," Anne said quickly. "But you know how cops are. If I didn't do my own police work, I wouldn't know anything."

The girl nodded and smiled. "Never around when your stereo's getting stolen, but always there if you've had a beer or two after work, huh?" She blew a long plume of smoke into the air and went on. "We went to the Lucky Strike, out near Brownsville. It's a dump. We got drunk. Same old, same old. There's not much to do around here but drink," she added, perhaps, Anne thought, to forestall any maternal moralizing on Anne's part.

But she didn't care about her daughter's drinking. "Did you and Andy leave together?" she asked. It was the first time she had ever referred to her daughter as Andy, and the name felt strange on her lips, as if she were talking about somebody else.

But Kim was shaking her head. "No. Andy left before I did. She took off after she and Jay had that fight in the parking lot."

"Were you in the parking lot with them?" Anne asked, and Kim shook her head again. "Did Jay say where she was going when she left?"

"Nope. Just that she was pissed off at him."

Anne was starting to build a scenario. Jay Miles, the goateed man — the kind of person who would fail to check on his girlfriend when he didn't hear from her for a week — had somehow lured Miranda out into the parking lot. Maybe they were going to smoke a joint, or have sex, but something went wrong —

132

"Where is this bar?" she said.

"The Lucky Strike, out on Route 51. It's a real dive."

"So why go there, that night?" Because maybe he'd planned it, maybe it was next to a ravine or somewhere that would be good to dump a body —

But Kim only smiled. "Same reason we always go there. Seventy-five-cent mixed drinks and two-dollar shooters."

"Are there woods nearby?" Now Anne saw Miranda with garish blond hair, lying alone in sun-dappled woods. Half-covered by leaves, one pale hand turned up toward the sky.

"It's in the middle of a cow pasture."

The sun-dappled woods and the pale hand blinked away, and Anne began to breathe again. "When they went outside," she said, "how long was Jay gone?"

"A couple of songs. Maybe three or four."

Fifteen minutes, then? Maybe less. Was that enough time? A new scene formed in Anne's head: a dark gravel parking lot, loud music and voices from inside the bar. The heady smell of grass and manure from the pasture. He would have had to do something with her body after he'd killed her. Put it in the trunk of his car. She asked Kim if Jay had driven to the bar that night.

"No, he came with Andy. I had to give him a ride home after she ditched him."

The trunk of *her* car, then. Just because Miranda wasn't in her car when the police found it didn't mean she hadn't ever been there.

Kim continued. "I was sure she was going to come back, but she never did. And then she didn't show up for work on Monday." She paused, and then the words came out in a rush. "Look, I didn't know her all that well — it's like I said, she hadn't been here that long, and we mostly hung out at work. But she was kind of moody, you know?"

"I know," Anne said.

"And there were all these people that she didn't talk to anymore. Like this one night, we saw one of her ex-boyfriends out and he said hi — just being a nice guy, you know? Andy turned right around and walked away like she didn't even see him.

133

When she didn't call me, I figured she was pulling the same shit with me. And I'm not going to put up with that."

"Who was her ex-boyfriend?" Although, Anne realized, she didn't really care. She had already decided that whatever had happened to her daughter had been Jay Miles's fault.

"I don't know. Some guy. I forget his name." Kim stubbed her cigarette out on the underside of the picnic table. Then she seemed to see Anne, and her face softened. "Look, she's probably fine — just being Andy. I'm sure nothing really bad happened to her."

Miranda stared up at them from the picture on the picnic table, looking drunk and slightly manic but definitely *alive*. With one of her arms around Jay Miles and the other around this girl, Kim, who was also definitely alive. How could it be, Anne thought, that Kim was sitting right here, at this very table, but Miranda was gone?

"Are you?" Anne said. "I'm not."

She called the detective from her car. He picked up the phone before it even rang on Anne's end. "Romansky," he said, his voice blunt and unfriendly.

"Detective Romansky?" she said. "It's Anne Cassidy."

There was a moment's pause. Then he said, "Mrs. Cassidy. How are you?"

"You talked to Kim Larkin yesterday," Anne said. "Did she tell you about Jay Miles?"

"Kim Larkin?" Romansky's voice was guarded. "Why do you think I talked to her?"

"I'm at Boylan Distribution. I just talked to her, too."

Romansky sighed. "I wish you hadn't done that."

"Did she tell you about Jay Miles?" Anne repeated.

"She did," Romansky said, "but —"

"Did she also tell you that he was the last person to see my daughter alive? That the last time she saw Miranda she was headed out into the parking lot to have a fight with this guy?"

"Mrs. Cassidy." God, she hated that tone of his, the one that implied that she was far too simple to understand the vast complexities involved in finding her daughter. "I understand you're very concerned about Miranda —"

Anne cut him off. "I think he did something to her. I think something happened in that parking lot, and then he put her in the trunk of her car and hid it until he could get rid of her." When Romansky didn't answer, she added, "Because he didn't have his car with him that night, and *her* car had to be gone when Kim came out of the bar to make it look like she left on her own."

Faintly, Anne heard the rustling of papers. "This is the Lucky Strike that we're talking about?" Romansky said.

Anne confirmed that it was.

"I know that place," he said. "That picture you showed me? There's a bullet hole in the paneling. It happened a couple of years ago. I took the call." He cleared his throat. "It's not a classy place, Mrs. Cassidy."

"So Miranda had lousy taste in bars."

"Well, she was a regular at this one. Look," he said, "I went out there yesterday afternoon. Talked to the bartender."

She waited, but the detective didn't continue. "What did he say?" Anne asked finally.

"Mrs. Cassidy, I promise you that the minute I have something concrete —"

"What did he *say?*"

Romansky's voice was sharp. "Nothing. He said nothing. He recognized Miranda because she used to come in every Thursday night for happy hour, and sometimes on weekends. But he doesn't remember seeing her that weekend. Not specifically. There were just too many people."

"Kim saw her there. Kim was with her."

"While I understand your concern," he said, "nothing happened in that parking lot. On a Saturday night, on a three-day weekend — which is what we're talking about, if we're talking about the fifth of July — that parking lot is packed solid. And people are constantly going outside, for whatever reason." He paused. "Some of those reasons are not exactly nice."

"The bar doesn't matter," Anne said, exasperated. This was

like a house of mirrors, she thought. Everything she said echoed off the pane of glass in front of her, and she couldn't find a way out.

"All I'm saying is there's no way anything could happen in that parking lot without witnesses — without a whole *crowd* of witnesses. And even if Jay Miles did manage to do something without being seen — how long did Kim say he was gone?"

"Fifteen minutes or so." Anne wished angrily that she smoked, so that she could do something — anything — during this conversation other than sit and listen while Romansky explained all his excellent reasons for not finding her daughter.

"The place where we found your daughter's car is a good twenty minutes' drive away from the Lucky Strike. And if he ditched the car, he'd have to walk back, right?"

Sounding as ugly and mean as she felt, Anne said, "So he ditched the car somewhere close and came back to move it later. Don't tell me you still don't have enough reason to talk to him."

Mildly, Romansky said, "Actually, I talked to him this morning."

Christ. "Well, what did he say?"

Romansky ignored her. "There's one other thing you're not considering. If Jay Miles did something to your daughter — without leaving a single drop of blood in her car, by the way — why would he bother going to all the trouble of leaving those messages on her answering machine?"

Just then, the door to the warehouse opened, and Kim Larkin came out. Anne watched as she walked to her car, which was parked a few rows away from the door. "Because he was covering his tracks," she said slowly. Kim was walking quickly, looking nervously at the cars around her. "He might not even remember killing her. Maybe he repressed the memory."

Detective Romansky said, "I think that's a bit farfetched, don't —"

Kim stopped next to a battered foreign compact and started fumbling in her purse. Anne cut Romansky off again. "I have to go. I'll call you later."

She hung up and ducked down low, so that Kim couldn't see her. There was only one exit from the parking lot. Kim's car would have to pass behind hers to leave. She heard an engine start and listened as the sound came closer, moving behind her car and toward the highway.

Anne sat up. The car waiting to pull out of the lot had rusted fenders and something dangling from the rearview mirror — something bigger than an air freshener or a rosary, maybe a bridal garter or a graduation tassel. As it pulled out onto the highway, Anne started her car and hesitated. She was thinking of the way she'd stood in the shower that morning, picking up Miranda's abandoned shampoo, conditioner, and soap, one by one. Gently, as if they were fragile. She took note of the names of the stores on the water-wrinkled price stickers, opened the plastic tops and inhaled deeply: this is what her daughter had smelled like. She put each bottle back exactly where she had found it, with the label facing in exactly the same direction. There was a pale blond hair stuck to the bar of soap. Anne was careful not to disturb it.

This was why she had left the house where she had lived with Nick. She would come home with groceries, start to put them away, and end up crying over the plastic tubs of chocolate milk mix and jars of pickled Vienna sausages that she had bought for him when he was still alive. He had forgotten his razor the last time he'd gone flying, and Anne had all but put a glass dome over it to protect the glob of dried shaving cream and dark stubble stuck to the blade. Finally she realized that she was treating the entire house like a shrine — a stray sock found under the bed, the pile of sports pages she was saving for him — and that was when she knew she had to move. Nick's death was a question that nobody was helping her answer, and she had given up. Nick was lost to her, that was all. Until she started going to spirit communication seminars in Sedona, that was where he stayed. Lost.

Not this time, she promised herself as she followed Kim onto the highway. Not Miranda.

· · ·

Nick's best friend, X-Ray, has been a part of Anne's life as long as Nick has. X-Ray is his call sign from flight school; his real name is John Excidies. He was among the group of men Nick was with on the night Nick and Anne met, and he'd hosted the party where Nick had taken Anne on their first official date. It is X-Ray who calls her from Central America to tell her that Nick is dead, and who flies home two weeks ahead of schedule to bring her the personal effects that weren't in the plane with Nick when he went down. His Saint Joseph of Cupertino medal is not among them, which means that he was wearing it when he crashed. Some good-luck charm.

One of the things X-Ray brings her is a T-shirt with a crude drawing on it of a buxom blonde lasciviously licking at a distinctly phallic lollipop. The slogan over the girl's head says *I got sucked off at Big Bob's Three Lizard Saloon! Home of the original three-shot tequila sucker!* Nick bought the shirt in Tijuana. Anne has always hated it. It occurs to her when she sees it that at least she will never again have to walk down the street next to a man wearing this shirt. This doesn't help.

So, two months after Nick's death, she calls X-Ray, and they meet at a bar near Agony County, and they order cheeseburgers. X-Ray is a lean brown man, with a sandy crewcut and squint lines burned deep into the corners of his eyes. Like Nick, he is always hungry. When the cheeseburgers arrive, he picks his up and takes a huge, enthusiastic bite.

Anne watches him quietly.

Staring at his plate of French fries, still holding the burger in both hands, his chewing gradually slows. He appears to have some difficulty swallowing. Finally he puts the burger down. He takes a swig from his bottle of beer. He meets her eyes.

"Annie," he says. She is Annie to all Nick's friends, as she was to Nick. "I don't know what to tell you."

"Tell me what happened," she answers. "Tell me what happened to Nick."

He looks away. "We don't know. He took off and he never came back."

"Did they look for him? Did they use sonar?"

"It's a big ocean, Annie, and Nick was due to fly over an awful lot of it that day."

"Radio contact, then," she says. "Distress signals. Locator beacons — don't you carry locator beacons with you when you fly?" X-Ray shakes his head, but Anne is insistent. "There must be some way to find out where he was. Modern planes don't disappear."

"They do in Central America." X's voice is grim. "You've never been down there. It's like another world."

"You're American pilots flying American planes for an American company —" Anne has already had her fruitless conversations with Rush and the aviation lawyer, and she knows that what she is saying is only technically true. Still, she wants to hear what X will say.

He interrupts her. "No. We're not. Not down there. Down there, we don't exist. We're ghosts." He shakes his head. "Even if they found the plane, it wouldn't matter. Nick's gone, honey. They're not going to find him, and nobody's going to search twenty square miles of ocean floor for a thousand pieces of scrap metal the size of your finger. It's goddamned unfair, and I'm sorry, but that's the way it is." X-Ray's eyes are such a pale brown that they are almost yellow. They are disconcerting and feline, and he is aware of their effect on people. He is using them on Anne now, staring at her fixedly.

But Anne knows X. He's eaten lasagna baked in her oven, and she's eaten steaks charred on his backyard grill. She has seen those animal eyes laughing and angry, and once, after an unhappy love affair and many bottles of beer, she has seen them crying. She is not intimidated by X's eyes.

She reaches into her purse and pulls out a white envelope. "I asked for a copy of the NTSB report on the crash," she says, and pushes the envelope across the table. "I got this."

He opens the envelope and unfolds the single sheet of paper inside. As his eyes move over the report Anne can see it in her memory: a government-issue form bearing the Federal Aviation Administration insignia, most of the spaces to be filled out blank and white and final. There is Nick's name, and Western

Mountain's; there is the crash location (*Pacific Ocean*). And near the middle of the page, in the box listing the determined cause of the incident, are two words: *pilot error.*

X-Ray stares at the form for a long time. "Throw that garbage away," he says finally, and tosses the report back across the table. He is angry. "Nick was good, Annie. There was no pilot error."

"You just said you didn't know what happened to him," Anne says softly. "Maybe it was that simple. Maybe it was his fault." Again, she does not believe what she is saying.

"No."

"Maybe he got tunnel vision, or blacked out —"

"Fuck that." X lifts his beer to his lips and drains it. "He flew the plane they gave him where they told him to fly it and did what they told him to do, just like he always did. The hundreds of times he does it well, nobody even notices, but the one time he doesn't come back at all — well, shit, must be his fault, must be pilot error." X shakes his head. "Let me tell you something, Annie. Every rivet in your plane could suddenly let go, and you could have six hundred witnesses with goddamned movie cameras filming the whole thing, and some paper-pushing shithead will still say, 'Well, sure, but shouldn't the pilot have expected the rivets to fail? Sounds like pilot error to me.' If the pilot doesn't make it, all the better, 'cause there's nobody to argue. No harm, no foul." He picks up the report, crumples it into a ball. "Nick was my best friend, Annie. I miss the hell out of him. You think I wouldn't have done anything I could to get him back home to you?"

"Gosh, X," she says softly. "That's nice."

He flinches. "I'm just trying to say that I know how you feel, that's all."

"Do you? Because I feel like I'm being lied to."

He looks down at the table. She gauges the grief inside her and decides that it will be safe to reach across and lay a hand on his arm, although when she does so the arm under her hand feels strong and smooth and is covered with crisp, masculine hair. It makes her think of Nick's arm, and it's all she can do to hold on.

"Am I being lied to, X?" she asks gently. "Are Miranda and I being lied to?"

It's a calculated move. X-Ray adores Miranda, in all her tempestuous glory, and he stares at the table for a long time. When he looks up, his eyes are filled with tears and for a moment he doesn't seem to be able to speak.

"I need another beer," he says finally.

Anne takes her hand away.

Trailing Kim turned out to be harder than Anne had expected. On the highway she felt relatively invisible, but when Kim turned onto a two-lane road, Anne had to follow. Then all Kim had to do to see her was look in the rearview mirror.

All the while, Anne was wondering if she was crazy. Going to Boylan was one thing; even haranguing Detective Romansky over the phone seemed okay, although her theory about Jay Miles's repressed memory probably approached a fairly weird place. But now she was *tailing* the girl, for god's sake. What if it was illegal to follow someone in your car? What if it was *stalking?*

But, damnit, Kim had acted strangely. She'd had a huge pile of paperwork on her desk and given the definite impression that she couldn't leave until it was finished. And yet she was out in the parking lot not ten minutes after talking to Anne. Looking around. Driving fast. Seriously fast, in fact.

As the road twisted and dipped through rolling farmland, Kim's little car zoomed along; she knew the road better than Anne did, and could drive faster. Anne could barely keep sight of her. They left the fields and pastures behind, and now both sides of the road were heavily wooded. Anne caught occasional glimpses of buildings through the thick undergrowth, but most of the land was undeveloped. She concentrated on the tiny compact's bumper, trying to memorize Kim's license plate number. Her eyes kept returning to a faded bumper sticker pasted to the chrome that said VIRGINIA IS FOR LOVERS!

The girl didn't seem like a killer.

Suddenly Kim's brake lights came on and her turn signal flashed. Anne could see a wide gravel road ahead on the left.

When Kim turned, Anne continued straight ahead, closer to her quarry than she had been at any time since leaving Boylan. Close enough to hear the country music coming from the girl's car stereo; close enough that if Kim chose this minute to look in her mirror, there was no way she could fail to recognize Anne. But Kim's gaze never left the road.

Anne turned around, backtracked, and discovered that the gravel road led to a trailer park. Some of the trailers looked almost permanent, with tiny lawns and carports and flowers. Others were propped on cinder blocks in lots scattered with bicycles and plastic toys. Most of the cars parked in front of the trailers had seen better days, although there were a few glossy, expensive trucks, which seemed out of place in the modest surroundings.

Kim's car was parked in front of a neat but plain trailer. Although there was no front lawn, Anne saw a fenced-in area in back. It was like Miranda's apartment: nobody had made any attempt to turn this place into a home, either.

Quickly Anne pulled in under the carport of a deserted-looking trailer with drawn curtains. Turning off her engine and getting out of the car, she went to the corner of the building and peeked around at Kim's trailer.

She felt absolutely ridiculous. But Kim had acted suspiciously, she told herself. She left work early, and she drove fast, and she seemed nervous. *I am right to be doing this. I am right.*

Somewhere a door opened and a dog barked. A moment later a bouncy, caramel-colored puppy charged into the fenced-in area behind Kim's trailer. There wasn't much space in the enclosure, but the little guy ran around its perimeter several times anyway, as fast as he could. The grass was high and Anne couldn't see much more of him than his ears and his wagging tail as he sniffed his way into the middle of the enclosure and squatted.

Kim had a new puppy. That was why she rushed home. She wasn't worried about the body in her trunk; she was worried about her carpets and her furniture.

Anne felt dull. Deflated.

Kim's voice called, "Roscoe!" and the new puppy bounced toward his unseen owner, and out of sight.

She was acting suspiciously, a small, petulant voice inside Anne said. *She was.*

"No," she said aloud. "She wasn't."

That night, as she was brushing her teeth — Miranda's frayed and bone-dry toothbrush staring up at her from the bathroom counter — Anne's elbow brushed against a bottle of lavender oil that was sitting next to the sink. Anne used the oil on her pulse points when she had trouble sleeping, as she had lately, which she supposed was no surprise.

The bottle fell to the tile floor and shattered, the oil soaking into the cheap mortar between the tiles like water into a sponge. And although Anne had made it through the cold receptionist and Detective Romansky's careful dismissal and even through the cop-show car chase fiasco, this was too much.

In the small bathroom, now filled with the sharp woodsy scent of lavender, Anne sat down on the toilet and cried.

eight

MIRANDA KEPT HER COFFEE grounds in the freezer. Anne, sitting at Miranda's tiny kitchen table the next morning with a mug of hot coffee in front of her and a blunt insomnia headache above her eyes, wondered who'd taught her daughter to do that.

Outside, in the apartment hallway, she heard a door shut and keys jingle. She heard footsteps passing Miranda's apartment, someone who didn't know anyone was inside, who didn't care. It was eight-thirty. Miranda's neighbors were heading to work. How many mornings had passed like this, with Miranda's neighbors walking past her empty apartment and never noticing she was gone?

The clock ticked. Anne's coffee cooled. Her hair, wet from her shower, dried.

What she had never expected from the news stories she'd seen about missing people was the *boredom*. The waiting. The pointlessly frustrating futile waiting. The mind-numbing, all-consuming sitting and thinking while absolutely nothing happened.

Anne jumped to her feet. She grabbed her car keys.

At the library, Anne looked at all the missing-person Web sites she could find. After that she spent another, far grimmer hour looking at pictures of unidentified corpses. She hadn't known you could find such things on the Internet and waited with her heart in her mouth for each page to load. The corpses came from places like Fresno, California, and Yuma, Arizona. All of them were sad and blank, like the dead man in the Sedona parking lot had been. None of them were Miranda.

Then she went to a drugstore and bought a notebook, because all the Web sites had suggested keeping a notebook for important information. It took her a while to choose one. She didn't think it would be appropriate to buy anything too fancy — although the ones with prismatic metallic covers caught her attention, because they reminded her of Miranda's makeup — but the plain ones were so boring. So not-Miranda. She pondered the notebooks for what seemed like an hour, and then abruptly realized that she hadn't actually had a concrete thought in some time and was just standing blankly in the aisle. People would think she was crazy. Fine. She didn't care.

Finally she decided to buy a hard-covered black one. It came from the office-supplies side of the aisle, not the school-supplies side. She imagined herself holding the notebook during serious discussions with official-looking government types, FBI maybe; the black notebook would make her look serious, capable, together. In the car, she peeled the price tag off the cover — would it make a difference to her hypothetical FBI agents that she had paid only three dollars and forty-nine cents for her missing-daughter notebook? — and dutifully wrote Detective Romansky's phone number onto the first page. After a moment's consideration, she also wrote down the date when she'd reported Miranda missing and labeled it. *Reported Miranda missing.*

She could think of nothing else to write.

The Web sites had said to make a note of everything, because you never knew what would turn out to be important. But Miranda's vital statistics, her job, what little was known about her disappearance — all of that would be in the police files. The things that Anne wanted to make notes about were the things that nobody else would care about but that were new and remarkable to her.

Things like this: Miranda had learned to like blue cheese. Anne had never been able to get her to eat anything other than processed American slices when she was a child, but now a half-used bottle of blue cheese salad dressing sat in her refrigerator. Of the three rented (and long overdue) movies on top of the television, two were thrillers and one was a children's fantasy from the seventies — *Bedknobs and Broomsticks* — that Anne remembered watching with Miranda as a child. If one were to judge Miranda's priorities by the contents of her apartment and the amount of money that she had spent on them, the things that she cared about were fabric softener, alcohol, and toilet paper. The things she did not care about were peanut butter, dish soap, and frozen vegetables. Her laundry detergent was Mountain Spring–scented and her deodorant was Shower-Fresh. The most-used lipstick in her makeup bag was called Soft Raisin; the least, Purple Nurple.

Life, Anne thought, could be seen as nothing more than a chain of used toothbrushes, the bristles of one touching the handle of the next: green leads to blue leads to pink, cheap leads to scientifically molded leads to electric. You always had a toothbrush. Life lived in its own details. Happy marriages were built on days when the towels were hung up, divorces on days when they weren't; happy childhoods were about unspoiled milk and reliable sandwiches. Anne thought that if somebody cared enough to make you a sandwich with the kind of jelly you liked and cut it the way you liked, then chances were you could trust them to listen to you and talk to you and help you when you were hurt, because they wouldn't bother if they didn't love you.

Miranda preferred her sandwiches with twice as much

strawberry jam as peanut butter, and she liked them cut diagonally. She liked them best with plain tortilla chips crushed between the bread slices, although potato chips would do in a pinch.

Anne knew this about her daughter. In the last twenty-odd years, she had prepared a thousand peanut-butter-and-strawberry-jam sandwiches for her. None of them mattered, she thought, staring at the empty notebook; nobody cared how Miranda had liked her sandwiches, and the knowledge would not help Anne bring her home.

Anne finds life simpler when Nick is away. This is not to say that she enjoys his absences — she misses him terribly, of course — but rather that most couples do not get the opportunity, on a six-week cycle, to see what life would be like if they were on their own. Certain things are harder, and just knowing that nobody is available to help her solve the hundreds of small domestic problems that arise each week is daunting at best. But if she wants to buy new curtains, she buys new curtains, and they're exactly the curtains she wants. If something breaks, she hires somebody to fix it or fixes it herself, and does not have to nag, or wait, or keep quiet.

When Nick comes home, he is often edgy for the first few days. In this mood it is easy for him to find fault with what she has done. He won't come right out and say that he doesn't like the new curtains, not once she explains the old ones had been so riddled with dry rot that they'd disintegrated when she'd tried to have them cleaned; he'll just pretend the new ones aren't there.

Home repairs are worse. If he knows that something has been repaired, he will also want to know exactly how it was done, in excruciating detail: What repair service she called, if she called one, and how much it cost, and if she called any other companies to compare estimates; where she found the instructions, if she fixed it herself, and what tools she used, and where she purchased the materials, and how much she paid. She tries to be generous with him, but it rankles her to take care of their house and daughter alone for six weeks and then never to have done anything quite well enough. She knows — or at least she tells herself she knows — that he is not really finding fault with her. It is hard for him, she is sure, to come back to this life after flying all over the world and living however it is he lives in Honduras (Anne doesn't know, and imagines some sort of barracks, or sterile on-base housing like X-Ray's house at El Toro). If pressed, he will say only that sometimes, when a man comes home, he likes things to be the way he remembered them, and Anne can understand this. It must be disconcerting to walk into your own house and not recognize it. And so she tries to be patient.

But if it is disconcerting for him to be home, it is just as disconcerting for her to have him there. Miranda is six years old and Anne still feels like the little girl is an extension of her own body. When Nick is gone it is just the two of them. In the mornings, Anne makes oatmeal for breakfast and braids Miranda's hair. During the day there is school, and meals to be planned and cooked; at night, she provides Miranda with a clean nightgown and a bedtime story.

Then Nick comes home, and Anne still does all of these things — except the bedtime stories, Nick gets those — but Miranda's thoughts are elsewhere. As far as Anne can tell, Miranda sees her father as a dreamy combination of Santa Claus and Mike Finn, the hero of her favorite television show. She would happily follow her father all day like a spaniel if allowed. For his part, Nick is happy to be followed, but he hasn't ever quite gotten the knack of being both husband and father. Either Anne gets his attention or Miranda does, and he doesn't seem to know who should get what and when. When the three of them are together, she sometimes finds herself wanting to shake him and scream, *Look at your daughter! She's right there!* Or, sometimes: *Look at your wife! I'm right here!*

But when Miranda does have his attention, she has it in a way that Anne is not sure she has ever had. When he has Miranda's, it's the same way. The two of them will tell each other things they won't tell her. She scolds herself for minding, but she cannot keep from eavesdropping. If she just happens to be a room away from where they are, on the other side of an open door or around the corner, then there is surely no harm in listening. After all, they are the people she loves most in the world, and she wants to feel that there is no mood or vacillation they can suffer that she doesn't understand.

And so one night, when Nick and Miranda are watching television together in the living room, she spends an extra-long time cleaning the kitchen counters. From the kitchen she can hear everything that happens in the living room. There is a Pirates game on, and for most of the evening Nick has been watching that. So has Miranda, because she likes doing what her father does. But tonight is *Emerald Idol* night. Nick and Miranda have struck a deal: he watches the baseball game without interruption until Miranda's show comes on, at which point they watch *The Emerald Idol* but turn back to the game during the commercials. At the end of the third inning, a half an hour before her show is due to start, Miranda comes into the kitchen, ostensibly in search of a cookie. In a slightly anxious voice, she asks Anne if she thinks they'll really change the channel when it is time to watch Mike Finn. She *needs* to watch, the little girl explains, especially this week: it is the second part of a two-parter, and at the end of the last one Mike Finn was being held prisoner in a secret dungeon.

Anne smiles. Nick might be the conquering hero, but Miranda is never entirely sure that he understands the local customs — like that cookies are okay for breakfast on Saturdays only, not during the week, and Wednesday is always *Emerald Idol* night.

It's petty, but she finds this satisfying. "Dad promised, didn't he?" Miranda nods. "Well, then. I think you're pretty safe. Your dad always keeps his promises."

"Okay," Miranda says dubiously, and goes back into the living room.

Nick keeps his promise, as Anne knew he would. Now father and daughter are in the living room watching *The Emerald Idol.* Anne considers joining them — the actor who plays

Mike Finn is tall and blue-eyed and sheepishly handsome, and Anne has been looking forward to seeing how he gets out of the secret dungeon. But just as she is about to go into the next room, she hears Miranda say, "Is that what it looks like where you fly, Daddy?" So she hangs back. Nick will not talk to her about his work.

"A little," he says. "But there are more mountains where I fly."

Miranda is silent for a few minutes. From the sound of it, Mike Finn is having some trouble. There are punching noises, grunts, breaking glass. Then Anne hears Mike Finn's plane taking off. So much for the secret dungeon, she thinks.

"Did you ever fly a seaplane like that?" Miranda asks.

"Once, but the planes I fly now are bigger. You remember when we flew to Florida, you saw those big green planes at the airport?"

"Uh-huh." Miranda sounds distracted. Anne smiles. Something interesting must be happening on TV. No matter how much she loves her daddy, the girl still has the attention span of a six-year-old.

"The ones I fly look like that."

"Oh."

Anne hears a spatter of gunfire from the television.

"Did you ever get shot at, like Mike Finn does?" Miranda asks.

Nick laughs. "Mike Finn's got nothing on your old man, baby girl. I get shot at all the time." He says it casually, as if it's no big deal.

Anne goes cold. Suddenly she can think only in broken pieces of thoughts: Shot at? Her husband? Flying a cargo plane?

"Really?" Miranda sounds excited. He has her full attention now. Anne can imagine her eyes, huge, awestruck. "How come?"

But there is a place deep inside Anne that knows, isn't there? Somewhere she knows that Nick's world, where a tool as lethal as a machete costs slightly less than three dollars' worth of American chocolate, is not what he tells her. She wipes the final crumbs from the counter into the palm of her hand and thinks, *I do not want to know this. I do not want to.*

In the living room, Nick answers Miranda's question. "Sometimes you fly over places, and the people on the ground don't want you flying there. Maybe they don't want you seeing what they're doing. Maybe they think you're snooping around. So they shoot at you. Kind of like you'd throw a rock at another kid who was in our yard."

Shocked, Miranda says, "Throwing rocks is bad. You can hurt somebody throwing rocks at them. And not just ouch-hurt. *Bad* hurt."

Nick laughs. "That's right. Absolutely no rock-throwing allowed. Never, ever, ever."

Anne washes her hands at the sink, dries them on the towel, and goes into the living room. "It's Mike-Finn-o'clock," she says cheerfully — more than a little surprised at her own calm — and Miranda smiles. And she knows that could be the end of it, but as soon as Miranda is asleep, Anne tells Nick that she doesn't like Miranda hearing things like that.

"Like what?" he says. They are sitting on the couch, watching the late movie. "No rock-throwing?"

"You know what I mean."

"Throwing rocks is *bad,*" he says in a credible Miranda imitation. "Somebody could get *hurt.*"

"Nick, stop."

He laughs. "You know, Annie, when I was a kid, we had rock fights all the time." *Silly Annie,* his tone says. *Silly Annie with your silly rules.*

But Anne will not be deflected. "Don't tell Miranda you get shot at. Especially if it isn't true." Which, of course, is his cue to say, *Silly Annie, I don't get shot at.* And then she can go back to not knowing, and everything will be fine.

But he only grins. "Come on, Annie. I can't let her think that bullshit Mike Finn is cooler than her old man."

Cool, she thinks incredulously, and shakes her head. "Great," she says. "So a month from now, when Mike Finn gets shot down and captured and tortured by the bad guys, you'll be here when she wakes up screaming from a nightmare at two A.M. to explain that nothing like that is going to happen to you."

"I hate when you do that," Nick says. He is still staring at the television, but his voice is suddenly flat and smoldering.

Anne is angry, too, because the nightmare-ridden face she sees in her imagination is not her daughter's. It's her own. "Hate when I do what?" she says. "When I try to tell you how to be a parent?"

"Goddamn it, Annie," he bursts out. "Don't fucking do that. Don't throw it back in my face that I'm not around more. You always do that." His jaw is clenched and the arm resting on the back of the couch ends in a white-knuckled fist. He is genuinely angry.

But he is wrong. She doesn't do that. She wants to scream at him, to throw things: she never complains. She should complain. She deserves to complain. *You leave me here!* she wants to shriek. *You leave me!*

She takes a deep breath. "Okay," she says. "Let's stop."

They sit quietly for a moment, each not looking at the other. Anne finally says, "I'm not asking you to be around more. I'm just asking you not to make things harder than they already are —"

"Hard! All you have to do is sit here and play with Randa and I'm out there —"

"— by scaring our daughter." She tries to pretend that she hasn't heard what he's just said. "By acting like I shouldn't have changed the curtains that were rotting into dust. By telling her you get shot at." *Just tell me you don't,* she pleads with him silently. *Just tell me you don't and I can go back to not knowing. I don't want to know.*

Nick fails her. "I do fucking get shot at," he says. "What I do is important. If it weren't for me, and people like me, you know what would happen to the world? You know what kind of place it would be?"

Something — her patience, she wonders, or her tolerance? Her nearly endless capacity for self-deception? — snaps. "Well, then, go," she says. "Go save the world. Leave us alone." She shakes her head. Why can't he just lie to her? "I swear to god, Nick. Sometimes I think I can do this alone more easily than I can do it with you."

And for a moment they stare at each other, because this is something that has never been spoken aloud between them. Anne herself is shocked by what she's said, and at the truth of it. Nick is wearing his Marine face, the one that shows her nothing. The Saint Joseph medal glitters from his bare chest, as if mocking her: she might leave Nick, he might leave her, but he will always go flying.

Her stomach lurches. Suddenly she is afraid of what he is going to say.

But then the Marine face softens. "Hey," he says, and takes her hand, pulling her to him. "Don't say that. Don't ever say that."

And in her relief she lets herself be pulled, and kissed, and soon it seems as though everything is right again — although it isn't, although they will have this fight many more times before his death. But still, there is nobody that Anne loves more than Nick, when she loves him, and she loves him that night.

Detective Romansky's suit was wrinkled, and his eyes looked tired. Still, he wore the same practiced and blandly pleasant expression as always, and Anne thought that it must be a hard job, spending all day pretending mild interest. As he filled a cup of water for her from the cooler, she imagined the evening that she was keeping him from. Was he married? Divorced? His left hand was bare, but he wasn't bad-looking, so she guessed divorced. An armchair, then, maybe a few cans of beer. She wondered if he had a dog and decided he did: a droopy-eyed, lazy old hound with a bad leg. On the weekends, he made chili and spaghetti sauce, those male culinary staples, and kept them in single-serving bags in the freezer. Maybe he played in a police softball league. She looked at his broad shoulders and heavy arms and thought, *Catcher.*

"So," he said, and smiled at her. "What's in the notebook?"

"Nothing. Your phone number," Anne said. She opened it up and showed him, and then told him about the Web sites she'd looked at that day.

"Not a bad idea," he said when she mentioned the notebook. "We'll have to get you more to write down." His voice was kind, as if finding Miranda would be as easy as going to the store for more paper towels. Anne knew he was humoring her. It would have annoyed her if she hadn't needed it so badly. For the first time, she found herself almost liking him.

She smoothed the pages of the notebook, as if getting ready to write. "What do you think about contacting the media?" she said. His jaw instantly tightened and she added quickly, "I think it's a good idea. Maybe somebody saw something that night, and they'll recognize her if they see her picture on the news."

Romansky shook his head. "Oh, sure," he said. His voice wasn't kind anymore. "They'll recognize her. Every lonely, attention-starved wacko between here and West Virginia will recognize her. Reporters are wolves, Mrs. Cassidy. They won't do you any favors."

"And all cops care about are doughnuts, and all New Age bookstore employees sleep under pyramids." Anne shook her head. "You'll have to do better than that."

"Okay," he said. She marveled at how he could so quickly build her goodwill and then shatter it again. "How's this? They might not even cover your daughter's disappearance. For you, it's a tragedy. For them, it might not even be a story. When your missing kid is four, it's easy to get press coverage — at least at first — but with adults you need a hook. You need to be a movie star or a billionaire or a sweet old grandpa with Alzheimer's." He took a sip of the coffee in front of him, grimaced, and went on. "Now, maybe you could be the hook, if they want to play it that way. Concerned mother coming across the country to find her daughter, that's not a bad story. But I have to warn you, they probably won't play it that way. They'll want to know about your history and Miranda's history — everything you can think of. For starters, when they hear that the last time you saw your daughter was three years ago, you're not exactly going to look like mother of the year. And then there's Miranda herself." Anne opened her mouth to protest, but he cut her off. "Four jobs and three apartments in eighteen months, tattoos all over everywhere, hangs out at places like the Lucky Strike — and she's visibly intoxicated in the only picture you have of her. Hell, they might even find out that she abandoned her cat and use that against her."

"None of that should —"

"Matter? No, probably not, but that doesn't mean they won't call your daughter a tramp on the evening news." Then, more gently, Romansky said, "I'm just telling you what I've seen in the past. The press worries me, because we can't control it. And I was serious about the wackos."

"And you'll be the one who has to deal with them."

"Who? The wackos or the reporters?" He shook his head before she could answer. "Doesn't matter. The answer to both is yes." His eyes were frank.

After a pause, Anne said, "I looked at another Web site today. It had pictures of dead bodies that hadn't been identified — actual pictures of dead people. John Does and Jane Does, right?" He nodded. "There were warnings on some of the pages, that they might be disturbing to look at — because they were so decomposed, I guess." She looked up at him. "There weren't any warnings about being disturbed because one of them was your daughter."

Romansky was silent. Then he said, "I question the wisdom of that kind of Web site."

"Why?"

"Because people are ghouls," he said shortly. "I just keep thinking about some creep who killed a girl logging on every night to look at her morgue shot." He sighed. "Mrs. Cassidy, do you know what I think?"

"You're going to tell me."

"I think your daughter just moved on." He shrugged. "I think she got sick of her job, sick of her boyfriend, sick of the Lucky Strike. I can understand that. I've been sick of it myself a time or two. Spent a few years in North Carolina, just for a change of scenery. You know what I mean," he added. "You left, too. You went all the way out to Arizona."

"That was different."

"It's always different," he told her. "Everybody thinks they're the first person ever to feel like chewing off their own leg just to get out of the trap."

Anne thought of the greed in Agnes's eyes when the older woman had asked her for Miranda, and even now felt the faint echo of the black rage and panic that had bloomed in her at the very idea. "No. That was really different."

Romansky gave her a careful look, his face suddenly closed off and official. "This sounds like there's something you haven't told me."

Wincing, Anne said, "That's unfair. There are a lot of things I haven't told you. I haven't told you about my first kiss or my childhood dog or my wedding night, either. Does that make me a liar?"

"It might, if your first kiss, your childhood dog, or your wedding night has some bearing on your daughter's disappearance." The official look never flagged.

Anne shook her head. "This isn't like that. It's nothing to do with Miranda. At least, not now."

Romansky sighed. "Mrs. Cassidy, the suspense is killing me," he said: still flat, still neutral, but his lips twisted ever so slightly with something that might almost have been disappointment. *Here it comes,* that twist said, and Anne realized that on some level he had expected her to disappoint him, that he had never expected her to be anything other than a liar. It reminded her of somebody — no, not of *somebody.* Of Miranda.

Anne shifted in her chair. "Miranda's father was a pilot. Twenty years ago his plane disappeared in Central America." She stopped, trying to figure out how to explain, and then said, "Have you ever seen pictures of what the forest looks like after a forest fire?" Romansky nodded wearily. "Well, that's what I felt like after Nick disappeared. Burned out and empty. And his parents — they live in Shadyside, or at least his mother does — they started making noises about how *hard* it must be for me, what a *challenge* it was going to be to raise Miranda alone." She stopped.

Romansky waited, and then said, "You were afraid they'd try to take her."

Anne nodded, telling herself that it didn't matter if that suspicious twist on his lips stayed or went. He didn't have to like her. He only had to help her.

"And then?"

She looked at her hands. Shrugged. "And then," she said, "I guess I ran away. I packed Miranda into the car with everything I thought we'd need to survive and off we went to Arizona. I didn't even take the furniture."

Romansky nodded. "Let me guess. You didn't send your in-laws a change-of-address card when you got there." Anne shook her head. "Have you spoken to them since you've been back?"

"I called," Anne said. "My father-in-law is dead, I guess, and Agnes — his wife — is sick. She has a home nurse. From what the nurse said, I'm not terribly popular in their house, but I don't know if they ever filed a report about it or anything."

"I'll check," Romansky said. "That must have been a tough time for you."

Anne smiled thinly. "In retrospect," she said, "I may have overreacted."

Romansky looked away. "They couldn't have taken her, you know. Grandparents hardly have any rights under the law, and they had even fewer back then."

"I figured that out eventually," Anne said, "but by then it just seemed to be too late." She raised her hands, and then let them fall. "How do you go to the two nice old people whose only relative you stole out from under their noses years before and say you're sorry?"

"Call long distance." Anne didn't answer, and Romansky sighed. "That was a joke. Not a good one, I guess." She shook her head. "Well, if you don't like that one, I've got a million of them. Here's another: it wasn't illegal for an adult to move without leaving a forwarding address back then, either."

"That's more a joke in the cosmic sense, isn't it?" she said. They smiled at each other, Anne through her misery and Romansky through the faint suspicion that had almost, but not entirely, faded.

nine

L OOK," ANNE SAID an hour and a half later to the thin, sour-faced woman who couldn't be anyone other than Agnes's nurse, Roberta. "I know you don't want to talk to me. But I'm here anyway."

After leaving the police station, she had realized that before she went to see the reporter Romansky had reluctantly told her about, she had to see Agnes. She had terrible visions of the old woman sitting down for the daily news, learning about Miranda's disappearance, and dropping dead from a heart attack.

Now, standing on this stoop under the maples, looking at the ceramic address tiles that Miranda used to trace with her finger, was surreal. Over Roberta's shoulder, Anne could see the gilt-framed landscape in the entryway and the study doors, half opened. "Slam the door in my face if you want," she said to the nurse, "but at least tell Agnes I came."

Roberta's lips were pursed. For a long moment she stared, steely-eyed, at Anne, and then she relented. "I'll tell her you're here," she said. "I can't guarantee she'll want to see you."

Then she did close the door in Anne's face, but it was a close, not a slam, and that seemed like a reasonably good sign. In a few minutes — minutes that Anne spent sitting on the steps, trying to decide how long she should wait for the nurse to return, and whether if she made it into the house she should lead off with the apology or build up to it — she was back. This time she opened the door all the way.

"Come in." Roberta's tone was now several shades friendlier. "Sorry for the wait. She wanted to get up."

Of course she did, Anne thought. Agnes would want to be up and dressed, so that she could receive her wayward daughter-in-law in the study. The interior of the Cassidys' house was old-fashioned and fancy, with stained glass windows and crystal doorknobs. *My mother's house is one big doily,* Nick had told her the first time she'd come here. It was always his mother's house, never his. Never his father's. Anne could picture even then the racing kind of teenager that Nick must have been, and during the car ride home she'd asked with no small amount of wonderment how he had possibly grown up in such a fussy place.

Hell, he'd said, laughing, *the thing I remember most about that house is being shooed out of it so I wouldn't break anything.*

"Did you find Miranda?" Roberta asked quietly.

Anne shook her head. "I'm going to a television station. It might be on the news." She paused. "I don't know what they'll say."

Roberta nodded. "Agnes doesn't watch the news."

"Good," Anne said.

As predicted, the nurse led Anne into the study. Agnes was sitting on the powder-blue sofa, leaning forward slightly so that she wouldn't disturb the lace antimacassar over the sofa's back. Her silver hair was shorter than Anne remembered it, and cut in a smooth pageboy that looked easy to care for. She was dressed in a green skirt and floral blouse, with a matching scarf knotted around her throat.

Nick's flight school photograph — his film-star hair Marine Corps short, his uniform formal and his eyes uncharacistically serious — stood on the mantel. The too-serious eyes from the picture were Agnes's eyes, slightly unfocused now but still snapping. Her chin was held high. Anne had never before seen her without makeup.

"She had a stroke two years ago," Roberta said quietly from behind Anne. "It affected her speech center. Just be patient when she's talking, she'll get it out." To Agnes, more loudly, she said, "Do you want me to leave you two alone?"

"Yes," Agnes said. The word came out slowly and deliberately. Roberta nodded, told Anne to call her if she needed anything, and left.

"Sit down, Anne." Agnes pointed to the other end of the sofa, and Anne complied. She felt as if she were sitting in the principal's office, waiting to hear about Miranda's latest catastrophe — and in fact Agnes's manner was cool. "Good to see you," she said. There was a brief pause between each word, as if she were choosing the one she needed from a mental list. "You look good."

"So do you," Anne said hesitantly. "I like your scarf."

Agnes touched the bright silk at her throat. "It's silly. Nobody sees me but Rob. But —" She shrugged.

"If it makes you happy, you should wear it."

"You're here to see Miranda?" Agnes asked. "How is she doing?"

Agnes didn't know. The nurse hadn't told her. Anne opened her mouth to speak — fine, clearly the correct answer was that Miranda was fine — but found that she couldn't do it. "Agnes," she said instead, pushing the words out of her mouth in a rush, "I want to say I'm sorry, about leaving and taking Miranda and everything. I should have called, or written —" Nick, young and serious, stared at her from the mantel. He seemed to be daring her to finish, and so she said it all: "I thought you wanted to take her."

Agnes's eyes narrowed. Then, unexpectedly, she laughed. "We did," she said, reaching out a thin hand to pat Anne's knee. "We were — angry at first, but too old to stay mad. Knew where you were, anyway."

Confused, Anne said, "What?"

Agnes struggled for a moment. Anne could see her frustration at not being able to find the word, in her eyes and the set of her jaw. "Arizona," she said finally. "Phoenix. Miranda sent us a Christmas card."

"She did?"

Agnes pointed at the secretary in the corner and said, "Still there. Top drawer. Go look."

Anne did, and there they were: a whole stack of cards in colored envelopes, all tucked together in a candy box. She fanned through them. The writing on all of them was Miranda's, in various stages of proficiency.

"Bring the box," Agnes said. When Anne did, she pulled a red envelope from the bottom of the stack. The old woman held it for a moment, stroking the bright surface with her thumbs, and then handed it to Anne. "This was first."

The card inside the envelope was handmade, with a childish picture of a Christmas tree stamped in tempura paint on the front. Miranda's name was written on the back in neat adult handwriting. A school project, then. On the inside, Miranda had written, *Dear Nana and Papa, How are you? I am fine. We live in Arizona now. It does not snow here. I miss the snow. I do not like Arizona very much. I hope you have a Merry Christmas. I think if Daddy comes home he will come to your house so tell him I am here please? Merry Christmas love Miranda.*

Anne's throat started to ache.

Ignoring Agnes, she flipped through the stack and pulled out another envelope. The writing on this one was more practiced. *Here is my last report card, like you asked, and a story for Papa to read. It has dragons in it but the teacher gave it an A anyway. My class went on a field trip to an observatory in the mountains and I saw a bear track. It was neat.*

And another. Now the handwriting was stylized, careful. High school. Miranda had received her driver's license — *You should see the picture, it's really goofy* — and wanted her own car, which she never got. There was no hint of the angry, stomping teenager that Anne had known, no mention of the combat boots, the dyed hair, the loud, rage-filled music. No mention at all of her furious battles with Anne, about anything and everything.

It would be great to see you, too, this unfamiliarly mature daughter wrote, *but please don't bother Mom. She is having a really hard time with her new job and it's only two years until I can come back there for college anyway.*

Anne remembered that job. It had been at a bank, and the teller next to her had been a bully. She didn't remember Miranda noticing that anything was wrong.

Anne looked up. Agnes was watching her sympathetically — but was there a tiny glint of satisfaction there, in those hazel eyes? "You didn't know," the old woman said, and when Anne shook her head, Agnes reached out and took the box back. "She was a good correspondent. Brought a lot of comfort to — Martin and me."

The smile Anne gave Agnes felt thin even from the inside. "I'm glad she wrote to you. At least one of us wasn't an idiot." She looked back at the picture of Nick on the mantel. *Tough little Randa,* his eyes seemed to be saying. *Won't let other people make her decisions for her. Good girl.*

Agnes followed her eyes. "That picture. Do you want it?"

"I couldn't," Anne said.

Agnes shrugged. "I have another. That was before you knew him, of course. Before you, before — Miranda, before Vietnam. My handsome son," she said, her voice still brimming with pride; even though her handsome son had not lived to see forty, even though her handsome son had driven her crazy and been driven crazy by her. Anne suddenly heard, in her memory, Agnes's voice, still sharp and quick after Nick had let slip some vulgar piece of slang in her earshot, saying, *If you're going to be crude, Nicholas, then do it somewhere other than my house. Come back when you can speak decently.*

"Very handsome," Anne echoed.

Agnes made an encouraging gesture. "Take it."

Anne went to the mantel, took the picture. "Agnes," she said suddenly, "do you know Miranda's boyfriend? Jay Miles?"

"Miranda never mentioned him," Agnes said.

Just then there was a light tap at the door, and Roberta came in. "Maybe that's enough," she said quietly to Anne, and then, more loudly, "Agnes? Are you tired?"

Agnes waved a hand dismissively but didn't answer.

"I should go anyway," Anne said, holding the picture of Nick, not letting herself look at the box of letters that still sat next to Agnes on the sofa. She would happily have traded one for the other — the young man she'd never known for the daughter who'd kept her at arm's length — but Agnes had a protective hand on the box. Anne wasn't brave enough to ask for it.

She crossed the room quickly, leaned down, and kissed Agnes's soft cheek. "Come back," the old woman said. "Bring Miranda."

"I will," Anne promised, and turned to leave, but found her progress impeded by Agnes's hand, surprisingly strong, on her arm.

"Don't feel bad about — Arizona," she said. "She came back to us anyway. In the end." And this time there was no doubt about the satisfaction in her eyes.

In the car, Anne let the engine idle while she waited for the air conditioning to kick in, putting the photograph on the passenger's seat. From within the tacky decorator's frame, Nick stared up at her impassively. Anne turned the picture over so she didn't have to look at him. "I never liked your mother," she said to the air.

She had been so careful, since her arrival, not to disturb anything in the apartment, not to interfere in Miranda's life. But now she turned the place upside down. The truce was off. She tore open boxes, dumped their contents on the floor, emptied drawers and filled them again. In the cardboard box that served as the nightstand, she found what she was looking for: a rubber-banded packet of letters, written on lilac stationery in Agnes's frilly, perfect handwriting.

Anne started at the top of the stack and worked her way down.

164

Miranda had been smart. Anne remembered explaining to her, very gently, that although Nana and Papa loved her, they believed some things that were different from what Anne believed, and so it was better for them not to know where Anne and Miranda were for a while. So when Miranda began to write to her grandparents, she had asked them to send their letters to her friends' houses. It was only when Anne began to let Miranda stay home by herself after school that the Cassidys had sent their letters there, where Miranda could take them herself from the mail carrier and make sure that her mother didn't see them.

But honestly, had Anne been paying that much attention? How often had she let days pass between trips to the mailbox, certain that the mail held nothing but advertising circulars and bills with distant due dates, and not wanting to deal with either?

Your photography class sounds nice. We would love to see some of your photographs! I just read in the newspaper that St. Mary's has built a beautiful new photography classroom. If you came to visit, you could tell me how it compares to the one at your school.

Miranda's high school photographs were bleak and monochromatic: rocks, dead birds, the skeleton of a coyote that she'd found in the desert. Anne doubted very much that Agnes and Martin would have found them appealing.

I am so sorry about your fender-bender, but so glad you weren't hurt. Papa says to tell you that your father went through three different cars before he graduated from high school, but I think he is exaggerating. I remember your father always being a very careful driver.

There was nothing, absolutely nothing, careful about Nick, Anne thought.

And, finally, the prizewinner: *You know that you can come and stay with us any time you like. I am happy to call and speak to your mother about it for you. I am sure that the two of you have grown very close out there by yourselves, but I know that she would want you to be happy above all else. That is what all mothers want for their children.*

During Miranda's senior year of high school, she and Anne had a fight that had ended with Miranda screaming, "You are so fucking difficult to live with!" Anne no longer remembered what had started the fight, but she remembered the scene clearly: Miranda, her fists clenched, so frustrated that she couldn't even look directly at her mother but instead yelled the words at the ceiling. Anne had said in response that Miranda was an absolute delight to be around, and the argument had ended with slammed doors on both sides. Anne had not known then that Miranda had an alternative. If she had, she wondered now, what would her reaction have been? Would she and her daughter have been gentler with each other? Would they have talked more, valued each other more? Would Anne have had Miranda on the first plane back to Pittsburgh?

That night Anne lay across the unmade bed, holding her crystal pendulum above her head as the light from the overhead fixture reflected off its facets and played over the striations in the stone. The stone twisted. Anne stared.

For all the times that she had striven in vain to empty her mind of thought, this time the sensation seemed to have come on its own. She felt like she had been drained. No — unplugged. Like she was waiting for somebody to turn her back on.

Dillinger, lying next to Anne, reached a tentative paw out toward the crystal and touched it, ever so slightly. She thought of Livingston the cat, who was staying with Rhiannon in Sedona, and wondered idly if she was supposed to be learning some sort of cosmic lesson as she searched fruitlessly for her daughter. Or maybe it was just something bad that happened, the way things sometimes did. Maybe somebody had to be there at the side of that road, in the wrong place at the wrong time. She could blame Jay Miles — and, in fact, did — but who was to blame for Jay Miles? Maybe he had spent the first ten years of his life locked in a closet.

This was not an entirely new line of thought for Anne. Late at night, when her mind echoed with isolation, she would lie in bed and trace a chain of badness backward, trying to find the source. Pick a tragedy: My Lai, Kent State, Tiananmen Square.

Did you blame the men who fired the guns, the men who built the guns, or the men who invented the guns? Did you blame the men who had put those particular guns in the hands attached to those particular trigger fingers? When Nick's plane crashed into the ocean off Honduras at a speed which turned the ocean to unyielding stone, was it Western Mountain's fault, for sending him out? Nick's, for going? Anne's, for letting him? Did you blame the human beings who had made such a world possible, or the world that had made such human beings possible?

The answer, she thought, lying now in her missing daughter's bed (Was it Miranda, for pushing a limit any time she saw one? Anne again, for uprooting her so callously, for failing in some way to adequately console her after her father's death?), was that you had two choices: you could blame everybody, or you could blame nobody. Either the random, evil deeds in the world were warp and weft in a tapestry too all-encompassing to see, or the world itself was evil and random — but Anne found the second option too horrible to contemplate. She wanted to believe that everything had meaning: every day, every life, every death. Every car crash and plane crash, every plume of smoke, every person who breathed. She had managed to convince herself over the years that Nick's disappearance had taught her invaluable lessons about life and death and the nature of love, but when it came right down to it, what were those lessons? Life was a nightmare, death was worse, and love — love didn't even matter. Love didn't feed you when you were hungry or warm you when you were cold. It didn't bring back the dead. It didn't even bring back the living.

She thought of Rhiannon, who spoke of love as if it were an enormous undercurrent that was always there, waiting to be tapped into. "I'm learning to embrace the love in my own heart," she might say, or "My mother doesn't understand love" in the same tones she would have used to say that her mother didn't understand Urdu.

Had Anne learned to embrace the love in her own heart?

She had. Twice: once in a bar on Carson Street, when she

met a handsome pilot with hazel eyes and film-star hair, with his blood type tattooed on his chest and the dirt of Southeast Asia still under his toenails, and the other time in her own bathroom, when she'd learned that she was pregnant. Love had seemed to her not an undercurrent but an ocean's worth of a breathable substance like air, vast and dazzling and wonderful.

Anne had read somewhere that most of your internal organs had no pain receptors, that they were wired to other parts of your body: your heart to your left arm, your diaphragm to the joint of your right shoulder, and so on, to let you know when something was wrong. First, she wondered, what awful experiment had established such a thing? Second, it was bullshit, anyway. She knew it was bullshit, because her heart hurt.

ten

ANNE FOUND THE LUCKY STRIKE the next day. As Kim Larkin had said, the bar sat in the middle of a cow pasture. As she had also said, it was a dump.

The building was made of prefabricated aluminum with a painted bull's-eye fading into shadow next to the front door. The weather was humid, the sky overcast and burned-looking, and the four cows standing near the gravel parking lot — there was no fence — stared stupidly at Anne's car as she parked. The rest of the lot was empty, and the door was locked. It was not quite noon.

Behind the bar, the pasture sloped up a steep hill to a thick stand of trees. Anne climbed the hill and walked along its edge, keeping watch for poison oak and wishing that she had worn more practical shoes. Her sandals were perfect for an Arizona summer; less so for hiking in the woods.

It had been a wet summer. The ferns growing in the shade

were thick and lush despite the beer cans and — ugh — used condoms that littered their roots, and the woods smelled like earth and mushrooms and growth. It would have been pleasant to walk there, despite the heat, if Anne's motivation had been less dark.

She wasn't looking for a body, she told herself. She was just — looking.

When the leather thong of her sandals began to rub uncomfortably against the skin between her toes, she stopped and looked down over the pasture. The weathered building and the pale gravel surrounding it looked innocuous, as if the owners sold linoleum or small appliances. At night, though, she knew the scene would be different. Anne pictured the small lot filled with cars, parked haphazardly because there were no painted lines. The music would be loud, she thought, and the voices louder. Standing where she was at eleven o'clock on a Friday night, the noise from inside would run underneath the quiet like a river over the next hill: a river with a throbbing bass line, punctuated by the shrill laughter of drunken revelers.

People would stand outside in groups, smoking and talking and making out; others would come, others would go. Like Miranda had. Anne could almost see her, leaning against somebody's car with a plastic cup of beer in her hand — of course the Strike would serve their beer in plastic cups — smoking like everyone else, laughing, talking. Maybe kissing or being kissed by the man from the picture. He would be bigger than she was, pressing her against the side of the car while his mouth bit at hers, his hands gripping her shoulders or her waist or her hair. Miranda would think she was just being kissed. Just having a good time. She had never been careful enough about that kind of thing. (Anne remembered driving past the coffee shop in Tempe where Miranda and her friends hung out and seeing a tall boy — a man, with his beard he looked like a man — kissing a slight girl with long green hair. *Wasn't me*, Miranda said later, not bothering to hide the hickey on her neck. *And if it was, so what?*)

And then — what? A walk, maybe; perhaps even the walk Anne had just taken. Or a drive.

Anne's eyes suddenly stung. She blinked to clear the imagined night from her mind and in the hazy daylight saw that another car was parked next to hers in the lot.

Behind the now-unlocked door, the bar was dark — no windows — and smelled of stale cigarettes and disinfectant. Music played, but not loudly. Cheap paper decorations hung from the ceiling, palm trees and garlands and pineapples; near the door a life-size cardboard cutout of a girl in a red bikini smiled and offered Anne a beer.

The guy behind the bar was young. He wore a Ramones T-shirt and cargo pants, and a steel ring looped through his left eyebrow.

"That your car outside?" he said when he saw her, and Anne nodded. "It's early. You want something to drink?"

"No." Once more Anne pulled out the picture, a gesture that was starting to feel futile. "Do you know this girl?"

He gave the picture a cursory glance and then looked quickly at Anne. His eyes were watchful. "Andy. Cops came by a couple days ago to talk about her, but I wasn't here. Who are you?"

"Her mother," Anne said.

The bartender winced. "Sorry to hear that," he said. "Wish I could tell you something. All I know is that she always drank Captain and Cokes and sat over there in the corner booth with her friends."

"These friends?" Anne waved the picture in the air, holding it with the blank side toward her so she wouldn't have to look at it again.

"Yeah." He pointed to the picture. "That's Miles. His first name's Jay, I think. The other girl — I don't know. Kristy, Caitlin, something like that —"

"Kim."

"Kimmy. Right. She was a cool chick," he said, and then quickly added, "Andy, I mean. Not Kimmy."

"Thanks," Anne said, although she wasn't sure that was the appropriate response.

"You want something to drink?" he asked again.

She asked for water, and when he gave it to her — in a plastic cup — she took it to the booth he had pointed out. She had never been in an empty bar before. She found herself thinking of parent-teacher conferences and school Christmas pageants, of how strange it always felt to be in a place at night that was so clearly intended for the day.

The bullet hole in the dark wood paneling, which Romansky had pointed out in the photograph, still scarred the wall about two feet above the table. Other than that, there was no sign at all that Miranda had ever been there.

Suddenly Anne felt exhausted. She realized that she was tired of chasing ghosts that used to be people she loved and now seemed never to have existed.

For the first time since she'd bought it, her cell phone rang. The default ring tone was the theme from *Mission: Impossible*. She opened it. Said hello.

"Is this Andy's mother?" a man said, his voice nervous and somehow familiar.

"This is Anne Cassidy," Anne said, instantly alert. "Miranda is my daughter."

There was a moment of silence before the voice spoke again. "Mrs. Cassidy, this is Jay Miles."

When she told him she was at the Strike, he said he'd meet her there. Two other people came in while she waited: both men, both wearing the same resigned look. They settled down on stools at the bar, and the bartender greeted them as if he knew them. Anne thought that they would probably be here until closing.

When Jay walked in, she knew him instantly, from the picture and from her imagination. He wasn't as tall as she thought he would be — not much taller than Anne herself, in fact — but he was big, with a soft face like a baby's and a sandy crewcut. He wore long shorts and a machinist's union T-shirt that had probably been free. He still looked like the high school defensive lineman that he had probably been, the kind of guy who cruised happily through high school and then sputtered

172

to a stop without ever really managing to accomplish anything else. And yet Miranda had dated him, had gone out on the town — such as it was — with him and with the equally unremarkable Kim Larkin. The friends of Miranda's who Anne had known in the past were the sort of people who were too smart to be happy, but this crop seemed as if they weren't smart enough to be anything else. How had her daughter changed since they'd last lived together, so that the people surrounding her were so far from what Anne expected?

And then, of course, there was the strong possibility that the man coming across the bar to meet her, with the commonplace features and the giveaway T-shirt, had been the last person to see Miranda alive and might have killed her. Perhaps, Anne thought, she should have called Detective Romansky while she waited.

"Are you Andy's mother?" he said. He seemed nervous. A faint dew of sweat shone on his forehead.

Anne nodded.

"I'm Jay." He put his hand out awkwardly for her to shake. Anne ignored it. He swallowed hard, wiped the palm on his jeans, and asked if she would wait while he got drinks. When a bottle of beer sat on the table in front of each of them and he was sitting across from her, he took a deep breath. "Kimmy Larkin gave me your number," he said. "She said you came out to Boylan to talk to her yesterday afternoon."

"You were the last person to see my daughter alive," Anne said. She did not bother trying to make the words sound friendly.

Jay nodded and took a long pull from his bottle. His fingers went to the label and began to pick. "That's what the cops said. This detective guy came out to talk to me yesterday morning." His nonpicking hand gripped the beer so tightly that his knuckles were white. "I never been in trouble with the police before. Got pulled over for DUI a couple of times, but nothing like this."

He mentions that so casually, Anne thought. Jay shook his head. "I got to tell you, it's some scary shit."

"Is that why you called me?" Anne said. "Because you're scared?"

Jay took another drink. His bottle was now only about half full. "I guess so. The cops showed up at my door yesterday — I wasn't even awake yet, you know? It was freaky. I had to ask them —" He swallowed hard again. "They let me put on my pants first."

"Did you kill my daughter?" Anne was amazed at the way the question came out: so calm, so blank.

"No." Jay's voice was trembling with emotion. Both of his fists were clenched. "That cop yesterday, he said it was always the boyfriend when a woman turned up missing, but I wouldn't hurt Andy. I wouldn't hurt anybody. You can ask anyone. I don't even get into bar fights."

"You got into one. With Miranda. On the fifth of July."

Jay shook his head. "That wasn't — that was nothing. That was just a stupid fight. That was how come I was so mad when she never called me back, you know?" ·

"Right," Anne said. "The answering machine message."

Jay's face turned red. He looked at the table. "I'm ashamed of that," he said finally, in a small voice. "I shouldn't have done that. But — listen — you got to understand, we have this stupid little fight that's just like all the other stupid little fights we have every day, you know? And then she just — shuts me out. Doesn't ever call me back, or nothing."

Anne's hands gripped the edge of her bench. "And it never occurred to you that the reason she never called you back was because she never made it home that night?"

"If I'd known —" he said. "You got to believe me. If I knew something bad happened to her that night — it was just this stupid contest they had at the bar. Like a beach party thing, a wet T-shirt contest, sort of. Andy got pissed off. I went out into the parking lot with her, thinking she'd cool off, but she just kept getting madder and madder. She wanted to leave."

"But you didn't."

"Look, it was stupid," he said. "But she was so mad. And not even about the contest. It was like she was suddenly just

174

mad, like at everything, and there was nothing I could say to make it better." He shook his head. "So she left. Shit, she wasn't making any damn sense. I let her go."

"Then what?"

Jay threw up his hands. "I don't fucking *know*." He sounded desperate, and near tears. "She got in her car and drove away and I never heard from her again. I wouldn't have done anything to her. I liked her." His hand was shaking as he picked up his beer. "I loved her, even."

He'd used the past tense. Suddenly the torrent of rage and bitterness inside Anne — Miranda's disappearance and Agnes and now this — rose up inside her like bile and spilled out in a vast, hateful flood. "You did not," Anne said. "I love her. Her father loves her. Her goddamned *grandmother* loves her."

His face turned red again. "I did. I loved her."

"I live three hours from the nearest airport," Anne said. There was a rushing in her ears and it seemed as if she could see nothing clearly but Jay's stupid face across from her, sweaty and bland and dumb. "It's a six-hour flight from there to Pittsburgh — unless you connect in Denver, which I did, in which case it's more like ten. And then I had to drive an hour and a half to get here." She put her palms on the table and leaned toward him. "I haven't spoken to Miranda in three months, but I traveled fourteen and a half hours to see her because she wasn't answering her phone. I hate this place, I hate this town, I hate this fucking state" — the obscenity was harsh and satisfying on her lips — "but I love her, so I came. Do you understand me? I love her, so I came to make sure she was okay."

Jay's eyes were filled with tears. He opened his mouth to speak. Anne cut him off, spitting the words at him like shards of ice. "So when you say that you loved my daughter and that you didn't hurt her, I don't believe you. Because I can only imagine one set of circumstances where somebody I loved could suddenly stop answering the phone and I wouldn't at least stop by to make sure they were okay. And that would be if I didn't need to make sure they were okay, because I already knew they weren't."

She made herself lean back, forced herself to lace her fingers together on the table so they wouldn't reach out and grab Jay Miles by his puffy linebacker's throat. When he spoke, there was a catch in his voice that was almost a sob.

"I didn't do anything to her. I swear I didn't. Fuck," he said, and dashed at his eyes with a clenched fist. He drained off the rest of his beer in a long gulp. "Everyone thinks I did. Kimmy, the cops — hell, even my own mom was looking at me funny after they left. But I swear to you, I didn't. Why would I call you if I'd done something to her? Why would I be sitting here?"

"Maybe you're a good actor. Maybe you're a sociopath."

He stood up. "I need another beer," he said curtly, and went to the bar.

Anne waited at the table. She did not bother trying to breathe the spiky black feelings out and the cool blue feelings in. Everything inside her was white-hot rage, burning clean and pure, and the heat it gave off was almost like elation.

I am talking with my daughter's killer, she said to herself. *I am talking with the man who killed my daughter.*

When Jay came back he seemed calmer. He sat down and said, "Look," as if Anne could do anything else but look, trying to peel away the layers of flesh to see into the mind of the man who had killed her daughter. "I'm not what you said. A sociopath. I'm an asshole, yeah, but that's all I am. I'm not a murderer, or — or whatever else you think." His voice close to hopelessness, he said, "I did call. I called her."

"I know," Anne said evenly. "I heard."

He squirmed in his seat. "I said I was sorry about that."

"That helps."

"Good Christ," he burst out. "Give me a break, would you, lady? You're right, I didn't check up on her, and I should have. Especially with us being out at a bar and everything. But I did try, you know? I might not have tried very hard, but I tried." He shook his head. "You said you hadn't talked to Andy much lately, right?"

Anne didn't respond.

"So maybe you didn't know her the way she is now," he

said. "You think Kimmy and me are bad friends because we didn't go check up on her, but you didn't know her. She was always on the lookout for something better. Better job, better apartment — except the way she talked, they never seemed to *be* better, you know? I mean, her last job was answering phones at this appliance repair shop, and then she went to Boylan — and hell, a monkey could do what she was doing there, it was a cake job, but she was already talking about leaving even though she'd only been there a few months. Said she was sick of it."

Anne remembered telling Miranda before she left for college that life wouldn't be any better in Pittsburgh than in Arizona. In the dark, stale bar with Jay Miles, Anne heard Miranda's response all over again, as if the girl were sitting next to her: *It doesn't have to be better. It just has to be different.*

Jay went on. "So it wasn't much of a stretch to figure she'd just ditched us, me and Kimmy both. Different job, different apartment, different friends." He was drinking as he talked, and his second beer was disappearing even more quickly than the first one. "It just seemed like her, you know? Cutting us off completely like that."

And that rang true as well. After all, hadn't Anne's own relationship with Miranda faltered in much the same way? Miranda had come to Sedona and they'd argued. After that, every time Anne called, Miranda took longer and longer to return the call. Eventually, calling her daughter had come to seem like one of those pointless but necessary tasks that had to be done every so often, like getting the carpets shampooed. It was the way that you fell out of touch with old friends; you looked back wistfully, wishing that it hadn't happened that way but knowing on some level that it was inevitable. But this time the old friend was her daughter. Anne thought of this and felt ashamed.

And if Jay had the foresight and intelligence to fake the phone calls, he would have tried to make himself sound more sympathetic. Hadn't Romansky said something just like that, the last time he and Anne had talked about Jay? The white-hot rage in Anne cooled, withered, and became something small and deflated. "You didn't kill her," she said dully.

Jay shook his head.

"And you don't know where she is."

"I wish I did," he said.

Anne sat quietly for a moment. She took a sip of her beer. It was cold and salty and mild. "How long did you know my daughter?"

Jay thought for a moment. "Five months. I met her in February."

"Tell me about it," Anne said.

"We met at a bar. Not here at the Strike, somewhere else. They had a black light on the dance floor and it made her hair glow." And then somebody had told him that she was from Arizona, but when he asked her about it she said she wasn't from anywhere, and did he want to dance or play twenty questions? They had gone back to her apartment that night.

"We were drunk," he said, blushing.

"It doesn't bother me," she said. But inside, she wanted to grab her vanished daughter by her ungrabbable shoulders and shake her. *So maybe it wasn't him,* she thought, *but it was someone. You're never careful enough.*

Jay smiled faintly. "That's right. Andy told me. You're the hippie." Then immediately, "I'm sorry. That wasn't nice."

"It's okay. Hippie is okay. Or at least," Anne said, with a wan smile, "it's an improvement on some of the other things she's called me over the years." Jay looked ready to apologize again. Anne stopped him before he could. "Did your mom ever meet Miranda?"

Jay nodded. "It's funny hearing you call her that. She hated being called Miranda."

Anne had never called her anything else. Maybe that was why she hated it. Nick had usually called her Randa. "Did your mom like her?"

"No."

"Why not?" Anne asked, but she already knew why not. A guy like Jay, who was — maybe not stupid, but simple and uncomplicated, would have a mother who was much the same: a mother who would want a nice girl for a prospective daughter-in-law, somebody who would bring the grandkids over and take them away again on a nice, responsible schedule. She would want stability for her son, and safety. Not Miranda.

But Jay said, "She thought she spent too much time on herself — you know, the hair, the tattoos. She used to say that she didn't think Andy would ever be satisfied, that if she won a million dollars in the lottery she'd wish it were two million, and if she was queen of the world she'd want to be queen of the universe."

He paused. Then he said, "It was hard dating Andy. We got along okay and all, but it was sort of like — nothing I did was ever good enough. Nothing I *was* was ever good enough. You know?"

"I know," Anne said.

The last time Anne sees Miranda in the flesh is three years before the girl's disappearance. She begs Miranda to visit her in Sedona, making — and paying for — all the travel arrangements. Miranda is supposed to pick up the rental car that Anne reserved for her at Sky Harbor Airport in Phoenix and then drive up to Sedona. She is a day late and offers no explanation for the delay.

It has been over a year since Miranda's last trip to Arizona. They have four days to spend together. Anne wants to use the time to get to know her adult daughter, and to give her adult daughter a chance to know her. She is hoping that they will be able to meet that way, as adults, and find something that they like about each other. So Anne takes Miranda to Red Rock State Park, Oak Creek Canyon, and the Chapel in the Rocks. She takes her to the Infinite Void and introduces her to Zandar. Miranda accepts this show-and-tell session passively, with only the occasional twist of an eyebrow betraying any opinion at all. Because she says nothing, it is easy for Anne to fool herself into thinking that the trip is going well, and on the last full day of Miranda's visit she decides that the two of them will be able to stay peacefully together at the little pink house, and talk. Reconnect. Bond.

She makes tea and watches with pleasure as Miranda — her hair candy-apple red and nearly waist-length this time around — lazes on the couch with Livingston the cat, who is only slightly more rickety than he was during Miranda's adolescence. After a while, Miranda informs her mother that she needs to pet Livingston more. Pet him and play with him. The only way to keep him active, she says, is to play with him.

There is some reproach in her voice. Anne is tempted to tell Miranda that the cat isn't arthritic because Anne doesn't play with him; he's arthritic because he's seventeen years old, which for a cat is ancient. But this trip is about reconnection, not recrimination, and so Anne says nothing. In fact, in a burst of overcompensation, she even offers to let Miranda take the cat back to Pennsylvania with her. They can send him on the plane, she says, although she loves the crotchety old cat and doesn't really want to let him go. Or Miranda can keep the rental car and drive back to Pittsburgh.

Miranda slides her hand over the dozing cat's curled body, says, "He *was* mine, to start with."

This time, what Anne doesn't say is *Right, that explains why I've spent a thousand dollars on vet bills for him in the last two years.*

But Miranda continues. "He's too old, though. It's not fair to make him adjust to a different place." She sounds decisive, and a little regretful. "What's with that guy Zandar?"

Anne is still wondering if the comment about adjusting was a rebuke — hadn't Miranda herself had to adjust to a different place after her father died? — and is caught off-guard. "What do you mean, what's with him?"

"Well, for one thing, is that his real name?"

"It's not the one his mother gave him, but I think it feels real to him."

"What *is* his real name?"

Anne feels as if she has spent the weekend holding the proverbial greased pig and it's suddenly starting to wriggle away from her. "I don't know," she says, keeping her voice casual. "I never asked."

"You act like my life is a mess because I move occasionally, but you work for a guy whose real name you don't even know? Nice." Miranda's lip twitches. "He has a thing for you, doesn't he?"

"Don't be ridiculous," Anne says, choosing to ignore the comment about Miranda moving. (She doesn't think that. Why would Miranda think she thinks that?) But Miranda is still watching her closely. More seems to be required, so Anne adds, "I met him in a class I was taking."

That sparks some interest. "What kind of class?"

Anne doesn't want to say, but she can't lie. "Spirit communication."

Miranda laughs. "Spirit communication? Isn't that when you pay hundreds of dollars to sit in a dark room while some chick in a corset hides under the table making knocking noises?"

"No." Although Miranda isn't far off about the hundreds of dollars. "It's when you try to communicate with the spirit of someone who has passed over. Through meditation," Anne adds quickly. "Soul journeys."

Miranda rolls her eyes. "Passing over," she says. "That's nice. Is that anything like kicking the bucket? Keeling over, taking a dirt nap, biting the big one?"

"Oh, Miranda," Anne says, exasperated. She is surprised to hear her voice slip back into the same mother-will-soon-weary-of-this tone that had carried her through Miranda's adolescence. Her head hurts just thinking about it. "You asked."

"Did you ever think as the hearse rolls by, that someday in it you will lie?" Miranda's voice is serious but her eyes are laughing, and so it goes until Anne points out that somewhere, Miranda's own father is dead too, and suddenly the girl's playfulness vanishes.

"Jesus, Mom," she says. "Don't start that again."

"Don't start what?"

"The government conspiracy crap. The CIA. All of that."

In Anne's head her lost Nick chokes on a lungful of dirt,

kneels before a fresh grave with a rifle to the back of his head. Hangs — perhaps from his thumbs — in a dark, dank room.

"It's not crap," she says, hearing the ice in her voice and feeling her hopes for the weekend fall out of the sky like a crippled airplane.

"It is crap," Miranda says, and Anne can tell from the poison in her voice that somehow they've stumbled into a well of something deep, and old, and toxic. "It's crap and you're delusional. What do you think, that Dad's sitting on a cloud playing a harp somewhere and saying to himself, 'Gee, I really hope Anne finds herself some fucking crystals and dream catchers so I can tell her about how I fucking died'? You think this is some garbage summer thriller and you get to be the grieving widow on the fact-finding mission?"

"You weren't there," Anne says. "When I talked to those people. You don't remember."

Miranda laughs. It is an ugly sound.

"I remember coming home from school one day and finding my teddy bear packed into the car," she says. "I remember not being allowed to call Nana and Papa. I remember leaving behind every single thing that had anything to do with Dad because you couldn't get your shit together —"

"What was I supposed to do?" Anne is almost crying.

"Be my goddamned *mother!*" Miranda's voice is loud and cracked with emotion. Her anger is like a jackhammer; it shakes the whole room. "This whole fucking thing, Anne. It's all about you, isn't it? Your crystals, your conspiracy theories, your poor dead husband. None of it has anything to do with Dad anymore, and you don't even fucking realize it because you're obsessed with all your stupid questions and you will never be able to answer them, okay? Never."

Later Anne will wonder what questions Miranda means — questions like the ones Western Mountain and Nick himself refused to answer, questions like the ones the lawyer told her would never be answered, or questions like those she asks of her pendulum late at night (did he go down in the water? Did he suffer? Could they have saved him? Did he die instantly?

Did he *die?*) — but right now she tries to sound calm. Emotionally she is in a flat spin and the solid lethal ground rushes up at her with a threat that is almost audible, but she tries to sound calm. "I did the best I could," she says, and then repeats, "you don't remember. You don't understand what it was like."

Miranda fixes her with a cold, unsympathetic stare.

"I understand that one day I had a happy childhood, and the next my dad was gone and my mom was crazy," she says. "I understand that I needed a grownup and there weren't any around."

"Let's not do this to each other," Anne says, but even she knows it is futile.

Miranda crosses her arms and glares.

"This isn't the way that I wanted things to be." Anne can hear the desperate, pleading note in her voice. Maybe Miranda will hear it, too, and they can both back down. Maybe this will still be okay.

But Miranda only barks a laugh into the suddenly stale air. "Yeah?" she says. "Join the goddamned club."

She packs the few things she has brought with her while Anne sits at the kitchen table, crying and holding a resisting Livingston against her chest for comfort. The only thing Miranda says to her before she leaves is, "Take care of my cat."

In the three years since then, Anne has spoken less to her daughter than to her daughter's answering machine.

Hey, it's me. You know what to do.

But Anne doesn't.

She called Romansky to ask if they could talk. He met her in the police station lobby and started to lead her back through the maze of hallways — heading, she thought, toward the same windowless room they'd occupied during their previous conversations. She thought of that room — the cold furniture, the old-coffee smell — and said, "Can we go outside to talk? Or is there some police rule against that?"

He shook his head sternly. "Strictly prohibited," he said.

"Section 121.8." Then he smiled. "There's a bench out front if you want. Got a great view of the bypass."

The bench was squeezed between the brick wall of the station and a bed of struggling yellow flowers. It did indeed overlook the six-lane bypass. Anne and Romansky sat together and watched the cars zooming by.

"Have you ever been to Arizona?" Anne asked.

He shook his head. "I told you, I spent a few years in North Carolina. Other than that, I'm a Pennsylvania boy. Arizona's too hot for me, anyway."

"Not in Sedona," she said. "There's a state park near where I live — Oak Creek Canyon? It's so wooded and alive. You can sit on a rock in the shade, listen to the wind in the leaves. Watch the fish in the creek. It's beautiful."

His fingers went again to that place near his jaw. "Sounds nice. I'll have to try and make it out there sometime. What made you think of that?"

Unexpectedly, Anne laughed. "The bypass. It's sort of like sitting next to a river, isn't it? A loud, smelly river." She sighed. "I met Jay Miles today."

"Did you?" Romansky said. "I wish you'd called me first. What did he say?"

"He wanted me to call off the dogs."

He stared down at the highway. "So what did you think of him?"

Anne rubbed her eyes, which felt like hot, hard balls of glue in her head. "Not much. But I don't think he killed Miranda."

"Okay," he said. "Anything else new, while we're sharing?"

"Just that I went to see my mother-in-law."

"Speaking of which, I did some checking. There were two very calm, very neutral missing-persons reports filed about you and Miranda in 1984. There was almost no follow-up."

Anne nodded. "Miranda wrote to them."

Romansky cocked an eyebrow. "So they knew where you were the whole time. How did your mother-in-law take it when you showed up on her doorstep?"

"As well as can be expected. She had a stroke, and she has

184

some trouble talking." Anne smiled faintly. "Still has dead aim when it comes to scoring points off me, though."

For a moment they were silent. Miranda's file lay on Romansky's lap, rustling gently in the breeze. He had a hand on top of the closed folder to keep it from blowing away. Anne couldn't stop looking at it. It was so thin.

"Okay," Romansky said. "I'll tell you what we know. It's not much." He flipped through the file and pulled out a piece of paper. "Miranda went to work on the Fourth of July, just like she was supposed to. She got off at twelve and went to a barbecue at Jay's mom's house. Got pretty drunk, according to Mrs. Miles. But that was no big deal, since according to Mom, everybody there got pretty drunk. Jay drove Miranda home in her car and didn't come back. Called his mother and told her he was staying at Miranda's.

"The next day, Miranda calls Kim Larkin at about five in the afternoon and makes plans to meet her at the Lucky Strike that night, which they do. Jay says he got pretty drunk but Miranda didn't, and Kim confirms that. Jay also says that at some point during the night they had sex in her car, in the parking lot. We did find some body fluids in the backseat, but no blood, which is a good sign. Apparently, there was some sort of contest going on."

"The wet T-shirt contest," Anne said.

Romansky grimaced. "Actually, it was" — he checked his notes — "the Lucky Strike Summer Beach Party Big Tit Contest. Like I've been telling you, it's a classy joint," he added, seeing Anne's expression. "And I'll tell you something else. I've got a couple of nieces who aren't ever going there again. Anyway, Jay said Miranda wanted to leave pretty much as soon as the contest started, which says good things about your daughter. They ended up having an argument about it in the parking lot and she left in a huff. And that's where things start getting a little fuzzy, because nobody remembers Miranda coming back into the bar after the fight." He gave her a wry smile. "With half a dozen topless girls standing onstage, I'm not really sure anybody would, but people will probably remember the contest, so at least we have a chance. I'm going to go up there on Friday night and ask around, see if anybody remembers seeing a girl fighting with her boyfriend in the parking lot during the Big Tit Contest."

"You don't expect much," Anne said. He shook his head, and she sighed. "I didn't think so. If you thought anything would come of it, you wouldn't be telling me any of this, would you?"

"There are still a few possibilities. We found her car on a toll road, so maybe PennDOT has some film from the booths — but it's not likely. Not from two months ago." Romansky closed the folder and laid his hand on top of it again. "Look, I wish things were different. I really do. For what it's worth, I don't think Jay did anything either, but the truth is, we've got nothing."

The detective sounded unhappy, and Anne gave him a wan smile. "It was easier when I thought I knew exactly what happened."

"It always is," he said.

At the local television station, Anne waited an hour to have a fifteen-minute conversation with a bored-looking production assistant. He asked some questions and scanned the photograph of Miranda — truly dog-eared now — into a computer. When she asked when the segment would air, he shrugged.

"Tonight, tomorrow," he said. "She's been missing awhile, right? So time's not crucial. Maybe Thursday. Thursdays are slow news nights."

She bought a salad for dinner at a fast-food restaurant on the way home and was sitting alone in the kitchen, listlessly scraping thick, sweet dressing off mealy tomatoes, when she heard a knock at the door. She opened it and saw the neighbor who had given her the keys to Miranda's apartment.

"Hi," he said.

"What do you want?" Anne said, her voice cool. She still had not forgotten that first afternoon. She wondered if the police had talked to him.

186

He looked embarrassed and reached up to tug nervously at the silver ball in his chin. "I saw you come in." His black T-shirt had a large grinning skull painted on it. As he spoke, he looked increasingly uncomfortable. "Uh — Andy had my Sega, and I was wondering — but I can come back later," he added stupidly.

Anne considered telling him to get lost, and then shrugged. "Might as well get it over with," she said, and let him in. As he untangled the knotted wires underneath the television, she asked him his name, so that she could tell Romansky.

"Kyle," he said, wrapping a cable around his hand. "What's up with Andy? Did you find her?"

Anne shook her head. He sighed. "Shit. I'm such an asshole. Should have called the police. I figured she just moved on." He looked genuinely sad.

"It's okay," she said, although it wasn't. But as she watched him, she realized that he probably knew that. "Everyone else seems to have thought the same thing."

"And I was an asshole when I gave you the key before, too." He shook his head. "Andy was sort of a tough person to like. Cool, but not exactly — friendly. You know?"

"I know," Anne said. "You want this, too?" She held out the plastic case to the game she'd tried playing.

Kyle glanced at it and grinned sadly. "HP Four," he said, and shook his head. "That's Andy's. System's mine, game was hers." He pulled the television away from the wall and crouched down behind it, unplugging wires from their jacks. "She was a real badass, too. I mean, I'm good and all, but she was friggin' unbeatable."

"You played this together?"

Kyle nodded. "Whenever we were both sitting around with nothing else to do. Kill some time, kill some bad guys."

Anne looked down at the game, remembering the severed arm. She pictured Miranda sitting on the couch with a bottle of beer, her thumbs frantically working the controller and her eyes far away and excited, like they always were when she was consumed by something.

187

"Wait," she said, as Kyle freed the last of the cables and began to lift the console.

He looked alarmed. "What?"

"Show me," she said.

Two hours later Kyle threw the controller down on the carpet, rubbed his eyes, and said, "Damn, Mrs. Cassidy. You suck at this."

Anne's thumbs hurt. The ache was deep in the abused joints, the kind of pain that she knew only stillness and a long hot soak would cure. Her eyes felt dry and sticky. "Call me Anne, okay?"

"Yeah, right. Anne," Kyle said, and shook his head. "I mean, at first I figured you were just learning, but *damn*. You died more in the last hour than I have in my entire life."

"In my world, dying is something you only do once." Sometimes not even that, Anne thought, thinking of her crystals and pendulums, and smiled.

Kyle was silent for a moment. Then he picked up the controller. His thumbs moved aimlessly over the buttons. The look on his face was stoic as he said, "Do you think Andy's okay?"

"I don't know," Anne said, wishing it were that simple. Standing up, she gathered their empty beer bottles and carried them to the kitchen, where she dumped them into the sink and got herself a glass of water from the jug in the refrigerator. All of Miranda's food was still inside, except for the stuff that had smelled. Anne's purchases were crowded together in one corner of the top shelf. She told herself this was because Miranda could clean her own damn refrigerator.

"You know who would have liked this game?" she said to Kyle when she came back. "Miranda's father."

"She told me about him," Kyle said, distracted. He was playing the game again. Anne sat next to him on the couch and watched as he disintegrated bad guys with the evil vacuum cleaner attachment — a photon cannon, according to Kyle.

"What did she tell you about him?" Anne asked.

He shrugged. Onscreen there was a door that led to the next level. Kyle pressed a button and it opened. "Just stuff. That

188

he was a pilot who disappeared when she was little." The armored man tripped a mine — Anne had died in the same place at the end of her last game — and the screen turned into a fireball. "Shit. I totally knew that was there. He was in Vietnam, right?"

"Laos," Anne said. "It was before I knew him."

Kyle shook his head. He seemed reluctant.

"What?" she asked.

Instead of answering, he stood up and got another beer. He took a long gulp, not looking at her, and then said, "The thing is, I sort of got the feeling that a lot of what Andy told me was lies."

"What kind of lies?"

He wouldn't look at her. "She'd just tell me about all these adventures he had in the jungle and stuff." He shrugged. "It didn't sound *real*. I mean, I've got an uncle who's a vet, you know? And he doesn't talk about it much, but nothing she said sounded anything like what he says."

"Andy's father flew in a lot of different countries, not just Laos," Anne said, not knowing what to think. "But what did she say?"

Kyle looked pained. "This is going to sound stupid." He took another pull from his bottle. Hesitantly, he said, "When I was a kid, I used to watch this television show about this guy who flew one of those planes that lands on water —"

Anne laughed. "Oh, god. Not *The Emerald Idol*."

"Yeah, that was it." He sounded surprised. "You remember that show?"

"Every Wednesday night at eight o'clock for years. It was Miranda's favorite show."

"I was afraid of that," he said, "because the stories Andy told about her dad sounded like stuff out of *The Emerald Idol*. There was this one story about gold smugglers that I think I actually remember seeing, because the bad guys kept the gold in this huge kind of treehouse fortress thing." He smiled thinly. "When you're a little kid you don't forget treehouse fortresses. He was really a pilot, though?"

Anne nodded, suddenly numb.

"You know, I never minded, when Andy would lie to me. I just thought of it like — tall tales. Making up stories. It wasn't bad or anything." Kyle sounded relieved. He waited for an answer. Finally he said, "I should get going. It was fun playing Hollow Point with you, Anne," he added awkwardly.

Anne shook herself out of her reverie. "Sure," she said. "It was fun."

"You want me to leave it, so you can play?" he said. "I haven't had it for months. I can wait a little longer."

"No," Anne said. "You take it."

But Kyle shook his head. "I'll leave it here. You might need something to do. You know, other than sit around and wait for the police."

"That reminds me," Anne said, and told him about her trip to the television station and what Detective Romansky had said about the media. "So they might be around," she said. "Asking you questions."

"That's okay. If it helps find Andy." Kyle turned to leave. Then he stopped. "Hey," he said. "You think if we saw that show today, it'd still be any good?"

"*The Emerald Idol*?" Anne shrugged. "It was okay. A little silly, I guess."

Kyle shook his head. "Man, I hope they don't ever put it on reruns or DVDs or something. In my head it's fucking awesome. I'd hate to find out it wasn't." He left.

Later that night, the television station did a twenty-second bit on Miranda. They showed her picture, mentioned Anne's cross-country journey, and asked anybody with any information to call the local police. They did not dig into Anne's past or Miranda's, and they did not mention Miranda's tattoos or her abandoned cat. They did mention the Lucky Strike, since it was the last place she'd been seen, and showed a picture of a car like hers.

Just after the segment aired, Anne's mobile phone rang. It was Detective Romansky.

"I guess you saw the news," Anne said, putting the television on mute. "Are you working this late?"

"Nope," Romansky said. "Just sitting here on the couch, eating some cold pizza and thinking about all the fun we're going to have tomorrow, after that news report." He sighed heavily. "I should have been an accountant. Nice, safe. No crazy people."

"Everyone's a little crazy."

"Guess so. Well, come in tomorrow and we'll assess the damage."

"I think damage is a pretty relative term in this case," Anne said, and he said that he supposed it was, and they hung up.

"Well, I've had a good morning," Romansky said cheerfully the next day, handing Anne a cup of coffee and sitting down across the table from her. "Every time the phone rings, it's a new adventure. You never know what you're going to get."

Anne shook her head. "I won't apologize."

"I wasn't asking you to," he said, but she said, "Look, twenty years ago my husband died and I didn't ask enough questions. I'm not losing my daughter the same way."

Romansky rubbed at his jaw. Finally he said, "I'm sorry if I sounded flip. You develop a pretty bleak sense of humor in this business. Sometimes I forget to turn it off."

"Okay," Anne said.

He grinned. "My ex-wife used to do that. I'd say I was sorry, and she'd say, 'Okay.' Left me feeling about this big." He held up his thumb and forefinger an imperceptible distance apart.

Anne smiled: not because it was funny, but because his grin had not touched his eyes. Instead they held something human and forlorn. For some reason it made her feel less hopeless. "You said you had phone calls," she said.

"Do we ever." He flipped through the pile of paper in front of him. "Four calls from people claiming to have had dreams of Miranda's whereabouts, dreams or" — he gave Anne a dry look — "visions. Six from men claiming to have dated her, ten from people claiming to have seen her the night she disappeared. One from somebody claiming to be an ex-boyfriend of yours —"

"What's his name?" asked Anne curiously. Other than Nick, she hadn't had a boyfriend since high school. Romansky checked his notes, said the name. She shook her head. "Never heard of him."

"No kidding." His voice held an utter lack of surprise. "We've also got two general well-wishers calling to see if we found her yet, one guy who worked with her in an appliance shop in Latrobe, and a professor at Pitt. Apparently she was in his freshman comp class ten years ago. You didn't tell me Miranda went to college," he added.

"She never finished. Isn't it a little odd that those people would call?"

Romansky shrugged. "Not really. People mean well, don't realize it'll get them on the suspect list. Anyway, we're checking both of those guys out."

"Only those two?"

Romansky sighed. "No, we're checking them all out. I personally took four eyewitness reports just this morning from people who say that they specifically remember passing your daughter's completely forgettable domestic vehicle on a dark, rainy night two months ago. A morning well spent, if you ask me."

"One of them could be real," Anne said, sounding only a little defensive. "What about the psychics?"

"Two of them seemed embarrassed about calling," he said. "We can probably just chalk that up to seeing the news story and having it stick in their heads for whatever reason. One was a regular, she calls every time there's an unsolved crime. If you take her at her word, she's had special paranormal insight into every local abduction, hit-and-run, and armed robbery for the last fifteen years. She calls, has a nice chat with whoever answers the phone, and hangs up happy."

"Sounds lonely."

"She doesn't do any harm. Now, the last psychic, I don't know about," he said. "Nobody here recognized her name. She said something about seeing Miranda — and try not to be too stunned by this mystic crystal revelation — near a body of water. Also that she's dyed her hair since that picture was taken, but she didn't know what color it was now."

"Last I knew," Anne said, "Miranda was dyeing her hair about every two months."

"So that might be true?" Romansky made a note. "We'll check it out. Not that I think she really had a vision, but maybe she knows something we don't. Which brings us to the last guy." He pulled out a slip of paper with a name and a phone number written on it, and passed it to Anne. "Says he knows you."

Anne took the paper and smiled suddenly. "X. A friend of my husband's," she explained, seeing Romansky's puzzled look. "X-Ray was his call sign in flight school. He knew Miranda when she was a little girl." Her smile was the first in days to feel remotely genuine. "I didn't know he was still in the area."

"How would you?" Romansky said. "I talked to him myself. He wants you to call him. Said he was worried about Miranda."

"Of course he is." Anne was still staring down at the scrap of paper. "He was crazy about her."

"Crazy, huh?" Romansky said.

Anne looked up sharply at the tone in his voice. "No. Not X. X is a good guy."

"Well, he's a good guy with a rap sheet." Romansky turned to another page in his folder. "Two DUIs, one indecent exposure, and one good old drunk and disorderly."

"So he goes a little wild sometimes."

"Not to mention assault on a police officer, harassment, and a criminal trespass charge. Dropped." He glanced at Anne. "That last is a domestic violence violation. Stalking. Remarkable how many of those get dropped."

"None of that sounds right. X was never violent," Anne said slowly.

"Maybe he wasn't, back in the day." Romansky looked at her, his eyes serious. "Anne," he said. It was the first time he had used her first name. "I can tell by the look on your face that you're thinking of calling this guy. I have to recommend very strongly that you do not do so — at least not until we get a chance to talk to him."

"He's an old friend," Anne said.

"People change."

"He loved Miranda."

"Did he know she was here?" he said quickly. "Would she have gotten in touch with him?"

Shaking her head, Anne said, "There's no way she could have. I don't even know if she remembered him."

"You also don't know if he remembered her."

She could tell that he wasn't talking about X seeing the news report. Anne stood up.

"X-Ray didn't hurt Miranda," she said.

"You don't know that," Romansky said. "You weren't there."

Once, when Nick comes home, Anne asks him to change the light bulb over the garage door. One of the neighborhood boys had thrown a rock at it, and the stub of the bulb was broken off in the socket. Nick turns off the circuit breaker, goes up the ladder with a pair of needlenose pliers, and in just a few minutes wrenches the stubby metal nub free. Jauntily, he jumps to the ground from two steps up the ladder, and comes down hard.

Fourth metatarsal, the emergency room doctor tells him. A freak injury. He'll be in a cast for six weeks while it heals.

"June sixteenth," Nick says, and in response to the doctor's quizzical look, adds, "It has to be off by June sixteenth. That's when I go flying again."

The doctor says that he can't guarantee that. Nick only laughs and says that *he* can, since he knows how to use a hacksaw.

So now one of Nick's legs is in a cast to the knee, and the other is rippled with scar tissue from the motorcycle crash when he was sixteen. Anne teases him, calling him Peg-leg Pete and Gimpy McGimperson. He laughs, but she can tell that he is getting restless. The weather is beautiful and he is trapped, sitting in a chair with a heavy plaster cast on his leg and watching spring go by without him.

After four days, Anne calls X-Ray, begging for relief. He shows up in an hour with two boxes holding remote-control airplanes. When she sees them, Anne bursts into laughter. "What, you don't fly enough?"

Up to his elbows in packing material, Nick says, "Honey, there's no such thing as enough flying."

"Just make sure you wear that voodoo charm of yours," X-Ray says, pointing to Nick's Saint Joseph medallion. "We don't want you breaking your other leg."

Outside, the men have little difficulty getting the planes in the air, but just flying them isn't enough. Soon they're dogfighting, the red plane — which is Nick's — swooping and diving at the yellow and vice versa. Nick's leg, in its cast, is propped up on the porch railing. Miranda is at school, and Anne sits on the porch steps, watching them fly.

It's a position she's used to. She has watched Nick fly from runways and terminals and even their own backyard. When Miranda was a toddler, Nick spent a few months hauling water into brushfires — this was in California — and sometimes he'd buzz their rented house on his way back to the airfield. Anne came to recognize his engine approaching in the distance, and she would run out into the backyard with Miranda. *Wave to Daddy,* she'd say to the chubby little girl, and Miranda would squint at the sky and wave obediently at the roaring airplane over their house.

Poor little kid, Nick said after one such episode. *Probably thinks her daddy's a C-113.*

"I gotta hand it to you, X," Nick says finally. "This isn't any damn near as good as the real thing."

"No," X-Ray agrees, the skin around his yellow eyes crinkling in smile lines, "but cripples can do it from their front porches."

Nick swears at him and redoubles his efforts to knock X's plane out of the sky. The battle doesn't end until Nick's plane crashes into the top of a neighbor's maple tree and gets stuck. As the only able-bodied adult stupid enough to volunteer, X is elected to climb the tree to retrieve it. Nick and Anne watch from the porch as he scales the trunk like a tan, long-limbed monkey.

Nick calls out, "Careful there, buddy. Wouldn't want you to break a leg."

Faintly, they hear X answer, "Yeah, what kind of idiot breaks his damn leg?"

"Thank god those things don't come with guns," Anne says.

Nick's face lights up. "Now that's a good idea. Why don't they come with guns?"

Across the street, the red plane suddenly swoops out of the foliage, landing on the neighbor's yard with a thud. The maple leaves rustle as X begins to work his way back down.

Anne looks at the tree, then at Nick. "I can think of at least two reasons."

Nick grabs for her but she dodges out of reach. Then he asks for a beer. When she comes back with it, X-Ray has returned, with scratched arms and a leaf in his hair. The plane is undamaged — "I'd sleep a lot better if they made the big ones out of that stuff," Anne comments; "So would we," Nick answers — and by the time the school bus stops down the street, both planes are back in the air.

Soon Miranda trudges up the street from the bus stop, frowning. The frown disappears as soon as she sees X-Ray. "X!" she cries. She drops her bookbag on the grass and breaks into a run.

"Here, Annie," X says, and shoves his controller into her hands so that he can sweep Miranda up into a giant hug, crying, "The lovely Lady Miranda!"

"Hi, sweetie," Nick says, without taking his eyes from the little red plane.

Anne stares blankly at the controller in her hands, and says, "X?"

But X isn't paying attention. Miranda is all smiles now. "Hi,

Daddy," she says, and Anne makes a mental note to ask her about the frown later. "X, what are you and Daddy playing?"

"Airplanes," X answers, his voice as serious as if he were another six-year-old.

"Can I play?" she wants to know.

"Annie, you need to bank left, or you're going to hit what's-his-name's house," Nick says calmly.

"How do I bank left?" she asks, as X answers Miranda's question: "Nope."

For an instant the frown is back. "How come?" Miranda says petulantly.

Out of the corner of her eye, Anne sees X shrug. "'Cause it's boring. I was just playing to keep your old man from driving your mom nuts. I really came over to play with *you.*"

"I bet," Miranda says, and Anne smiles, because that tone of patient disbelief is hers, exactly. "Can we play squirt guns?"

X looks at Anne, who is still trying to keep from crashing her plane into her neighbor's roof. She nods. "Looks like that's a go," he says. "Lead on, Sarge."

The two of them disappear into the house. "Nick, I need help," Anne says when they're gone. At the last possible second, Nick takes X-Ray's controller from her and sets the yellow plane flying in a high, loose rotation. "Hold it there for a sec," he says, giving the controller back, and she does, keeping the controls exactly as he set them. Inside the house, the faucet is running and Miranda is giggling as she and X fill up her arsenal of water weaponry. As Anne's plane circles overhead, Nick lands his own. When he's ready, he says, "Okay, babe," and pulls her onto his lap.

As X-Ray and Miranda explode from around the back of the house, half-soaked already and — in Miranda's case — shrieking with joy, Nick puts his arms around Anne's stomach and shows her how the controls work. His head resting against her shoulder, their eyes on the small yellow plane buzzing its way through the sky, she flies.

IV

DARK WATER

eleven

IT WAS RAINING AGAIN. She took it as a personal affront. The sunny days of the past summer seemed like a dream, or a television show. Every morning, every afternoon, and every night brought the same cold, listless drizzle. Damn rain seemed to follow her everywhere she went.

And now there was no warm place, no dry place to which she could retreat. Jenny was in Tennessee, and the room at the Oceanside Arms was gone. The Pink Pearl was operating with a skeleton crew, and even Jimmy's Clam Shack was closed all but two nights a week. So there was only the van, and Rainier, and the glovebox.

Randa had spent two months in Lawrence Beach and seen Rainier a dozen times; but after the party at the Clam Shack he had suddenly been everywhere, or she had noticed him everywhere. She saw him at a bar, where he bought her barbecued shrimp. She saw him at the arcade, where they went head to head on Zombie Hunter. (She won.) She saw him at a bonfire, where in the smoky semidarkness at the edge of the firelight he started to make good on his promise to teach her to juggle. The first time she caught a pin the right way, he'd smiled at her.

"Not bad," he'd said. "Maybe next summer, you can be my partner."

"Maybe I can," she said, and threw the pin up again. She lost it in the darkness and it landed behind her, hitting the sand with a wet thump.

The atmosphere on the boardwalk during the final week of summer was manic. All the people who had been working at bars and seafood shacks and T-shirt shops quit their jobs to spend their last week working on their sunburns and hangovers. Pity any tourists still in town looking for a late-season deal, because all of Lawrence Beach was a wake: for the vanished summer, and for other things. Memorials to the five dead girls had sprung up on the boardwalk like late-blooming perennials, as if the death of the summer had freed Lawrence Beach to acknowledge that they were gone. Now, blurry photocopied pictures of April Agostino and the others adorned almost every block. They were surrounded by carnations and empty bottles of booze — although it was possible that the empties had been full when they were donated. Respect for the dead had its limits.

Randa thought she knew why the candles and flowers had taken so long to appear. During the summer, when everybody had been pretending not to be scared, placing a memorial would have felt — to her, anyway — like a jinx. She remembered her father saying that crashes happened when gravity noticed your plane. The memorials would have felt like that. Which was not to say that bad luck ignored you just because you ignored it, but there was no reason to call it down out of the sky. And hell — everyone who was alive to leave flowers had survived the summer, hadn't they?

Rainier's juggling partner had been the last of their friends to leave. Even the guy from the surf shop, the guy who was rumored to feed his dog boardwalk leavings — even *that* guy left. Rainier said, "No worries, we'll have that money for the mechanic in no time," and Randa left her room at the Ocean-side Arms to move into his van. Everything she owned fit into her backpack, and she had found herself standing for a moment at the door of the tiny room, holding her tiny bag and marveling at how small her life had become.

That first night, when she'd met Rainier at his van, he'd held up a bottle of whiskey and said, "Housewarming party." An hour later, wrapped in army-navy blankets and lying among the jumbled piles of juggling equipment and power tools, Randa told Rainier — her voice friendly, warm — that he had better not get any funny ideas about her sleeping in the van with him. "I'm using you for a ride," she said. "You're using me for van money. It's a fair trade."

He put up his hands in mock consternation. "Hey, I'm a good guy," he said. "You've got nothing to worry about with me." And true to form, it was Randa herself who, three nights later, lifted his blanket and crawled underneath it, ignoring the clove cigarettes on his breath and the slightly gamy smell of his body, to officially Make the First Move. It was not a passionate decision but a calculated one. Those first three nights had been awkward, with both of them trying too hard to avoid touching each other and then feeling eerily disconnected during the day. If they were dating, she reasoned, or at least ostensibly together, things would be easier.

For that first week — before the Pearl shut down, when there were still a few tourists around to throw money in Rainier's hat — things were easier. Despite the memorials, life still seemed like an adventure. The taco shack was still open and they could still afford to buy tacos. He met her at the Pearl and took her walking on the beach while they held hands. His feet were huge, immense; she could stand comfortably on top of them, arms around his waist for support, and he could walk the two of them up and down on the sand, stiff-legged like toy soldiers. Each evening they came back to the van exuberant and optimistic. Randa could already hear herself telling the story to some willing ear on a day that hadn't yet come: *We lived in his van, made love all the time, lived on tacos and ketchup from plastic packets. Then we drove to Key West together, and there we said goodbye. He was the one who taught me to juggle.*

And she could juggle, in a halting, hesitant way. He had given her three red-and-green particolored beanbags to practice with. At night, by the light of the streetlamp coming through the van's windows, he would lie on the cheap carpeted floor as she sat, cross-legged and naked, and practiced. "You're not using your left hand enough. Fluid motions," he would say, and poke her with a pale, hairy toe, as long as her little finger. "You're good at fluid motions." Her progress was slow. She had hand-eye coordination, sure; but it was the kind of hand-eye coordination that made her a badass at Zombie Hunter, not the kind of hand-eye coordination that made it easy to catch a ball in one hand while throwing one with the other.

"It's something you feel," Rainier said to her once. "You know where the ball's going to land, where it's going to go, and you're there to catch it." In the darkness she saw him smile, and felt his long fingers in her hair. "Like falling in love."

"I wouldn't know," she said.

But then the Pink Pearl let her go. The money in Rainier's hat at the end of each day dwindled, and dwindled, and vanished entirely. He found work hauling brush at the country club, which was taking advantage of the off-season to do some landscaping. She found a place a long way from the beach that let her tend bar for tips (never mind that she didn't like people), but the regulars were all locals, and they didn't tip well. It was the off-season for them, too.

Making enough money to live on had always been hard, but soon it was desperate. It was only a matter of days before Randa began to feel her sense of humor withering. The weather grew cold. The two thousand dollars that they needed to escape might as well have been ten thousand. All their money went into the locked glovebox. By the time the taco stand closed down, they weren't spending money on food anyway. Instead they ate crackers and jam and pizzas that they ordered over the phone and never picked up (the pizza place would throw them away, usually, and Rainier would retrieve them from the dumpster). Every cent had to be saved, and the effort of saving sapped their energy. Their nights became quieter.

And now it was raining, and as Randa walked the fifteen blocks from the bar back to the parked van, she felt chilly. She was wearing a pair of Rainier's jeans, belted tight at the waist, and a sweatshirt she'd bought on sale for ten dollars at the skate shop on the boardwalk. The sweatshirt was black and hooded, zipped up the front, and said *Locals Only, Go Home* on the left breast. It was soaked through and sat heavily on her shoulders. Her head hurt. She was getting a cold. She thought that if a stranger walked up to her right now and said, *Hi, I'm the beach killer and you're my next victim,* she'd probably ask him if his car had a heater that worked, and if she could take a nap on his couch before he smothered her.

The van was parked on a quiet side street in front of a closed café. There was an arbor in front of the café with a few benches underneath it — just the place to sit and wait for a table on a crowded summer afternoon — and that was why Rainier had chosen that spot: so they would have somewhere to go outside the van, to smoke cigarettes or give the other person some space. He was sitting there now, smoking.

"Asshole," Randa said when she saw him. "You bought cigarettes." She was only half joking. Rainier smoked cloves, and they cost a lot of money.

He flicked an ash in her direction. "I found a pack in the van. This is the last one." His hands were cut and bruised, and he held the cigarette stiffly, as if his fingers hurt. "After this, I'm out. How were the jerkoffs?"

"Somewhere other than in my bar," she said, and showed him the ten dollars she'd made in tips.

Rainier shook his head. "You could always get a real job," he said. "Something that pays more than tips. Hell, tend bar if you want, but there's gotta be somewhere that'll still give you shift pay."

"On a good night I bring in more money than you do and you know it." Randa stuffed the bills back in her pocket, and they sat in silence for a few moments. Eventually she said, "Can I have a drag?"

"You don't smoke." But he handed her the cigarette anyway. She put her lips where his had been and inhaled. The filter tasted sweet and spicy. Drawing the smoke into her lungs, she felt the burn of it all the way into her chest. Without warning, she started to cough: deep, racking coughs that made her stomach muscles work and her hands shake. Wet coughs. She could almost feel soft pieces of lung tissue tearing inside her, and a hard spear of pain drove itself through her sinuses.

Rainier pounded her on the back, his face a mixture of amusement and concern, and took the cigarette from her. "You shouldn't inhale on the first drag. Some people don't ever inhale on cloves," he said. "They just smoke on them like pipes."

"You don't do that, though," Randa said when she could speak.

"Nah." Rainier smiled for the first time that night. "That's pussy."

The inside of Randa's mouth and nose and the back of her throat were coated in that sweet, spicy smell. Suddenly, unbidden, she suffered a flashback of the bookstore where her mother worked, the one time she had visited her in Sedona. The air there had been thick with incense that was meant to be calming or something, but smelled mostly like cat piss to Randa.

She shuddered. "Well, I'm warmer."

"Baby, you're hot," Rainier said without much conviction. "With that ten bucks in your pocket, we're up to eight hundred."

"Great."

They sat in silence and watched the rain pelt the ugly gray concrete. Finally Randa said, "I'm going to go sit in the van," and Rainier said, "I'll be in later."

Inside, Randa stripped off her wet clothes and draped them over the vinyl seat. The van was a cargo van, with nothing in the back but a square of tattered indoor/outdoor carpeting and Rainier's juggling equipment. She retrieved her backpack from

under the front seat, dug out a T-shirt and a pair of dry underwear, and put them on. Wrapping herself tightly in a blanket,
she lay down. She rested her head on her backpack.

When Rainier came, not long after, he lay down next to her
without a word. For a time they didn't speak. The light from
the streetlights was orange and unpleasant.

Finally Rainier said, "Goodnight."

"Yeah," Randa said.

Her head and the back of her throat hurt and her skin ached.
As she fell asleep, Randa, who had kept that last hundred dollars from George in reserve at the bottom of her backpack,
began to wonder if perhaps she shouldn't spend it on a bus
ticket. Tennessee, maybe, to see Jenny. Or west; see how far a
hundred bucks could get her.

The next evening, Rainier bought a package of bouillon cubes
at the grocery store and mixed two of them with cups of free
hot water from the coffee bar at the gas station. That was
dinner.

Sniffling, bored, Randa said, "Tell me about your dad."

She was huddled next to him for warmth, and she felt rather
than saw him shrug. "Nice guy. Doesn't think much of my chosen profession. Yours?"

"Dead," Randa said briefly. "He was a pilot. His plane went
down off the coast of Central America. They never found the
body."

He squeezed her shoulders. "At least that's a more interesting way to go than eating yourself to death in front of the television, which is how my old man's probably going to kick it."

"What about your mom?"

"She's nice, too. Got a bum lot in life. They're not together
anymore."

"That's too bad."

"No, it's good. They kind of hated each other."

"Do you talk to her?"

"Sometimes. I don't like to call her unless everything's okay.
I'm a bad liar and she worries. What about you?"

"My mother? I haven't talked to her in — god, I don't know. Six months, I guess." Randa sneezed. "I haven't called her since I've been here."

"Why not?"

When Randa was in high school, she'd taken the honors classes, which during her junior year meant calculus. She'd failed miserably. The next year she'd signed up for calculus again, even though a fourth math class wasn't required for graduation, figuring that it would be easier the second time around and vaguely annoyed with herself for failing in the first place. But the first day, while the teacher took roll, she'd opened the textbook, flipped through its pages, and realized that calculus hadn't changed a bit over the summer, and neither had she. *Same old shit again,* she'd thought, miserable and defeated, seeing failure glowing ahead of her like brake lights in a traffic snarl. She'd dropped the class that day. "Don't know," she said now. "Guess we just lost touch."

"You miss her?"

She shook her head. The motion made her face hurt, and she squeezed her eyes shut. "Sometimes I miss other people's moms, though. Like right now," she said, "I kind of miss yours. She sounds nice."

Rainier was silent for a moment. "I bet your mom misses you, what with your dad being gone and all."

"Hell," Randa said, bitterly. "My mom doesn't miss my dad. She talks to him all the time. He lives in her crystals." She shook her head. "My mom has a cute little house in Sedona and a bunch of New Age hippie friends to burn candles with and whatever. She's happy."

Rainier shifted next to her. "Doesn't mean she doesn't miss you. You're still her daughter."

Randa shook her head. "She might miss other people's daughters, but she doesn't miss me."

They were quiet. Finally Randa said, "You know who I miss? I miss my cat."

"You have a cat?" Rainier said. "Who's taking care of him?"

"Don't know." In the darkness, Randa's eyes were distant, unfocused. "He ran away a week before I came here. Big old fat guy. I think he had a bunch of other people feeding him besides me."

"Maybe one of them was a catnip farmer and he figured, screw this Kitty Kibble shit."

She smiled. "I like that better than what I've been thinking."

"What have you been thinking?" Rainier asked, yawning.

"Roadkill."

He didn't answer. Sighing, she settled in closer and said, softly, "He used to bring me squirrels sometimes. Ripped the guts right out of them." She smiled, remembering. "It was horrible. He was so proud of himself."

"I had a python, once."

"Snakes are cool. Kind of like fish, though. Not really interactive."

They were silent again. Then Rainier said, "You feel like interacting with something right now?" and Randa sighed again, and said, "Not right now."

Randa slept most of the next day. Toward nightfall, still sick, she went to work. The manager told her they didn't need her that day, so she walked to the Pink Pearl in the growing darkness. If there were enough guests, Tom sometimes let her work for a day — mostly, she thought, out of sympathy for her increasingly bedraggled appearance — and he would tell her tonight if he needed her tomorrow. If he did, she'd be able to sneak a nap and a shower in one of the guest rooms. Tom had told her once that if she ever found herself without a place to stay, he'd let her crash in an empty room, but she suspected that was just a momentary lapse of reason and had yet to call him on it.

Maybe she could even take a bath, she thought. Her body ached just thinking about it.

The rain started again while she walked, and by the time she got to the motel she was soaked. She found Tom sitting behind the registration desk in the lobby — which had all the ambiance of the waiting room at the DMV — reading a magazine and looking bored. He raised his head when she came in.

"There you are," he said, and then, "God. You look like shit."

"I've got a cold." Randa pushed her dripping hair out of her face. "Do you need me to work tomorrow?"

He shook his head. "No, but your friend the accountant is back. He's been waiting for you."

"The old guy?" Randa said slowly. What the hell was George doing there? Waiting for her? She didn't want to see him. She remembered, after that walk on the beach, feeling quite sure that she shouldn't see him again.

But he had seemed better that night in the grocery store. And thinking of George made her think of his hundred-dollar bills. Her secret hundred wouldn't get her anywhere good — not and leave her with anything left over — but two hundred might. If she could get another hundred from him. If she could get him to give it to her. "You mean he's here? In the motel?"

"Room 11. I told him that you stopped by a couple times a week, and he said he'd wait. Look, Randa —" Tom rolled out from behind the desk on his chair, looking almost concerned. "I'll stay out of your life if you want, but I gotta say, the guy's a little strange. Pays cash, no car —"

Randa shut him out. Double-oh George, super-spy and super-weird — but with two hundred dollars she could take a bus to California, maybe. And add to that what she'd already contributed to Rainier's van fund, which he'd probably give back to her, she thought. If she was nice about it.

"Room 11?" she asked Tom.

He nodded. For the first time in weeks Randa felt something like hope. It was a small hope, and deeply qualified — what did George *want?* — but there'd been so little hope for so long that it felt as warm as whiskey inside her. Not even her solidly packed sinuses could block it entirely. She gave Tom a smile. "Tell Angie I said hi," she said, and left.

It was still raining, and she noticed a puddle of dirty water collecting in the bottom of the empty swimming pool. By the time Randa reached his room, she and George had already had their entire conversation in her head, and she was already on her way out the door with a hundred-dollar bill — maybe even two hundred-dollar bills — tucked into her pocket. The pink paint on the door, glossy with rain, seemed to shine with welcome, and she realized for the first time how truly desperate she felt.

George opened the door quickly when she knocked. "You're here." He sounded relieved. "I was afraid I was going to miss you. Come in." When she was inside the room, he fastened the chain lock and then turned around to face her. He was wearing a T-shirt and jeans for the first time since she'd known him, and there was a coffee stain on his right thigh. He had claimed on their trip down from Ratchetsburg that he often drove for days without stopping, but he had never looked it until now. "I'm so glad to see you," he said, and hugged her.

He smelled like coffee and sweat. She let him hold her for a minute — just long enough not to be rude — and then gently pushed him away. "Good to see you, too," she said, forcing herself to smile at him. There were two double beds in the room. Randa dropped her backpack on one of them and sat down beside it. Being on the bed made her feel uncomfortable. She wished the rooms at the Pink Pearl had chairs.

"You look terrible," George said.

She shrugged. "I've been sick. It's no big deal. Just a cold."

"Your hair is growing in brown. Where are you living now?" He sat down on the other bed. He really had drunk too much coffee, she thought: his eyes were nervous, flicking from her face to the floor and back again. "Still with your roommate?"

"Sort of. Different roommate." She decided not to tell him about Rainier or the van. Living in a van, she thought, seemed to be a pretty irrevocable sign that your life wasn't working. She needed George to think that her life *was* working, that there was no room for him there. Outside, of course, of a small and strictly temporary loan.

"Are you happy?" he asked her.

The same old question. She rubbed her forehead and tried to

decide what to say. "Not really," she said finally, because she knew that he would want to help her if he thought she was unhappy, but also because it was true, wasn't it? She was sick and cold and broke and *tired,* tired down to her very core of working so hard to stay alive.

"I see," he said, nodding. "Are you thinking about moving on?"

"Actually, I was thinking —" Randa tried to swallow, but her throat hurt. "I have this friend. In Tennessee. I was kind of thinking I'd go and visit her." She stopped, unable to keep going, to tell him that she didn't have the money for a bus ticket and it would sure be nice if he could float her a loan. It sounded too much like the kind of line you'd hear from somebody standing in a train station: *I just need seven bucks to get home, man. Somebody stole my wallet. My kids are at the sitter's. I'll send you a check, I swear it. I swear.*

Randa hadn't asked anybody for anything in years. Taken, yes. Asked, no.

George was staring at her, his face blank. "You want to go to Tennessee?" he said.

She stood up. "No," she said. "Listen, I've gotta go, George. It was good seeing you, but —"

"I'll take you to Tennessee," he said.

"I just said I don't want to go there."

"You must have had a reason for bringing it up."

"I was thinking about my friend, that's all."

She saw George's hands clutch together and release in his lap. "What if we went somewhere else? There must be somewhere you'd like to go."

The sound of the rain filled the room, beating down on the roof, the asphalt, the cars in the parking lot. God, it was cold outside. She shook her head and picked up her backpack, the padding on the sodden strap chilly and unpleasant in her palm. "I just came by to say hello," she said.

"Because I was thinking," he continued, as if she hadn't spoken, "that maybe you might like to go down to Florida with me. I'm going there next."

212

Randa, her hand already on the doorknob, stopped. Florida. Not in a week, not in a month, but tonight. She could go to Florida tonight.

Her bag was so heavy when it was wet like this.

"Tomorrow," George said as if he had heard her thoughts. "We'd leave tomorrow morning. We could go to the Keys. I think you'd like the Keys," he added. "Warm weather. Lots of jobs."

Blue water, white sand. For a moment Randa said nothing. Then she said, "You'd give me a ride?" She wouldn't go, she told herself. She probably wouldn't go. But if she did go, she'd do it with her eyes open. "For free? I don't have any gas money."

"The company pays." He said the words automatically, as if he didn't even need to consider it.

They were talking. Just talking. There was no reason to stand here holding her bag while they talked. Slowly she let it drop to the floor. "You want to leave tomorrow," she said. "So what happens until then?"

He stood up and sat back down again. "You look like you need food. And sleep. We'll eat, and sleep." His eyes darted away from her and back. "Are you still afraid of me?"

Randa shook her head. "It's not that I'm afraid. It's just that I'd like to have things out in the open this time."

"Out in the open." George nodded. "All right. I would like to give you a ride to Florida because you look like you need it, and it would be nice to be able to give you something that you need. I would like to see you in Florida. I think you would be happy there, and I would like to be the one that made you happy. I can make things better for you. I would like to do it."

He gazed steadily at her. Randa felt very still inside. She knew that if he took her hand now and pulled her down next to him, she would let him.

"I think a lot of people have made you sad," George said. "I'm afraid that one of them might have been me."

She sat down on the other bed. Their knees were almost

213

touching. She found her voice in the stillness and said, "How do you think you've made me unhappy?"

"I brought you here. I think your life here has been hard. And I made you worry about my — my intentions. I didn't mean to do that." George looked away from her and pulled at his hair. "It never occurred to me," he said softly, "that a woman like you would even think about — *that* — with a person like me."

The warm air from the window heating unit was blowing in her hair, down the back of her neck. The bed felt soft under her — how far she must have sunk when the beds at the Pink Pearl seemed luxurious — and George was watching her as if she were not just another semihomeless chambermaid but something unique and special in all the world. She pressed her palms against the bedspread as if trying to keep it at a distance and told herself that she could stay the night, maybe, and see how it went. If it felt weird in the morning, she could leave. She could always leave.

"I'd like you to come," George said. He reached out and touched her knee, and then pulled his hand back. "I'd like to take you."

She bit her lip.

"I'll think about it," she said.

In the meantime they had Chinese food delivered. George gave Randa money and asked her to pay when it came, saying that he needed to wash his hands. By the time he came out of the bathroom, the delivery girl was gone. Randa went straight for the broth in her wonton soup, her body crying out for something warm and easy and nourishing. George sat on the other bed and picked at his garlic chicken.

"You're not eating?" Randa asked when her soup was gone.

He smiled. It was a tense smile. "I guess I'm not hungry. I wanted you to eat," he said. "You looked like you needed to eat." He pinched a piece of chicken between his chopsticks and brought it to his mouth.

Randa noticed that his hands were trembling. "Are you all right?" she said.

"I'm fine," he said. "A little nervous, maybe. Ready to be on the road again."

"How long have you been waiting for me?"

He thought for a moment. "Two days. It's good that you came today. I'm not sure I would have been able to wait much longer. I suppose I could have left a note, but I really wanted to see you. I wanted you to come with me." He stopped. When he spoke again, his voice was shy. "Are you going to come with me?"

Randa nodded, and then shook her head. "I don't know." She should leave, she thought. Something felt strange about all this: George, his dirty clothes, the two days he'd waited on the chance that she might show up. Rainier would be waiting for her back at the van, anyway.

But the weather was nasty, she told herself. The food smelled good. The bed that she was sitting on was clean and soft and almost twice as big as her half of the van, and there was no Rainier, no smell of clove cigarettes and unwashed clothes. No juggling pins poking her in the back in the middle of the night. A good night's sleep — a *warm* night's sleep — might get rid of her headache. Make her feel like a human being again.

And he said he wants to make me happy, she thought, a bit defensively. *What's wrong with that?*

There was a knock at the door. George jumped. His chicken spilled onto his pants. "Oh," he said. "Can you get that? I need to —"

He went to the bathroom. Randa went to the door.

Tom stood on the other side of it with a newspaper held over his head. "You okay?" he said.

"Fine," Randa said. "Having some dinner." September or not, the air outside had that foreboding winter smell that meant it was only going to get colder.

"Where's your friend?"

"Bathroom."

"And everything's okay with you," Tom said.

Randa nodded. "Yeah, sure," she answered, with more confidence than, strictly speaking, she felt.

215

"*Are* you sure?" Rain was dripping through the paper over Tom's head.

"Goddamn it, Tom, I'm fine," she said. If she wasn't, if she was — it wasn't like Tom actually cared, she thought. He just didn't want to be the guy the cops came to if her body washed up on the beach. "This guy is my friend."

"Yeah, well." Tom's eyes were still searching the room behind her. "I was going to sleep in the office tonight, anyway."

"Great," Randa said. "So if I need anything, I'll call." Before he could say anything else, she shut the door.

"Was that the owner?" George said, behind her. The coffee stain on his pants had been joined by a chicken stain. "What did he want?"

"Just checking in." Then Randa remembered something Tom had said earlier. "George, where's your car?"

"I parked it in a public lot a few blocks away."

"Why?"

"Because discretion is the better part of valor," he said. "I promise that it's nothing you need to be concerned about."

Randa hesitated for a moment.

"You told him I was your friend," George said. His tentative smile was one Randa had never seen before. "Does that mean you're going to stay?"

Fuck, Randa thought wearily. What was the worst that could happen? She'd had sex with Rainier in exchange for an army blanket in a van. There was a speed-dial button on the phone that rang right into Tom's office. She could sleep here in this (incredibly soft, incredibly warm) bed, and in the morning she could reassess. If things felt at all strange then, she could leave. "All right," she said, and bent to take off her sneakers.

George smiled again, and this one was familiar, the huge brilliant smile that lit up his face. "I'm glad," he said. "I'm very glad."

"I'm tired," she said. "I'm going to go ahead and sleep now, if that's okay."

He nodded enthusiastically. "It's perfect. Get all the sleep you can."

216

"What about you?" she asked.

"I'm not tired," he said, turning off all the lights except the one in the bathroom and sitting down on his bed. "I might take a nap later. I've been sleeping a lot these last few days, waiting for you. I'll stay up and look at maps, maybe."

For a few moments Randa lay awake, listening to George breathe and feeling awkward and uncertain. But she really *was* tired, and the bed was comfortable. Soon she was asleep.

At some point during the night, she woke up to see George sitting at the foot of the other bed. The television was on. The blue light from the screen flickered on his face, making it seem haunted and unearthly.

The room was quiet. Randa fell back asleep.

It was still night when George shook her awake. The lights were now on. Blearily, Randa sat up, shielding her face from the brightness with an arm. Her head felt foggy. "I'm sorry," George said. "But we should go. We shouldn't wait any longer. To beat the traffic, I mean." He pressed her shoes and sweatshirt into her hands. His face was flushed and his breathing heavy, as if he'd been running. "The car's outside. I'll go turn on the heater. You can go back to sleep as soon as we're on the road." He was moving quickly around the room, collecting the things he had there: a jacket, a small overnight bag, a leather satchel.

With numb fingers, Randa pushed her feet into her sneakers and tied the laces. She had never been an easy waker, and the world slid and shifted around her as if she were drunk. By the time she finished with her shoes, found her still-wet backpack, and put on her sweatshirt, George was gone.

Sitting on the edge of her bed, still dazed, Randa saw the remote control lying on top of George's bed. She picked it up and pressed the power button. The room lit up with bright light: one of the cable news networks, a too-polished woman staring seriously into the camera. There was no sound.

Suddenly George was back, and the television was off. "Come on," he said. "We have to go."

twelve

W HEN ANNE SPOKE to X-Ray on the phone, he sounded uncertain and nervous, as Anne thought anybody would when speaking to an old friend they hadn't seen in twenty years. He said that he was sorry to hear about Miranda, and Anne said that she was, too. She asked if he wanted to get together, and he said yeah, sure, that'd be fun. But not tomorrow. Well, maybe tomorrow. It was hard to say, he told her; maybe she should call him the next day and see.

Romansky said, "If you're going to meet with him, at least let me know where and when, so I'll know where to start looking when you don't come back." And in truth, Anne could already hear the voiceover from the television documentary, the severe baritone reserved for true-crime stories: *Despite his criminal record, and against the advice of the detective working her daughter's case, Cassidy made contact with her husband's former colleague — a decision that would have tragic consequences.*

But for god's sake, it was X-Ray they were talking about. Gawky, boyish X, with the wild animal eyes and the ready laugh. When she thought about X, she thought about him and Nick and Miranda running wild through the yard with squirt guns or water balloons or — god forbid — slingshots, tumbling and crashing like a litter of lightly armed wolf cubs, and Anne herself standing in the middle, trying to keep the world on the saner edge of chaos. Or she thought of his lanky frame draped over a lawn chair, holding a beer and slapping at mosquitoes, grinning and tag-teaming some horrible story with Nick that made her laugh and cringe at the same time — ice on the wings, dead engines, no fuel, nowhere to land —

And this was the person Detective Romansky didn't want her to contact, the person who was too dangerous for her to see alone. This person, who was the only living remnant of the life that she had lived then, back when her husband and her daughter were both alive and she'd never been plagued by thoughts about the world as anything other than a backdrop for their lives, never thought about it as limited or limitless, lonely or loveless. Back when the world was where they lived and what they saw; when *astral* meant stars and *plane* meant flying, and *spirit* was what you called it when your daughter stamped her foot and wouldn't wear the stupid pink dress no matter what you said, and your husband laughed and said let her go naked if she wants to, even the kid knows my mother doesn't have any damn taste.

She tried to imagine an X-Ray twenty years older than the one in her memory. Would the lines on his face reach a little farther? Would his rail-thin body have gained any bulk over the years, his eyes lost any of their fierceness? She couldn't blame X for being nervous. She was nervous, herself. The last time she'd seen him, she'd still used a curling iron, worn lipstick, owned a pair of high heels. She had been Nick's Annie, cheerful and wifely and just spunky enough to make him laugh; and now here she was, her feet couched in ergonomic sandals from Sweden and her only jewelry — other than her wedding ring — the ankh around her neck. She thought she had worked hard to become the person that she was, but now she saw that she had become that person in a vacuum, with nobody from her old life around to hold her to the person she used to be. This scared her.

But it also made her want to see X. She wanted to see him and see how much, if any, of Nick's Annie came out to meet him. Maybe Anne and Annie could have a little chat after lunch and see where they stood with each other.

X-Ray sounded less nervous when she spoke to him the next day. They made plans to meet for lunch at a chain restaurant not far from Boylan. She had expected a moment of uncertainty when she first saw him, but she recognized the thin figure standing across the parking lot instantly, even at a distance. X stood straighter than he did in her memory, held himself differently; his face looked only slightly more weathered, and his sandy hair was so closely cut that she couldn't tell if it was thinning or not.

Anne stood by her car without moving. She had just realized that it was not age that separated them from their younger selves, but years: lonely years, happy years, years that had run roughshod over them with steel-toed boots. All at once she was not sure that she was ready for this.

Then he turned, saw her. "Annie!" he cried, and lumbered toward her — had X-Ray *lumbered,* back in the day? She didn't think so, and as he came closer she saw something was wrong with his right leg. She met him halfway, and he hugged her enthusiastically. His arms around her felt wiry and tense, and that was familiar. X had never been very comfortable with hugs. (Except with Miranda — he had hugged Miranda all the time.) He smelled like chewing tobacco and too much cologne.

"Hi, X," she said when he let her go.

For an instant he looked confused. Then he laughed. His laugh was nervous and didn't seem entirely genuine. "Haven't heard that in a while," he said with embarrassment. "Most people these days call me John, when they call me anything at all."

"I guess they would," Anne said with a smile that she didn't feel, thinking, *Discarded nicknames, experiences, years.* Then she remembered what some of X-Ray's experiences had been, according to Detective Romansky, and the smile suddenly felt even worse.

"Well, you know." He laughed his nervous laugh again. "It's a little hard to explain to people that you want them to call you the same thing as what their dentist does to them."

They went inside. X held the door for her. When they were sitting together at a table and the chirpy waitress had been and gone with their drinks — Anne ordered a glass of white wine, X ordered orange juice — X said, "I'm so sorry about Miranda, Annie. I recognized her from her picture. I didn't even have to hear her name. Those eyes." He shook his head. "I never realized how much she looked like Nick."

Anne nodded. "You should see her when her hair's not dyed. It's uncanny."

"I used to think she looked just like you," X said. "A little baby Annie with dark hair." He sipped his orange juice through a straw without picking up the glass, like a child. His yellow eyes were fixed on her. "Have the police found anything yet?"

"Nothing very useful." Detective Romansky had suggested, very politely, that if she was determined to go against his advice and her own better judgment and meet with this person — who was now effectively a suspect, by the way, even if he didn't know it yet — then at the very least she could refrain from passing along any specific information about the case. And he'd also appreciate it very much, he continued, if she'd call his mobile phone when she left the restaurant, just so he'd know that she wasn't dead. "Although it might be a lot less trouble for me if you were," he had added.

"Your jokes are not improving," she'd said.

X picked up the paper wrapper from his straw and pressed it flat against the side of his glass, where it clung to the condensation. He took his hand away and the paper stayed where he'd put it. "They found her car by the side of the road, the news said?"

"Something like that." Anne wanted to squirm but willed herself to keep still. "I'm not exactly sure of the details." She told X about the dead man in Sedona and not being able to reach Miranda on the phone afterward. That much, at least, would be safe; most of it had been on the news, anyway.

"He died right there in the parking lot?" X asked.

Anne nodded. "A brain aneurysm. Quick and painless."

He shook his head. "God's mercy," he said. "We are rewarded with the deaths we deserve." His voice was serene, as if he spoke from experience.

Watching him carefully — the tone in his voice was somehow familiar, and she couldn't remember X-Ray ever saying the word *god* when it wasn't followed by a *damn* — Anne said, "I suppose. Although if my daughter had her throat cut in the woods by some psycho, I have a little trouble believing she deserved that."

He cocked his head. "Is that what they think? Do they think that somebody killed her?"

"They don't know."

"I remember when the two of you disappeared," he said suddenly. "After what happened to Nick — I thought for a while that something bad happened to you."

"Nothing too bad," Anne said. "I moved to Phoenix."

"Starting over?"

"You could say that." She tried to smile. "You could also say that I ran like a scared cat."

He nodded. "Starting over is important. I've started over a couple of times myself."

The waitress came back with a pad and pencil. Anne ordered pasta with artichoke hearts; X asked for a garden salad and a bowl of soup. Glad at last to have something light to talk about, Anne said, "I'm disappointed. What happened to your famous appetite?" This time her smile came more easily. "Nick used to say it was something about the altitude, the way you two ate. I remember at the memorial service, I was worried about two things: Miranda, and running out of food. We almost did run out of food."

X laughed sheepishly. "My bottomless pit days."

Anne shook her head. "I remember the days when a large

order of French fries and a slab of chocolate cake could be dinner. What terrible things age does to us."

"Not age for me so much as gravity." X was wearing a plain blue shirt buttoned up to his neck. Now one of his hands went to his collar, undid the first two buttons, and pulled one side of the shirt aside. The skin underneath was pink and twisted and glossy with scar tissue.

Anne's heart sank, because there was usually only one explanation when a pilot ended up with burn scars. "Oh, X," she said.

Buttoning up his shirt — the scar tissue actually extended above his collar, Anne saw now, although she probably wouldn't have noticed if she hadn't been looking for it — he said, "I went down a year or so after Nick. The painkillers did a number on my appetite. Can't fly anymore, either." His tone was light, but there was pain in his eyes. The X Anne knew had loved flying more than anything. Nick used to say that he had feathers on his chest instead of hair.

On impulse Anne reached out and touched the hand holding his orange juice. "I'm so sorry, X-Ray."

"I wish you wouldn't call me that. My name is John," he snapped. Anne jerked her hand back as if she'd been the one burned. Immediately X smiled his unreliable smile again. "I'm sorry. I overreacted. I just — don't really think of myself as that person anymore."

Carefully, Anne said, "That person wasn't so bad."

"He wasn't so great. I suppose the police told you about my record." X-Ray — John — half laughed. "*His* record, I should say."

"The world takes us to strange places, sometimes," Anne said.

"And sometimes we take ourselves there. Were you surprised?"

"A little."

"Why?" All at once X was leaning forward, his voice intense and a little frightening, his eyes ablaze. "Because Nick's old buddy X-Ray wouldn't have done those things?"

"Maybe," Anne said, startled. "Yes. I guess so."

X sat back. As quickly as his anger had come, it left his face entirely, replaced by that disquieting serenity, and Anne began to consider the possibility that Detective Romansky had been right, that she never should have come here.

"He did other things, though," X said. "Things you didn't know about. Things you wouldn't believe. Nick's old buddy X-Ray" — his tone filled with contempt — "wasn't a very good person, when it came right down to it."

Their food arrived. Anne stared down at her pasta and could not even conceive of eating. When the waitress was gone, X continued. "I'm glad you came. I wasn't sure, but now I'm glad to have the opportunity to sit here and talk to you, face to face. I've been wanting to talk to you for years." He picked up his fork and began to spear pieces of lettuce from his salad, one by one.

"Anything specific?" she said.

He nodded. "Nick shouldn't have married you. He had no business dragging you into the mess that our lives were back then. A couple of the guys, they tried to tell him, but he wouldn't listen. You couldn't do what we did if you were married," he added. "They wouldn't even offer you the job."

"He warned me, remember?" Anne said. "I knew what I was getting into." As Nick had reminded her on a regular basis, every time she complained about his absences. *Not my fault you married me. I tried to tell you. You're just so damn stubborn.* And then he would laugh and kiss her.

Nick's voice was very clear in her memory today.

"No, you didn't," X said. "You thought you were marrying a pilot who wouldn't be home as often as you'd like. You didn't know you were marrying a criminal."

Anne went cold. "Nick wasn't a criminal."

But she was remembering the aviation lawyer she'd talked to after Nick vanished. *They fish in some pretty dark water,* he'd said about Western Mountain. *They're untouchable.*

Anything, he'd said. Nick could have been doing anything.

"Sure he was. We all were." X waved his fork in the air.

"And those that shall lead the righteous into sin, let them be thrown into the sea with a millstone bound about their neck. Do you know what that means?"

"Nick was a good person," Anne said. "You were a good person."

X smiled and shook his head. "We thought we were," he said. And then he told her his story.

They flew out of Honduras. Mostly they flew supply runs between that country and a disparate array of others: Israel, Portugal, Colombia, Panama. Supplies for what, nobody asked; sealed crates, usually unmarked. Some of the pilots knew more than others, but all of them — said X-Ray — all of them knew that there was a war going on, a secret war, an exciting one. The good guys were fighting the bad guys, that was all they cared about. One day, X said, he saw two sunsets in the same day, and then a sunrise four hours after that. After all these years Anne still saw the wonder in his eyes that such a thing was possible.

This was the kind of flying that Nick told her about, and that Western Mountain told her about: supply runs. The question that nobody would ever answer, at least not with any degree of honesty, was what kind of supplies. Anne asked X this question now, and he said, all the usual kinds needed for a war — guns, explosives, soldiers, assassins — and some less usual, because this was a secret war, and funded in secret ways. "International currency," he said, "the powdered kind, sold by the kilo." He added that the Tower Commission dragged all this out in '86, anyway, and with a bitter smile said that the Tower report was only mostly lies, if she ever wanted to read it.

But back then, in Honduras, he had still believed that the lines were clearly drawn, with good on one side and bad on the other, and that he and his fellow pilots were all firmly on the side of the good. One of the pilots he and Nick flew with — a grizzled old veteran who had flown for Chennault in China — used to say that they were the guys in the tall white hats, the ones who never missed and never had to reload. X-Ray told Anne that he'd never wanted to be anything other than a pilot. It was all he'd ever known. He'd been shot at on the first mission he ever flew, in Southeast Asia, and after that everything else felt boring.

And because she could not wait, Anne asked him then if Nick had been shot down.

"I don't know," he said. "All I know is that I took an empty ship to Portugal, and when I brought it back full our chief pilot told me he'd ditched out over the ocean and they hadn't found him."

Was the chief pilot lying? she asked. Steady, her voice was so steady.

"Probably. I don't know," X said again. "All I know is what happened to me."

He had been flying a surveillance mission over Nicaragua in a twin-engine King Air 90 with a camera hidden in its belly. Sometimes they flew the King Airs low, trying to draw fire and trick the enemy into revealing their positions. Who the enemy was, why they were firing — none of this mattered. It was like a game, and either their fear was replaced by adrenaline or they grew to confuse the two.

But this time they wanted only pictures. The camera worked automatically. All X had to do was keep his eyes open and fly. When he saw the puffs of gray smoke in the forest beneath him, felt the ship shudder, he knew that even that — flying — was soon going to be beyond his reach.

"*You* were shot down," Anne said.

He nodded. "Straight down."

There was an electrical fire in the cockpit. When he pulled himself from the pile of metal that used to be an airplane, a thing of grace and liberation, his left side was burned from the middle of his neck to just below his shoulder. The right side of his body was smashed. His shoulder, his knee, and his ankle all felt like they were full of red-hot molten glass, glass that somehow screamed. And there he was, broken to hell, with the wreckage of his ship sending a plume of jet-black smoke four stories high into the sky.

226

The scene X described was one that Anne had seen before in a hundred nights of haunted dreams, where Nick screamed and writhed in the burning cockpit as men with ugly, crude machetes made their way through the jungle to him.

But X-Ray was lucky. He had a radio transmitter on board that sent out a beacon signal every hour on the hour. And so he hid, and waited, and tried to stay alive.

All the pilots who flew for Western Mountain had private code names that existed in only two places: crash envelopes, locked in the bottom drawer of the dispatcher's desk, and their own heads. This was done so that nobody who found your body in your wrecked aircraft could pretend to be you and lure your still-living compatriots into an ambush. X-Ray's code name was Desperado, which he'd chosen because of the Eagles song. When he heard another engine overhead, and saw the second King Air through the clearing his own plane had made coming down, he turned on his transmitter and said that Desperado was tired of riding fences and wanted to come home. The King Air's pilot — Stukey, they'd called him Stukey — patched him into base, and X told them where he was. Told them to fucking come and get him; and did she, Anne, know what they said?

Anne didn't know.

They said that his location was insecure and they'd send someone in as soon as they could. "Insecure," he said, and the bitterness in his voice was palpable even through the thick layer of serenity that he forced on top of it. "Of course it was insecure. It was fucking enemy territory. That's why I was *there*."

When Stukey signed off, there had been a false note of ease in his voice, X remembered, and he should have known then. But still he waited, with his broken shoulder and broken ankle and broken everything in between, in agony from his burned skin. For all that day, and all the next, he waited. The cockpit fire went out and he took shelter in the burned-out fuselage, where he waited another day, another night. He drank the moisture that dripped down from the trees above him, and he ate his own pain. Once a day, Stukey — or somebody — flew overhead: *Just checking in on you, buddy, hang tight — keep it together.*

This is Desperado, he'd say. *You guys should come on down, visit for a while.*

But they didn't. Couldn't. Orders.

Every time the sky darkened, he resigned himself to another eight hours of waiting, because nobody ran search and rescue ops at night. Every time the sky lightened, hope filled him again. For surely this would be the day; today was the day, they would come for him and take him home. He spent no small amount of time thinking of Nick. Did he wait, too, in a life raft on the open ocean or floating in a life jacket, for a rescue operation that never came?

And in the restaurant, Anne — who was, of course, thinking the same thing — said, "Would they have left you there to die?"

"Of course," X-Ray said, and below the creepy serenity Anne sensed a deep, blazing rage. "Easiest way to deal with the situation."

On the third day he heard voices speaking a language that he didn't understand, and so he crawled out of the fuselage and hid in the ground cover. He pulled a piece of brush behind him so the speakers would not see the drag marks. When they emerged from the forest into the clearing, they were desperate, ragged-looking men, but there were only two of them, so X assumed that they were just a search party. Whoever they were, they were excited to find the plane. Carefully, they examined every inch of it, but they took nothing. After about an hour — or so it seemed to X, lying in the undergrowth with his breaks and burns screaming — they left.

But after they were gone and his relief faded, he realized that they would soon be back with reinforcements. There was no more waiting; this was the end. So he dragged himself back to the plane and found the camera in the wreckage. It was demolished. The film was a melted black lump.

X returned to his radio, anyway, with its drained batteries. And the next time a King Air flew overhead — *Death watch, they're on fucking death watch,* he thought — he told them that the film survived, that he took it out of the camera and was holding it on his person to keep it out of the hands of the desperate men with machetes. He knew that the people who ran Western Mountain would be more concerned with the disappearance of their film — with the possibility of it getting into the wrong hands — than they would be with its actual destruction. Even back then, there were plenty of reporters sniffing around Central America. "They knew something down there stank," he told Anne, "and nobody wanted them finding out that what stank was us."

They sent a helicopter for him in four hours.

He spent a long time recuperating in a civilian hospital — not the American hospital, but a Panamanian one that asked fewer questions — and then, when he could travel, Western Mountain sent him back to the States. They arranged for him to see a private doctor who specialized in reconstructive orthopedics and was told that he'd been in a car crash. They rebroke some of his bones, rebuilt others, and eventually put him back together again.

Except that he couldn't fly. There was nerve damage in his right hand and no range of motion in his right shoulder. Because of the pain in his leg, he couldn't sit long enough to make even a short trip. I'll take anything, he told Western Mountain — give me a desk to fly, a broken engine to repair. Just give me something to do. All I know is flying.

But the worst part about sitting broken on the ground in Nicaragua for all those days hadn't been his company's refusal to come and get him. It had been his knowledge, from the beginning, that they had no intention of coming. It was what he'd signed up for. They'd never said anything different, not from that first day in Vietnam, when all the unmarried pilots had been pulled into a room and offered immediate discharges, civilian jobs, good salaries, no questions asked now and forever. You go down, you're your own problem, was the attitude; good luck and keep your mouth shut, and the cyanide pills are in the second cabinet on the left. All that mattered was the operation, and the trick he'd pulled with the King Air film had put the discretion of the operation at risk for something as small and insignificant as his life. By doing so he had revealed himself to be made of less dedicated stuff than was necessary for the job. In the jungle, when his death had been imminent, the choice had seemed clear; in the hospital, he realized that he was a traitor. Worse, he was a coward.

And so he was not surprised when no desk job could be found. When Rush visited him after his last surgery to tell him that his medical bills would be paid and his pension initiated — and also to remind him of the binding confidentiality agreement he'd signed all those years ago in Vietnam — the cool politeness in the older man's tone made it clear that Western Mountain was finished with X-Ray and they expected him to be finished with them.

Shamed and shaken to his core, X meekly agreed to everything Rush said. Nick, he told Anne, used to say that the only way to keep from looking like a coward was to go down in flames. Talking to Rush made X realize that his friend had been right. He used to be a pilot, worthy of Rush's respect; now he was just an unemployed chickenshit in a hospital gown.

When he could work again, he set about finding a job, *any* job, that his nerve damage and limited mobility would let him do. His pension was almost enough to live on, so he didn't need much. Eventually he found work at a lumberyard, where he could get up and walk around sometimes to relieve the throbbing ache in his leg. He would drag himself around the dusty yard, feeling like a bird scratching in the dirt for worms. It was a helpless, hopeless way to live.

He tried being married, to a nice girl who worked at the grocery store. "I was thinking of you and Nick," he told Anne. "The way you used to look at him. I thought that if I had somebody to look at me like that, maybe I wouldn't feel so — rotten. Things would be better. But it didn't work out that way." The way that it did work out was that he drank more and more and became angrier and angrier with the failure of everything in his life to be what it once was. Finally there came

a night that ended with the nice girl who was his wife screaming and his own fist landing on a policeman's jaw. More ar-
rests. Trips to the police station. Dropped charges, misery, guilt.
Cowardice. Shame. And more, and worse. And on and on.

"It was a difficult time," he said, as if he were describing
a particularly nasty tax audit. "It was a dark tunnel. But I've
come out the other side. I've been reborn." He smiled. "I'm not
that person anymore. I've left him behind."

And suddenly Anne realized why the cadence of his speech
seemed familiar to her. He sounded like one of the zealots who
sometimes came into the store in Sedona. Not the normal people with strange ideas, like Zandar or Rhiannon or Anne herself, but the real crazies, the ones who put their infants on fasts
and chanted over them when they were burning with fever.

Because the story continued: the story of how his ex-wife
— who still loved him, and whom he loved to this day, even if
he would never again inflict himself upon her, even if he wasn't
allowed within one hundred feet of her — had started going
to some holy-roller church, and how she'd nagged and nagged
him to go. How he'd almost been to the point where he'd told
her not to call him anymore because he was that sick of hearing about it.

But then one Saturday afternoon she called. He had just woken up and was more or less sober. She said, *Baby, there's going to be a man at the church tonight. A healer. I want you
to come.*

He told her there was no way in hell.

But then she said, *What's the worst that can happen? You
hurt right now, don't you?*

He did; down to his bones, he hurt.

*So come and see this guy tonight. And afterward, if you
want, I'll buy you a bottle myself. Maybe you're right and it
won't help. But maybe it will.*

And so he had gone. The church was out in the woods, down
in Fayette County near the West Virginia border. Anne could
see it in her mind's eye: the metal folding chairs, the fluorescent
lights, the plain white walls. She could hear, as X described it,

231

the voice of the man with the pompadour who stood at the front of the room, shouting brimstone and damnation into a microphone. She heard the voices of the congregation, calling out responses to the healer's prayers; saw the shuffling line of people headed toward the altar. Their eyes were glowing, their faces lit up with the wonder of the possible, that sense of magic, of mystery, of hope. She could see X sitting there among the joyful, looking like himself but with the unfocused eyes she associated with the chronically intoxicated.

"And I felt an opening inside me," X was saying, his voice dreamy and elated. "Like a door I'd never noticed, opening to an empty place that had been there all along. Imagine living in a house for years and never noticing that it had a basement. That was what it was like. Suddenly there was this deep, dark place inside me, crying out for light."

And so, barely aware of what he was doing, he had risen to his feet, joined the slow shuffle of the tired and the sick moving toward the altar. When he went closer, when there were only a few rows of people between the healer and the place where he stood, he saw sweat flying from the healer's brow, and suddenly he was consumed with fear: the healer was too tired, his gift too limited, and this special open moment, this *possible* moment, would be lost forever. He had hesitated, and now he would lose; and that glow of magic and mystery and hope that he had seen on the faces of the congregation — that glow that looked like flying had once felt — would be lost to him forever. Lost to him. Hope. Lost.

And then somebody's arm was across his shoulder, somebody else's hand upon his arm, and he was being led through the crowd, which opened before him, smiling faces, warm, welcoming. Inviting him to be here, to take part, to be *of* them — and there was the healer, whose string tie hung askew beneath his collar, whose face was pale with effort. And X was brought before him, and the healer's red eyes focused on him.

You've got pain, the healer said. *You've got pain down in your very soul.*

X could only nod, because yes, he did have pain, and it was

everywhere, everything for him. The healer took his hands — his damp, doughy hands, his hands that were hot and sticky with sweat — and he put one of them on each side of X's face, gripping tightly as if he must fix the source of the pain, must pin it down. And then he spoke, and his voice trembled with power, trembled with faith: *In the name of the Father, the Son, and the Holy Spirit, with the mercy of God on his almighty throne, with the love of Jesus Christ that burns through all of us like a mighty, mighty flame — in the name of God and of your own salvation, be thou made whole! Be thou made whole! Be thou made whole!*

X had felt a great push that had come not just from the hands upon his head but from something inside him that was at that moment breaking free, coming alive —

And he fell backward, and there were many arms waiting to catch him —

And he was made whole.

Listening to him, Anne had her doubts.

She was calm: a profound calm, stainless, glasslike. It reminded her of the way she'd felt in the days after Nick's disappearance. After the tears passed, before the anger began, she had felt this way, when there were memorial services to plan and legal documents to file and Miranda to feed. Quiet; numb. And in this state, she was able to look critically at this person named John who used to be Nick's best friend, X-Ray, and take the measure of the deep places that he had locked away behind his tale of healing and rebirth.

Because when John had talked about being a pilot, he had sounded like a pilot. The words he'd chosen, the cockpit-radio nonchalance that pilots use when they talk about their flying machines and the misadventures they have in them. More to the point, he'd sounded like a pilot she had known, and known well. He'd sounded like X-Ray.

When he talked about being made whole, he sounded — broken.

She said the only thing she could. "I'm happy for you, John."

233

He smiled — the wide flat smile of the converted — and nodded. But incongruously, impossibly, the words that came out of his mouth were "It killed you when Nick was lost, didn't it, Annie? Ripped the heart right out of you. I saw that it did. I can still see it. You can be happy for yourself, too. You can leave all of that pain and agony behind." He leaned toward her, as if he were telling her a great secret, and said, "God can make you whole, Annie. He can make you whole."

It took all she had not to recoil. And of all the things that X had just said to her, there was only one that she felt able to grab on to, to make sense of and confront.

"My name is Anne," she said.

It is that moment again, that moment at the end of the world. Anne, kneeling on the kitchen floor, feels like she is two Annes in two universes. In one the phone has rung, and now dangles at the end of its cord. X-Ray's voice, ghostly, trickles out of the receiver. She is crumpled on the floor, eviscerated, torn.

In the other universe the phone never rang, and Anne is standing at the kitchen counter, slicing tomatoes and humming. This Anne has her petty grievances: her husband is gone too much, and when home is sometimes secretive and distracted. But if he didn't go away, he wouldn't be able to come back, and Anne loves when he comes back. She loves the feel of his arms around her, the sight of him with their daughter, the smell of him that is the smell of airplanes and altitude and flying.

But the Anne in the world where the phone never rang isn't thinking about her husband. She's thinking about her daughter, and the summer that stretches ahead of them, how lucky she is that they can spend it together, that she doesn't have to work. How there won't be many more summers like this one, because Miranda is growing up and will soon be a distant teenager. Anne is also thinking about how amazing her daughter is: how remarkable it is that such a creature would never exist but for her and Nick. How impossible it is to imagine a world without her.

What did Nick and I talk about before there was Miranda?

this Anne thinks to herself. *What did I think about? What did I do?*

The Anne in the universe where phones ring and living people become dead can see this other Anne as if through a window. Standing at the counter as if the world is safe and strong, as if the days will all be sunny and not particularly precious, slicing tomatoes for Miranda's grilled cheese sandwich without a care in the world. Oh, how she hates her. Stupid, vacant, unappreciative *bitch.* This Anne, the real Anne, pounds at the linoleum floor with her fists, as if she can break through and get to that other world, that world where things are still okay and she and Miranda will be having lunch at the table soon because everything is okay —

Suddenly, through her tears, Anne sees a puddle on the kitchen floor. Two puddles. Rain boot–shaped puddles, Miranda-sized puddles. All at once Anne is treated to a memory of her stunned daughter standing in front of her — a new memory, something that has just happened, Miranda standing there and Anne opening her mouth and screaming —

She is up. On her feet as best she can, stumbling and crashing through the house as if drunk because her legs will not seem to hold her. She opens her mouth to cry out and hears herself, a tear-choked croak — *Miranda!* — but the little girl is not in her bedroom, not in front of the television, not on the front porch, not on the back porch. In her fear it somehow seems that if she cannot find her daughter, Miranda will be gone forever, and she will never see her again.

Not both of them, she pleads, talking to herself and to Nick and to the Anne in the safe universe and to whatever uncaring, malevolent force runs a world that has suddenly become incredibly cruel. *Please, not both of them.*

And when she finds the door to the garage she all but falls through it, gripping the doorjamb with both hands. Underneath the panicked rushing in her ears she hears a child's voice, small, crying. The door to the cupboard underneath the tool bench is slightly ajar.

Anne knows that she should move gently, that Miranda is

scared and confused — but Anne herself is scared and confused, and when she throws open the door it must seem to the little girl that the monsters are here.

Because there she is, tear-stained Miranda, sobbing and frightened. Holding something to her chest as if it is precious.

"Baby," Anne gasps, and then she is holding Miranda, and they are both crying. Soon Anne will have to tell her that her father is gone, but not right now. Not now, because Miranda is telling her own story, about cats and rescue missions and refrigerator boxes. She is holding the something in her hands out to Anne, and the something is a kitten. A half-starved, near-dead kitten.

Miranda's big eyes (which are her father's eyes, her vanished father's eyes) are gazing up at Anne with all the trust in the world, and all the hope, and she is saying, *Can you save it, Mommy? Can you save it?*

But Anne can only hold the kitten, and her daughter, and cry.

The solution, Anne decided on the way home, was to think of him as two different people. There was X-Ray, squirt-gun assassin, climber of trees, eater of hamburgers, and watcher of Super Bowls and World Series games. And then there was John, who had been twisted and broken and burned and finally, in some cut-rate church throbbing with the thumping of many misinterpreted Bibles, made blandly, horribly whole.

If that was what you called it, when you took everything that you were and locked it away, when you let your pain eat you alive.

She parked the rental car in front of Miranda's apartment building and took her phone out of her purse to call Detective Romansky. It rang before she could dial.

She opened it, pressed the talk button. "Hello?"

There was a pause. "Annie," X-Ray's voice said. His voice was thick, as if he had been crying, but it was unmistakably X-Ray.

"What's wrong?" she said.

"I think —" His tone was uncertain. "I think there's something I should tell you. I wasn't — but — can you come to my house?"

Anne scrawled the directions he gave her on a gasoline receipt and said that she would come, and he said maybe she shouldn't, after all. She told him that now she had to come, because she was worried.

"Are you okay?" she asked.

He laughed — not a happy laugh — and hung up. The line was silent.

X lived in a trailer in the woods. It was old-growth forest, and pretty: the sort of place where it might be nice to build a summer house. But the trailer itself was dismal. Long smears of dirt streaked its white paneled sides where the gutters had rusted through and the rain had brought the dust and soil from the roof back down to the ground. The windows were small and spotted, and weeds grew thick and tall around the cinder blocks on which the trailer rested.

X's car, a dingy brown truck, was parked in front. Anne smelled smoke, and some chemical. Lighter fluid, or charcoal. As she came closer she saw that the smoke came from a metal barbecue crouched in the driveway like a fat three-legged spider. The vents in the lid were open. Anne wrapped a fold of her skirt around her fingers and lifted the lid.

Inside, instead of a grill, there was a pile of frail, blackened lace that had once been paper. An envelope on top of the pile was deeply browned but almost intact, its striped edging still visible. Anne fancied that she could almost see writing on the envelope's face, and it was almost familiar.

Nick, she thought, and reached for the envelope — but then the fresh air from the lifted lid made the fire blaze, and the envelope was gone.

Anne put the lid down.

Two crudely built steps led up to the door, which was as grimy as the walls. She climbed them and lifted her fist to knock — but the door, unlatched, swung open at her touch.

"X?" she called, and then, "John?"

There was no answer.

The living room was dark and empty. But beyond the living room was a narrow hallway, and beyond the hallway was a bedroom —

And the bedroom was where she found him, as she had somehow known she would. Slumped down on his low single bed, the air thick with the smells of blood and gunpowder, his shirt torn open to reveal the horrible pink-scarred skin that he had shown her that afternoon. And something else.

Something on his chest: something small, and gold, and hanging from a chain around his neck. Something oval.

Anne was not afraid. It was only poor X-Ray, poor haunted X-Ray who had not been made whole, after all. She stepped forward, thinking vaguely of Detective Romansky — she would call him soon — and making sure not to step on anything that looked like blood. She reached out, touched the medal, read the writing around the edges that said *Saint Joseph of Cupertino;* touched his still-warm chest, and turned the medal over.

thirteen

THEY WERE BACK IN THE CAR. This time it wasn't raining. Randa's skin felt hot, even to her own touch, and she fell asleep as soon as the car started moving.

She awoke in stages: out of deep sleep when the car stopped moving, and slightly more aware when the car door opened and closed again. When she felt George's hands on her, tucking his dusty-smelling coat over her, she came almost all the way awake. His touch was careful and kind.

She felt the seat shift under her, sensed George moving closer, and heard him take a breath and let it out, slowly. His hand touched her hair, moved to the side of her face, her earlobe, her neck.

He paused. His fingers seemed to be trembling.

Then his hand moved lower, inside the neck of her sweat-shirt to her collarbone and then to the hollow underneath it.

Dazed with sleep and fever and moving as if on autopilot — thinking only vaguely that if they were going to do this, then doing it this way would be extremely slow — Randa took his hand and put it on her breast.

There was another pause. Then suddenly the seat shifted again, his hand was gone, and the space where he had been felt vacant. She opened her eyes.

George was sitting behind the steering wheel, staring straight ahead. The world outside the windows was still dark. It looked as if they were pulled over on the side of a road.

Completely awake, Randa thought, *Oh. Oh, no.*

"You're sick," he said, his voice flat. "You have a fever."

She sat up and pushed away his coat. All at once she didn't want it touching her. "It's just a cold."

"It's not right." George didn't look at her, and she realized that he was talking about more than her fever.

"George, it's okay," she said. *Nothing happened,* she told herself. *Nothing.* "It's no big deal."

Then he did turn and look at her, his eyes as fierce as they had been the night they walked on the beach, the night when he had taken her wrist and not let it go. "It's a very big deal to me," he said. He turned the key in the ignition and pulled onto the road.

For a long while they drove in silence, George palely illuminated by the lights from the dashboard and the radio silent, as it had been the first time they'd done this.

"I'm sorry," he said at last.

Randa sighed. "Don't be."

"I don't want things to change between us," he said, and that was such a normal guy thing to say that she laughed.

"They haven't," she told him. "They were weird to start with, and they remain weird. Status quo. How long was I asleep? Is this the turnpike?"

He cleared his throat. "No. We've done the turnpike. The back roads are more interesting anyway, don't you think?"

She yawned. "Not at night. In the dark they're all the same. What time is it?"

"Around four. We've been driving for about an hour and a half."

"Jesus, George," she said, staring at him. "Are you trying to beat traffic or what?"

He laughed. It didn't sound quite right. "There's coffee if you want it. In the thermos by your feet."

"Maybe later." Something felt wrong about this — something besides the strange aborted groping session, which already seemed surreal and dreamlike — and she remembered that something had felt wrong earlier, too. Not that anything about George had ever felt *right*, exactly, but this had been different. Sharper. She was going to think about it in the morning, she remembered. One night's worth of good sleep; she had been so tired, and her head had hurt so much. And then she was going to wake up and decide.

But he'd woken her up, and she had been dazed and exhausted, and she hadn't thought about it. And now she was here, in this car, and not very long ago she had been willing to let George fuck her for no better reason than that he'd put his coat over her while she was sleeping. She pushed away the trembling feeling that was swelling inside her and thought, *So what. We're going to Florida. We'll get there and I'll get out. Free ride. No harm, no foul.*

She leaned her head against the cold window. "We're going to Florida?"

"At least to start with. Then — who knows?"

"What do you mean, who knows?" she said.

"We could have an adventure. We could —" He stopped. Randa saw him bite his lower lip. "We could go to Cuba."

She looked at him. The trembling feeling found a nest in her stomach. She felt queasy. "I thought you couldn't get to Cuba from the United States. I thought it was illegal. Like with the cigars."

"That's true," he said, "but we could take a boat maybe. Or fly through some other country. Havana is supposed to be amazing. Great culture, food, music, architecture —"

"Sure," she said in disbelief. "That must be why all those people are willing to risk being eaten alive by sharks to get out."

"People are like that," George said. "The grass is always greener. You know how it is."

She scanned the dark world outside. There were no lights, no farmhouses. Nothing.

"George," she said. "I don't think I want to go to Cuba."

He cleared his throat. "Well, you don't have to decide now. We can talk about it later."

They drove in silence for a while. Finally George, staring impassively at the road, said, "I found your father's file. It's in the bag on the floor in the back."

Feeling less secure by the minute, she reached around the seat and found the satchel George had brought from the hotel room. It was stuffed full of loose paper.

"There's a folder," he went on. "You might have to dig."

She began pulling out pieces of paper at random. Most of them seemed to be computer printouts, maps and diagrams, although she could dimly see that some of the pages were made up entirely of columns of gibberish: numbers and letters mixed together, in no order, making no sense.

"George, what is all this stuff?" she said slowly.

"Just papers," he said evasively. "Look for the folder. It's in there."

She found it in an outside pocket, an ordinary tan file folder with no markings on its exterior. There were documents inside, but it was too dark in the car for her to read any of them. "Can I turn on the light?"

"Sure."

She flipped on the dome light, but she still couldn't read most of the pages. Some were written in Spanish, and others were so rife with abbreviations and acronyms that she could make no sense of them: *0800 Op 32106-J, Loc 82, id 6x T46-C, ap. 12XAA.* She looked for her father's name but couldn't find it. "What does this have to do with my dad?" she said.

"Those are his flight records. If you knew how to read them, you'd be able to tell where he was and what he was doing on any given day."

She flipped through a few more pages. "Do you know how to read them?" George shook his head. "Why not?"

His throat moved convulsively. He sighed and said, "Because I'm a computer programmer. If it was Visual Basic, I could read it, but —"

Randa's fingers froze. "You're a computer programmer," she said.

"Yes."

"For the CIA."

"The company I work for has a contract with the CIA," he said. "We build their databases. I didn't mean to lie to you." He sounded anxious. "I don't think I actually *did* lie."

She shook her head, mystified. "If you can't read any of this stuff, how do you know that it has anything to do with my dad?"

"I built the database," he said. "I know where the back doors are. And when I ran a search on his name, that's what came up."

"Nicholas Cassidy," she said, still not sure that she had ever told George her father's name. "You searched for Nicholas Cassidy."

He nodded. "Look for a memo," he said. "Some agent who thought he saw him in Costa Rica after he was supposed to be dead —"

She reached up deliberately and turned off the dome light. "You're lying."

But he went on. His voice was rushed, insistent. "They think he might have been working with some drug dealer who helped him fake —"

Randa cut him off. "I don't want to hear it. You've been lying to me for as long as I've known you. You said you worked for the CIA, but you don't. You said you didn't want to sleep with me, but you do. So no more bullshit." She pulled her knees up to her chest and wrapped her arms around them. She stared straight ahead of her at the black road.

"Miranda," he said.

"Shut up," she said. "Don't talk to me."

And he was quiet.

• • •

After a long time she reached out to turn on the radio. George stopped her hand with his. "Can we talk about this?" he said.

"What do you want to talk about?" she said. "The fact that you're a lying asshole who says nasty things about my dad?"

He didn't say anything.

"Move your hand or I'll break it," she said coldly.

"You couldn't do that. You're not strong enough," he said, but he moved his hand.

"Yeah, well, I don't have the benefit of your CIA training, do I?" she said, and turned on the radio.

It was tuned to a news station. She pressed the scan button over and over but couldn't find any music. "Where the hell *are* we?" she finally burst out.

"South Carolina," George said.

"Middle of fucking nowhere. Great." She turned the radio back to the news station. They sat silently, listening as the calm-voiced announcer told them about what the weather was going to be doing and which teams were in the running for the baseball playoffs and where the latest war was, and why it was, and who was ostensibly fighting it. None of these news items stirred either of them to comment.

During the commercial break, George said, "None of this is going the way I planned it," and Randa said nothing.

Then the announcer came back on, and in the same calm voice said that government and law enforcement officials in five states had just released a composite sketch —

— *of the so-called Coastal Killer, who has been blamed for the deaths of ten women over the last four months. The suspect is a white male in his late thirties, last seen driving a silver sedan* —

He snapped the radio off.

In Randa's head it was as if a key had turned in a lock. She stared at him, her body twisted so that her back was against the car door, shrinking as far away from him as she could. "It's you," she whispered.

"Miranda," he said, his trembling voice desperate. "It's not true. It's not." She felt the car's speed increase. "It's a coverup, a frame. Some of those papers are valuable — weapons schematics, production schedules. We can buy our way into Cuba. We'll have a good life there. The people your father worked for were not good people, Miranda."

"Stop the car. Let me out," she said, and noticed as if from an outsider's point of view that she was not afraid.

He said, "You could look at it like we're evening the score. Imagine all the ways that your life would have been different if your father had been in it — you'll be giving that to somebody else, some other little girl. I did this for you." He sounded desperate. "To make you happy."

Her skin was cold and her stomach was hollow, and suddenly she found herself thinking of a television show she'd liked when she was a kid, about a seaplane pilot in the South Pacific, and how whenever he was in trouble somebody would get worried and come looking for him. But there was nobody looking for her. Rainier and Tom would think she'd just moved on, and even if they wondered about her they would not find her on a back road in South Carolina. Not a soul on the planet knew exactly where she was right now, and nobody was coming to rescue her. And then it occurred to her that it would be awfully hard on her mom this way; first her husband and now her daughter, vanished, disappeared as cleanly as if they'd been erased from a page. As if they'd never been.

Then she thought that if she lived through this, the next place that she went would be somewhere that she'd always wanted to go, somewhere she had dreamed of going, somewhere that would mean something. She would not drift anymore, letting life take her where it did, and even if it was too little, too late, she would be damned if she'd go quietly along with George.

"I'm not going to Cuba with you," she said, and reached for the door handle, even though the speedometer was inching toward eighty.

George said, "No, don't," and there was a heavy click as he hit the door-lock button on his control panel, but she had already determined that she had let too many things happen to her and this one thing she was going to *do*. She grabbed the steering wheel and turned it as hard as she could.

George cried out. The car twisted and spun, and the guard-rail came at them fast and bright in the headlights. She just had time to think *Not again,* and then there was the sound, and the blackness, and the silence.

V

SAINT JOSEPH OF
CUPERTINO

fourteen

IT WAS HARD TO MAINTAIN hope; hard to get up every morning, knowing that the day would probably bring nothing at all and definitely bring nothing good, and still go through the motions. Anne's mind was constantly drawn back to her memory of X-Ray's dead body and the blood-spattered wall behind him. Not because it made her sad — although it did, in an angry, resigned way. She thought that the essential things that made X-Ray who he was when she and Nick had known him had died long ago. The X-Ray that she had known would not have liked the person he had become, just as the person he became didn't like the X-Ray that had been. In the end, the two could not coexist.

She kept thinking, though, of what he said to her — *We are rewarded with the deaths we deserve* — and wishing that he had been wiser, or that she had been.

But most of the time when she pictured X-Ray, she wasn't really thinking of him at all. She was thinking of Miranda —

plagued, in fact, by thoughts of Miranda's dead body. They'd always been there, these thoughts, but now they were front and center, demanding every ounce of her energy. How can it be, she would think as she stood at the bathroom sink and brushed her teeth, that I'm standing here scrubbing my teeth with my Ultra-Max tartar-reducing toothbrush and my Sparkle Mint gel, and my daughter's body is rotting in a shallow grave somewhere?

Worse were the moments when she thought about all the lives that were only slightly affected by Miranda's disappearance. Romansky, for whom she was probably just a case, sitting unsolvable in a pile with others just like it. Zandar and Rhiannon, back in Sedona, who were working extra shifts to cover Anne's absence. Anne herself, whose life waited nearly unscathed back in Arizona, like a pair of rain boots ready for the next storm. Miranda's killer, whose life had been waiting for him, too — Anne was quite sure that it was a man — as soon as he had finished cutting her throat, or smothering her, or whatever it was that he had done to end her life.

Anne had used her cell phone to call Romansky from the trailer and tell him about X-Ray's death. Three days later, Detective Romansky called her and asked if she wanted to meet for a cup of coffee. He was careful to say that he didn't have any news about Miranda, that he just wanted to talk. They met in a bookstore with a small café. The bookstore was a massive, warehouse-like space, fluorescent-lit and echoing, and the café was just a corner in the front of the store, behind a plate-glass window that looked out onto the parking lot. She found Romansky sitting at a table tucked away in a nook between the counter and the window, where nobody would be able to hear their conversation over the hiss of the espresso machine. There was something in a cup in front of him that looked and smelled suspiciously like a chai latte.

He rose to meet her. "I would have gotten you something to drink," he said, "but I don't know what you like."

"I'll get it." She draped her shawl over the back of a chair.

"This place gets a little loud sometimes," he said, "but it's the only place in town where you can get a decent chai latte."

"Where did you learn to drink chai lattes?" she said.

Romansky's mouth twitched. "Yeah, well, I had a dozen doughnuts to go with it, but I polished those off before you got here." He shrugged. "You know us cops."

She went to the counter and bought a cup of chamomile tea. It came in a paper cup with a cardboard sleeve, and the liquid inside burned her through the thin material. "You wanted this," Romansky said as soon as she sat down. He handed her a small paper envelope, the kind that Miranda's school had handed out for lunch money when she was little.

She broke the seal and dumped the medal out onto her palm.

"All the evidence was released when they ruled it a suicide — not that there was really a question about that," Romansky said. "His ex-wife came and got most of his stuff, but she said she'd never seen that before. In case you were interested." Anne closed her fist over the gold disk in her palm. Romansky watched her carefully. "I gather it's familiar."

She made her fist open and placed the necklace on the table between them. "It should be. I bought it."

"Those initials on the back," he said. "They're yours."

They were — hers and Nick's. *AC-NC.* Anne turned her head and stared out at the parking lot, at the rows of cars and the highway beyond. "When my husband's plane disappeared," she said, "there was no wreckage, no body, no nothing. One minute he was due home in a week and a half, and sixty seconds later he was never coming home again." She shook her head. "X-Ray shouldn't have had this medal. Nick never took it off. It should have gone down with him in the crash."

"Maybe he wasn't wearing it that day," Romansky said. "Maybe the chain broke or something."

"Then he would have carried it in his pocket." She looked down at her tea, which was pale and milky. "Either X took it after Nick was dead — which he wouldn't have done, except to give it back to me — or Nick gave it to him. And if Nick gave it to him —" She couldn't finish the sentence. "There's something I don't know," she said finally. "There's something nobody told me."

Realization dawned on Romansky's face. "You think he's still alive," the detective said. His voice was incredulous.

"I'll never know," Anne said quietly. "I'll never know, and it doesn't matter. My husband worked for the CIA. Not directly, but at some level. The guy who paid him was paid by a guy who was paid by a guy, you know? He did this for a living, long before I ever met him. He flew in Laos, Angola, Nicaragua — every nasty little war that America wasn't officially fighting." Anne sipped her tea. "You know, I think that at least in the beginning, he really believed that he was doing the right thing, that something terrible was going to happen to the world if he wasn't right there on the front line. Getting shot at and getting shot down and doing god only knows what."

Romansky was still.

Anne continued. "I have no doubt whatsoever that his plane went down filled with guns or bombs or cocaine or something equally horrible, because that's what he *did*. Every time Nick took off, somebody somewhere died because of it. Ten somebodies. A hundred somebodies. Revolutions and overdoses and land mines and just — the wrong place at the wrong time. So what I've been telling myself for all these years is that when he went down, the guns or the bombs or the coke ended up on the ocean floor, and so those hundred somebodies didn't die. I wanted to believe that he'd died to make it right somehow. What he'd been doing. It had to be *meaningful*."

With trembling hands, she put her paper cup of tea down on the table and laced her fingers together. "So now here I am, and nothing happened the way that I thought it happened, and nothing is the way that I thought it was. I've spent twenty years looking for answers that don't exist. And now all I can think about is how Nick was the lucky one, because it was *our* lives that were destroyed. Miranda's and mine. We didn't get to choose. We've had to live like this for twenty years because he was so convinced that he was doing the right thing, and he was *wrong*."

Anne stopped.

She tried to compose herself. She did not try to breathe out the spiky green anger and breathe in the cool blue calm. There was too much green, too many spikes. She felt full; for the first time in years, she felt full.

Finally Romansky spoke. "I've been on the force for twenty-four years," he said. "I can tell you stories that'll make your head spin. People are assholes, you know? Worse than that, they're stupid. That's what really gets me: not the jackass who beats his wife, but the wife who takes her two-year-old back into the house with him at the end of the call. I know what they say about battered women, how the violence gets into their head, how they don't feel like they have any choice. And maybe that's true, but it doesn't make it any less stupid to stay with a guy whose pet name for you is *cunt*, you know what I'm saying?" His face was calm, serene. "But there she goes, back into the house, and you know that you're going to be back there in two weeks, and you can't do anything to stop her. And all the while there's this wide-eyed little pumpkin in pigtails watching all of it go down, and you know that some-day some poor bastard's going to go on a call to *her* house, too, and you just hope like hell that bastard isn't you.

"People make stupid decisions. They think stupid things. There's nothing you can do about it. You just sort of have to hope that in the end it all adds up, because when you stop feeling bad about it —" He stopped.

Anne didn't speak. For a long time they sat together in silence. Anne's gaze was fixed on the medallion on the table, Detective Romansky's on the cars passing on the highway, but neither of them saw what they looked at, and the liquid in their paper cups grew cold.

Finally Anne said, "I think Miranda is dead."

"Don't say that," Romansky said, automatically. "You don't know that."

Anne smiled. It was a bitter smile. "When I looked at those Web sites," she said, "they all said that after the first forty-eight hours, the chances of finding whoever it is you're looking for decrease practically exponentially. How many forty-eight-hour blocks of time have passed since Miranda disappeared? Thirty, maybe forty? How many before anybody even noticed that she was gone?"

And that was it: that was the black bubble of feeling that was pushing its way up inside her. Because if one person could vanish without a ripple and leave the world exactly the same place that it had been before, if an individual life mattered that little, what was the magic number when it started to make a difference? One life obviously didn't do it. When Anne thought about Nick's planes full of guns and bombs and drugs it seemed to her that a thousand wouldn't either, or ten thousand, or twenty. And if lives were that meaningless, then it wasn't the lives that were meaningless: it was life.

Romansky leaned across the table. He grabbed her hand and clenched it, hard. "Things happen," he said. "Two weeks from now she could pop up on some computer screen somewhere, and the case could break wide open, and she'll be home by Halloween."

Anne shook her head. "I'm going back to Sedona," she said. "There's nothing for me to do here." She gave him a sad smile. "I'm finally getting out of your way."

He squeezed her hand. "You weren't in the way. You were just being a good mom."

"In a radical departure from the norm."

"Don't say that," he said again, with less conviction. Then he asked when she was leaving, and she said tonight, because she was driving. He told her to keep her phone on. "You never know when something might turn up," he added.

Anne took the medal and held it in the air by its chain as she would a pendulum. It spun slowly, clockwise and then counter, showing first the robed Saint Joseph with his cross and then the two sets of initials. Nick's, and hers. She had been so young when she'd bought it. "You mean the way this turned up?"

He smiled, and they stood up to go. As Anne draped her shawl over her shoulders, Romansky said, "I've never heard of that guy, Saint Joseph of — whatever."

"Saint Joseph of Cupertino. The patron saint of aviators and astronauts," Anne said, and shook her head. "Levitation was one of his miracles. I used to know the story. I don't anymore."

"Must be hard to find something like that," Romansky said, his tone conversational, and Anne answered, "It is. You have to go to a specialty store —"

And she started to cry.

epilogue:
be thou made whole

S HE WOKE UP in a hospital room. There were bandages wrapped tight around her ribcage and a cast on her left leg. Soon after she woke up, there were doctors with questions. What was her name? Did she have an address? Family they could contact? Known drug allergies?

She gave them the name she had used in Lawrence Beach and answered no, no, and no; then the police came with more questions. How long had she known George? Where had she met him? What had they talked about?

Slowly, she understood that while she had survived the crash, he had not. The knowledge made her faintly sad, but more than that, she felt as if a door had closed somewhere, and she stood on the other side of it.

After the police, there were other men, who never identified themselves but somehow managed to convey a deeper, more fundamental sense of officiousness than the police had. They, too, had questions for her. Had George had any papers with him other than the ones in the satchel? Had he mentioned that he had any others? Had he told her what he planned to do with them?

And that was one question that she could answer. Yes, she said. George had wanted her to go to Cuba with him, and he had said that the papers would buy them a new life.

"Was it him?" she asked. "Was he the killer?"

"Did he mention the murders?" one of them asked quickly.

She looked from him to his associate. "He said he was being framed. Because he stole those papers."

The two men exchanged a look that she could not interpret.

"It's possible that he was associated with the killer, or that he knew who the killer was," one of them finally said. "There are a number of possible scenarios. We're still investigating."

After they were gone, she lay alone in the room for a long time, watching cartoons, feeling the aches in her body and thinking about what to do next.

Finally she buzzed for the nurse and told her that she had lied earlier. "My name is Miranda Cassidy," she said, and gave them the last number that she had for Anne.

In Sedona it was a beautiful day. The morning sun was bright on the red rock monoliths, and the leaves of the cotton-wood tree that shaded the little pink house were rustling in a light breeze. The same breeze gently blew the wind chimes on the front porch, filling the yard with their thin metallic notes. When the phone rang, it rang into empty space. Nobody was there to hear it; not even Livingston the ancient cat, who was still staying with Rhiannon, and who had once been rescued from a refrigerator box.

The nurse told Miranda that there was no answer. She sighed and gave them Jay Miles's phone number, amazed that she still remembered it.

And so the nurse called Jay Miles —

— who called Detective Romansky —

— who hung up and let out a great whoop that made the detective working at the next desk jump. For a moment he sat still, tapping his chin with a pencil and smiling an immeasurable smile at nothing, or maybe it was at something that no-body else could see.

Then he picked up his phone again.

Somewhere in Oklahoma, in a rental car that was starting to feel like home, Anne's phone rang. It was still set to play the *Mission: Impossible* theme song, and as she fished it out of her bag, she thought to herself that she really had to change that, if she was going to keep the phone.

She pressed the talk button.

"This is Anne," she said.

ACKNOWLEDGMENTS

People are fundamentally good. The following people, however, win bonus points: my wonderful agent, Julie Barer, and equally wonderful editor, Heidi Pitlor, both of whom put up with me through six drafts and as many mailing addresses; my early readers, Lauren Grodstein, Amanda Eyre Ward, and Owen King (who gets extra-special dishwasher-loading, cat-feeding bonus points); and everyone at Houghton Mifflin — particularly Gracie Doyle and Brooke Witkowski, but also particularly Reem Abu-Libdeh, Nicole Angeloro, Suzanne Cope, Carla Gray, Ryan Mann, and Mark Robinson. Long overdue bonus points should be issued immediately to Charlotte Mendelson, Leah Woodburn, and all of the hardworking people at Hodder Headline Review, as well as to Lisa Dierbeck (whose novel, *One Pill Makes You Smaller,* should be read immediately by anybody who was ever a female human adolescent, or met one in passing), Joseph Gangemi, and Peter Straub.

Thankful and loving bonus points go to everyone who let me ask them questions (any errors are mine, not theirs): James Braffet, for his wealth of aviation knowledge and anecdotes; Casey Braffet, for explaining emergency medicine (it's good to have family members with interesting jobs!); and Dr. James C. M. Brust, who has once again proven an invaluable resource on human injury. I would also like to express my gratitude to Corporal Phillip C. Hipchen, Pennsylvania State Police, Retired, who patiently and enthusiastically guided me through the inner workings of police investigation; to Molly Braffet for introducing me to him; and most of all to Phil's family, particularly his wife, Sally Henry.

Finally, much love and gratitude is, as always, due to my family, but this time especially to my mother, Theresa Braffet, who *always* saved the kittens.